Praise for *Shades of Darkness*

"Destiny, death, dating, and daubs of paint:
Shades of Darkness perfectly captures the art school
experience with a dastardly magical twist that
will leave you hungry for more."
—Delilah S. Dawson, author of
Servants of the Storm and *Wake of Vultures*

"A. R. Kahler's *Shades of Darkness* is an eerie, wistful
meditation on love, sacrifice, and the demons
we struggle to leave behind. The arresting final
image is going to linger with me indelibly."
—Karsten Knight, author of
the Wildefire trilogy

"I love A. R. Kahler's writing and *Shades of Darkness*
is no exception. Mythical. Magical. Murderous.
But grounded in the real world. I devoured
this book and can't wait for the next one."
—Julie Kagawa,
New York Times and *USA Today*
bestselling author

Also by A. R. Kahler

Ravenborn, Book One: *Shades of Darkness*
The Immortal Circus trilogy
The Pale Queen trilogy
Love Is in the Air

Coming soon:
The Runebinder Chronicles

ECHOES OF MEMORY

A. R. KAHLER

RAVENBORN BOOK TWO

SIMON PULSE

New York   London   Toronto   Sydney   New Delhi

SIMON PULSE

An imprint of Simon & Schuster Children's Publishing Division
1230 Avenue of the Americas, New York, New York 10020
First Simon Pulse hardcover edition March 2017
Text copyright © 2017 by A. R. Kahler
Jacket illustration copyright © 2017 by Stina Persson
All rights reserved, including the right of reproduction in whole or in part in any form.
SIMON PULSE and colophon are registered trademarks of Simon & Schuster, Inc.
For information about special discounts for bulk purchases, please contact
Simon & Schuster Special Sales at 1-866-506-1949 or business@simonandschuster.com.
The Simon & Schuster Speakers Bureau can bring authors to your live event.
For more information or to book an event contact the Simon & Schuster
Speakers Bureau at 1-866-248-3049 or visit our website at www.simonspeakers.com.
Jacket designed by Regina Flath
Interior designed by Steve Scott
The text of this book was set in Janson.
Manufactured in the United States of America
2 4 6 8 10 9 7 5 3 1
This book has been cataloged with the Library of Congress.
ISBN 978-1-4814-3260-3 (hc)
ISBN 978-1-4814-3262-7 (eBook)

For my family

CHRIS

CHAPTER ONE

"What. The hell. Is going on?"

Ethan's words jolted me back like a bucket of ice water. I sat there, shuddering and numb, my blood sluggish in my veins and my brain a static cloud. But I was there. There, alive in the painted circle on the classroom floor. There, beside Jonathan, who was passed out or dead at my feet.

I was there, and Kaira was not.

"I'll ask again," Ethan said, stepping farther into the classroom. His eyes darted around the scene, taking in more than my scattered brain could: the shards of glass, the overturned desks. The body. Only one body. "What the hell is going on, Chris? Why was everyone running and screaming? And what is *he* doing here?"

Ethan gestured to Jonathan. The professor's body was sprawled on the ground beside me. He was twisted into a fetal position, his tattooed arms clutching his head like he was trying to keep out the ravens that were no longer there. Like he was hiding from what he'd done. But he wasn't hiding. He wasn't moving. Not anymore.

And I didn't give two shits.

"Did you see her?" I asked. I glanced from Jonathan to Ethan. Calm, composed, bohemian Ethan, standing there in the empty classroom in his pea coat like an actor trying to find his lines. "Did you see where she went?"

Ethan glanced around. His eyes kept snagging on the body beside me.

"Chris . . . what did you do? Did you—"

"Did you see her?" I asked, louder this time. I pushed myself up to my knees, but the ground began to sway as my head swam, so I didn't go farther. I kept looking around, like maybe the shadows were hiding her, maybe she was under a desk, waiting to surprise us both.

The emptiness—the silence—weighed down on me. It felt exactly like—

"Who?" Ethan asked. His eyebrows furrowed. I didn't like that look.

"Kaira!" I yelled. I kept searching for her. If she was here, she could explain what I saw. If she was here, she could confirm I wasn't sleeping. No, *no*, I knew I was awake. I knew what I'd seen. I'd held her while her eyes turned purple and something *else* spoke through her lips. I'd watched the ravens burst from her skin and carry her away.

It couldn't be real.

It *was* real. What did that make me?

"Chris, what the hell are you talking about?"

In answer, I forced myself to stand, forced myself not to wobble over, to trip on Jonathan's body. Because it *was* a body. He was dead.

I couldn't think about that right now.

Instead, I ran to the window, ignoring Ethan's question. Shattered glass covered the floor like snow: something had broken into the room. Something had come in, had changed my world forever. A murder of crows, screaming like the lost voices of the Underworld. And that something had transformed Kaira. That something had spirited her away.

She wasn't out there, wandering in the night. The grounds of Islington spread dark and heavy before me: a few academic buildings with their lights muted, a few streetlamps casting pale circles over the thick snow. Empty. No kids wandering between practice halls. No cars navigating the school's back roads.

No Kaira, standing in the snow, waiting for me to find her.

No ravens ripping my world apart.

I pressed my hands to the sill, barely noticing the sharp bite of glass under my palms or the warmth of blood suddenly pooling through my fingers. A cold breeze blew past me. But I was warmer. Warmer than I should have been. My hands felt like fire, and my blood beat magma.

"Where are you?" I whispered to the night air.

Ethan came up behind me, his feet crunching on the glass.

"Chris . . ." he whispered, much more tentatively. "What happened here? And why are we looking for Kaira?"

I tried to see farther in the darkness. Tried to make out her shape, tried to find a single damned raven. There had been

5

hundreds in the past few weeks, thousands in the last few minutes, *so where are they now?*

"They took her," I muttered.

"Who?" Ethan asked. He stood next to me, but he wasn't looking at the sky. He was looking at me. Like I was crazy. Like I had somehow done this.

Like he was scared of me.

My heart froze.

"The ravens," I said. The words sounded so stupid on my tongue.

"There aren't any ravens," he said.

He spoke in a voice I knew all too well. The voice of someone trying to keep someone else from exploding. The voice of someone talking a madman off a ledge. He wasn't worried for me.

He was worried about me.

"There were," I said. "Thousands of them. You have to believe me. They were here and then they took her."

"I believe what I see," Ethan replied. "And right now I see something that should have me calling the cops. Jonathan is dead, Chris. What the hell went on in here? Even if there *were* birds, that doesn't account for why he's dead."

I didn't understand how his voice could sound so calm, and so close to breaking, all at the same time.

I looked past him then. Over his shoulder and into the room. I really *looked*. What would Ethan see in here, and what were my memories?

He couldn't have seen the ravens swirling around the thick black circle painted on the floor. He couldn't have seen Kaira,

6

begging me to help her before she became something else. He wouldn't have the memory of Kaira and Jonathan squaring off in the middle of the room as the ravens burst in and turned everything on its head. He wouldn't see any of that, because there wasn't a trace of anything supernatural. There weren't even any feathers to make my case.

Ethan could only see what was left: the shattered glass, the overturned desks, the smeared paint on the floor. He would only see Jonathan and me.

Jonathan, who was dead.

And me, who was the only one around who could have killed him.

My heart suddenly remembered to beat. Now it was making up for it and pumping triple time.

"I didn't do it," I said. There was a voice in my head telling me to run. But I couldn't run—not from Ethan. He was my friend. Kaira's friend. He needed to believe me. If only so *I* could believe me.

He glanced back to Jonathan's body. We both stared for a while. Like we were waiting for it to move. As though this could all be one big prank.

"I checked his pulse," he whispered. "Nothing. And there aren't any wounds or signs of struggle."

It was the birds, I wanted to say. But I didn't. I held my tongue, partly because he seemed to be trying to think up an explanation. One that didn't involve me.

"I don't know what happened," I admitted. "But I swear to you, Ethan, I didn't hurt him. I came in here and—"

7

"Was he dead when you arrived?" Ethan asked, still watching Jonathan's corpse.

I shook my head. "I don't really know," I admitted. "I was too focused on . . ." But I trailed off. Kaira wasn't here. I hadn't lied, though—I wasn't focusing on Jonathan when I came in, when I'd pushed past all the screaming kids. I was too focused on Kaira, on keeping her safe.

"We should go," he said. His voice had a distant, haunted cast to it. He still didn't turn to face me.

I nodded slowly. Okay, okay. He didn't believe me. But if we found Kaira . . .

"You're right," I replied. "We should go. You have a car. We can find her."

"No, Chris. We need to *go*. Before someone finds him."

"But Kaira—"

He rounded on me then; his calm facade had finally snapped.

"Kaira isn't here, Chris!" he yelled. "You are. You and a goddamned body, and if you don't get your ass out of here, I'm going to call the cops myself and have them arrest you because you're lingering at a crime scene, and even if you don't think you did it, you're talking like an insane person and maybe you're just too fucking screwed up to remember killing him."

My breath caught between my teeth.

"I didn't—"

"If you want me to believe you, you're going to have to come up with a better story. One that doesn't involve nonexistent birds and a girl who isn't around. And you won't be able to do that if you're behind bars."

8

He started pulling me toward the door, mumbling to himself. Part of me wondered if I should resist; maybe he was taking me to the RA, or to campus security. But I was innocent. Jonathan's blood wasn't on my hands.

That was when I realized something that made me stop in my tracks.

My blood should have been dripping down the window, splattering on the floor. I had cut my palms deep. I had felt the blood ooze between my fingers. But when I looked to my hands, they were clean and smooth, the skin unbroken.

It is not right that you should bleed for her, came a voice. It simmered through my veins, familiar as my own shadow. I glanced past Ethan, to where the falcon perched atop Jonathan's broken body. *It is not right, when her blood is yours to spill.*

Get out of my head, I thought to the bird. When I blinked, it was gone, nothing more than a memory. Worse than a memory. A curse.

Maybe I *was* going insane.

Maybe they *should* put me behind bars.

"Hurry up," Ethan demanded. "It's like you want to be caught."

"We have to find her," I repeated. I felt like a broken record. But wasn't that about right? The whole world was broken. Why should I be any different? At least if I found Kaira, we could be broken together.

Islington no longer felt like home.

As Ethan guided me out of the academics concourse and

9

down the long, snow-swept road, I couldn't escape the feeling of being lost. This place—once the closest thing I'd ever had to feeling like I belonged—was no longer mine. The shadows were deep, and even the welcoming glow of the arts building up ahead couldn't pierce the darkness that seemed to linger everywhere. I wanted to break free from Ethan's grip, to run screaming Kaira's name through the woods and the shadows that had taken her.

The trouble was, I couldn't move. If not for Ethan pulling me along, I would have stood still, a statue of ice. Moving meant operating in this new world. And that meant believing what I'd seen. Or the alternative: I was going insane.

"You're going to tell me everything that happened," Ethan said as we walked. "What were you doing in there? And what happened to Jonathan?"

I wanted to squeeze out the images that pushed through the backs of my eyes—Kaira, running into the room and leaping over the circle, punching Jonathan just as the window exploded with black wings and razor beaks. Everyone screaming. Every-*thing* screaming. Before the silence. Before . . .

I am not Kaira, vessel of the Aesir. My name is Freyja.

"What the hell is going on?"

But it wasn't Ethan asking. It was me. And when I looked at him, I knew without a doubt that he had even fewer answers than I. If anything, he just looked scared. Scared that he wasn't the only one questioning my sanity.

We didn't stop until we were in the arts building. Normally, stepping in there would have felt like finding sanctuary. Tonight it was just a reminder of the demons I wasn't able to escape. Kaira's tarot card paintings still hung on the walls, the images connected by webs of silver thread. I'd stared at them for hours over the last few days, read her artist's statement over and over. Trying to figure out why she had such a pull on me, why this shadowed girl with streaks in her hair was an orbit I couldn't escape. I'd learned nothing. Only that she had been hurt—something she'd already told me—and that her past was as dark and clouded as mine.

Ethan tugged me along.

"Come on," he urged.

I didn't ask where he was taking me. I just let him pull me down the hall and up the stairs, until we were in a room I'd never stepped foot in before. Black-and-white photographs were pinned on the walls of the tiny studio; a single desk littered with papers and canisters sat beneath a small window.

"What is this?" I asked. My hackles rose the moment the door clicked shut behind us. It felt like a trap.

"My studio," he replied. I said nothing else, but he followed up quickly with, "All senior photographers get one. There aren't many of us."

I wanted out. I *needed* out. Kaira was out there. She needed me. I needed her. Before I was convicted for something I didn't do. Before Ethan turned on me. Turned me in.

But where is she? Where would she be? Or is she already dead and gone?

Somehow, though, I knew she was alive. I could feel her. Like a spark of warmth in the distant tundra, a barely perceptible beacon. She was there. And I would find her.

11

Ethan made a noise in his throat and dragged me over to the chair, forced me to sit. With the bare bulb above us, it felt like an interrogation chamber.

"Talk," he said.

I opened my mouth. No words came out.

He made another noise and then cleared a space off his desk, sitting down and pulling off his beanie. He worried it between his hands. His eyes didn't leave mine.

I'd known Ethan for a few weeks. I mean, I'd known of him for longer, but it wasn't until Mandy's death that we'd really become friends. I'd seen him stress out over paintings and laugh over Kaira's bad jokes and fawn over the loving glances of his boyfriend, Oliver. But I'd never seen him like this. He'd always been a little lighthearted, even when stressed, like he took himself so seriously it was almost a joke. Tonight, though, he didn't just look worried; he looked pissed.

"Tell me it wasn't you," he said. His voice was colder than the snow outside. It didn't sound like a request. With the light and the silence and the tone, I knew it was a command.

The knot in my chest loosened in an instant, dropping to my feet with a thud.

"What?"

"The circle. Jonathan. Tell me you were in the wrong place at the wrong time."

I knew without a doubt that he would report me if he thought I was to blame. I shook my head, the first tinge of feeling finally returning to my shell-shocked limbs. I had to convince him of something not even I was convinced of. I had to sound sane. None of this was sane. *The birds . . . Kaira . . .*

"I didn't do anything," I said. It felt like pleading. "I swear, Ethan. I saw Kaira run into the room. She was angry, yelling something. I followed her. That's why I was there. I don't know . . . I don't . . ."

"Kaira wasn't in there, Chris, and I didn't see her run out," Ethan said. "Just you. And Jonathan. What am I supposed to believe? That some birds magically came in and—"

"They took her!" I yelled, half standing in my chair. Ethan didn't flinch. He stared me down and waited for me to sit again. I did. If only because I was shaking too hard to stand.

I took a deep breath. It was clear he wasn't going to buy the story that I knew . . . that I thought . . . was true.

For some reason, my mind jumped back to the day I was hit by a car, to the time I learned when to hold my tongue. Learned to say the truth that the person wanted to hear so they could twist it into whatever narrative they wanted. No one believed I had died after being hit, or that I was brought back to life. My parents thought I was just begging for attention. But they *did* believe I was nearly hit, that I should stop playing by the road. And they believed I had an overactive imagination. That was enough to make them believe part of my story, to make them fill in the spaces they needed. It let me get by.

I didn't tell them, in the wake of my sister's death, that the gods told me she had died to pay off my life-debt. That if I hadn't been hit by that car and brought back to life, she would still be around. I knew they would think I was insane.

Just as I knew Ethan would think I was insane if I tried to push what I knew in my gut to be true.

So I looked at my feet, tried to look confused and scared. Neither emotion was hard to pull off. Neither was a lie.

"I honestly don't know what I saw," I said. "I followed Kaira in there. She . . . I don't know what happened. The window exploded and I thought it was birds, but I don't know anymore. Maybe it was just shadows. Maybe someone threw a rock in. All I know is, Kaira was there, and then . . ." *Then she became something else, something inhuman. Something with violet eyes as dark and unfeeling as space itself.* "Jonathan was dead when it all cleared. I wasn't even near him at the time. Look, I know this sounds crazy, but—"

"No," he interrupted. "Having to finish three different paintings on the same day sounds crazy. Applying to Islington knowing it's going to make your life hell is crazy. This is a fucking fairy tale."

"You have to believe me."

"I don't *have* to do anything." I glanced up at him, but he wasn't even looking at me. He was staring into the corners of the room, one foot tapping nervously. "Here's what I see, Chris: We took you to dinner, and rather than go to a movie after like we planned, you asked to be taken back to campus. Where I later find you in a room with a dead body and a circle like we saw before. Just like the circle around Jane's body. Which, come to think about, you didn't seem too surprised by when we found it. And when I find you tonight, all you can do is blabber about Kaira being taken, which is stupid, because we're in the middle of the woods and there's no one around to take her and she definitely didn't sneak out that window. So, to me, unless you can explain this away, it looks like you've had a hand in all this. Like maybe these deaths weren't so random or unexplained all along."

It was a death sentence. Hearing him say it . . . God, it sounded insane. If the roles were reversed, would I believe him? If I hadn't actually seen it with my own eyes? If I hadn't experienced everything I had?

What if she had never been in there? What if I walked in there and saw Jonathan dead and had some sort of nervous breakdown?

What if I—

"Please," I choked, forcing down that train of questioning. "I can't explain what happened. But I swear it wasn't me. I wouldn't hurt Jonathan. I wouldn't hurt any of them. You know me, Ethan."

"Actually, I don't." Ethan's words were like a guillotine, cutting off my rambling plea and any hope of winning him over. "I only know that you started hanging out with us when all this started happening. Which doesn't look very good either." He looked down to his hat then. "Jesus, Chris. What have you gotten yourself into?"

"Check with security," I said—it sounded so close to begging. "About the day Jane died. I was on the phone. There's a log, and my parents can tell you they were talking to me. I wasn't there for Jane's death, and I had no idea what I was walking into tonight. I'm just as innocent as you."

I paused. A new thought twisted in my gut along with the fear. A different sort of nervousness.

"Wait. Why were *you* there?" I asked. "You were supposed to be at the movies with Oliver and Elisa."

He looked away and shoved his hat back on his head. Like he was trying to hide.

"I didn't feel right." His words were small and uncertain.

"What do you mean?"

He sighed and looked back to me. "I mean, after we dropped you off, I didn't feel right about going back out there. Thought it was a blizzard coming or something."

"You felt it," I whispered. "The wrongness. Something is going on and you know it." It felt so stupid saying it, but to my relief, he didn't laugh.

"That's an understatement." His expression hardened. "Why should I believe you, Chris?"

"Because Jonathan wasn't injured. You said it yourself." I held up my hands then pulled the collar away from my neck. "And look. No bruising. No blood. How could I have killed a grown man without getting some sort of scratch?"

"You've put a lot of thought into that defense."

"Only because it's the truth." I slumped down. "I don't know what's happening anymore. I don't know what's true. But I know I didn't hurt him. Or Jane. Or anyone else." Then, because he still hadn't answered my question, I turned the questions on him. "Why did you stay on campus?"

He shook his head.

"No. No, this isn't about me. I said I felt strange. Which anyone would feel if they'd seen . . ." He actually shuddered. "They're stupid circles, but I can't get them out of my head.

16

Ever since Jane. It's like staring into the eye of Death himself."

"Something is happening," I pressed. "You know it. I can't explain it any more than you can. But I'm going to figure it out, Ethan. And to do that, I need your help. We have to find Kaira. She's"—*been taken, transformed into something else*—"in trouble. You know it too. And not because of me."

He didn't look at me when I said it, and I didn't feel the same accusation when he finally replied.

"I've been worried about her. . . . You swear you had nothing to do with what happened in there?"

I nodded. "I swear on my life."

Not that that means anything, since you're living on borrowed time.

"I'm not saying I believe you," Ethan admitted. "But I'm not going to report you. Not yet. Not unless you give me a reason to."

"We need to find her," I said. Now that the panic of him turning me in was fading, the fear of not knowing what happened to her took hold again. "Kaira. She's—"

"Probably painting," he interjected. "Unless you're telling me she jumped out that window and ran off."

"She didn't jump. She . . ." I trailed off. He didn't need to know she became a murder of ravens. "She was there. I swear. And I need to find her; she'll prove it."

"Are you on something?" he asked. He leaned in, like he was checking my pupils. "Seriously."

I pushed him back. "I'm sober. One hundred percent. I know what I saw. She was there."

Rather than answer, he pulled out his phone and typed in a number and held it to his ear. We sat in silence while the phone rang, my nerves on edge. Was he calling campus security? Should I be running right now? But he didn't look like he was about to turn me in; I watched his eyebrows furrow deeper. Finally, he perked up.

"Kaira?" he asked. "Oh, sorry Elisa. I didn't . . . Yeah, I wanted to see if she was around."

A pause.

"Okay, thanks."

Then he ended the call and leaned forward.

"That was Elisa; she answered Kaira's phone," he said. He looked me in the eyes. "You need to start thinking of a better cover story. Because according to Elisa, Kaira's sound asleep in their bedroom."

My chest tightened.

"That's impossible. I saw her . . ."

He held out the phone, Kaira's number already dialed and ready to be sent.

"You're welcome to ask her yourself," he said. "But let me warn you: She's a monster when woken up."

CHAPTER TWO

I didn't make the call.

I sat there staring at Ethan while my brain tried to kick into gear. *Kaira is safe. Back in her room. So . . .*

So I was going crazy. That was the only rational explanation. I was going crazy and Kaira was okay and what if . . . No, I didn't have anything to do with Jonathan's death. I knew that much. But the rest—the birds and the screams and the falcon demanding Kaira's life—I had no explanation for. *Something* had broken the window in that classroom. But what if it had been like that before? What if I really had just snapped, and Kaira had never even been in there? I'd walked in and seen Jonathan dead and . . .

"What's happening to me?" I whispered.

"Stress?" Ethan ventured. I hadn't actually expected him to answer. Stress didn't explain a dead professor or seeing Kaira in a place she couldn't have been. It couldn't explain what I'd seen happening to her. It had either happened, or I had snapped. There was no middle ground.

I ran my hands through my hair, tried to dig out the memories of the way she'd looked at me. The way her skin had burned like ice when I'd touched her, the gristle of feathers pushing through her flesh, the biting wind of a thousand wingbeats. I could still smell it, the tar of the feathers, the tang of fear. It burned in my nose, scratched in my brain.

No. I wasn't crazy. It was real. It had happened. But the only one who could confirm it was currently—apparently—asleep in her room.

Why would she have flown off, only to go back to her room? Why had she seemed so scared if she was returning to safety? It didn't make sense. None of it. My pulse wouldn't stop racing, because there was no way Kaira was just safe in her bed and it was all a hallucination. Kaira was out in the wilds somewhere, needing to be rescued. She had to be. She couldn't be back in her room. This couldn't have all been a delusion.

I looked down at my hands, to the smooth palms. No cuts, no shards of glass from the broken window.

Maybe it *was* a delusion. Maybe . . .

"You're sure she's in there?" I asked. There was a desperation in my words, a heaviness. A need. "It wasn't just some pillows under the blankets?"

"I didn't ask Elisa to clarify," he said, leaning back. I couldn't tell what his expression was saying. Confused? Concerned? "But again, you're welcome to call her if you want."

I shook my head. If Kaira was in there . . . what did it mean?

"In the meantime," he continued, "you need to think of a story. If there were others in there, like you said, fingers will

20

be pointed if someone remembers seeing you on their way out. You'll need an alibi."

"I don't have one. Not this time."

I watched the muscles of his jaw tighten as his eyes looked to the corners of his studio. I knew that look; he didn't believe what I was saying any more than security would. He needed the story to convince him as much as it would the cops.

"What about the kids who left?" he asked. "Do you remember who they were? Maybe they'd speak up. If we can get them to corroborate, maybe we don't have to worry about any of this."

"Maybe," I muttered. He gave me a look, like that answer was unacceptable. "What? I wasn't focused on anyone else, Ethan. If you'd have been there, you wouldn't have been either." I closed my eyes, tried to trace my footsteps back. Who had run out of the room screaming? "Erik," I whispered, pressing my hands to my eyes. I felt the edge of a headache approaching, one I doubted meds or caffeine would help. "And Tina. I don't really remember any of the others. And I don't know if they'd admit to being there."

"Do you think they did it?"

I knew he meant killing Jonathan. He wanted a scapegoat, someone who wasn't me. It was easier to point the finger at something rational than the truth I wanted to feed him. Jonathan hadn't died from a mortal blow. He hadn't just dropped dead, either. Those kids had summoned something, something I was positive Kaira was trying to fight. Whatever they had brought into this world, that had been what killed Jonathan. Just as it had killed Jane and Mandy. And that was something Ethan would never believe.

The fact that I even considered that made me wonder if maybe I *had* snapped. This was real life. Kids couldn't summon things.

And kids don't get brought back to life when they're killed.

"They had to. I mean, I don't know. It looked fairly ritualistic, you know? What if that's what this was all about? Human sacrifice or something?"

"There weren't any marks on him," Ethan reminded me. "So . . . was he alive when you ran in there?"

"Yes. I mean, I think so." I closed my eyes and tried to remember. All I came up with was screaming and ravens and Kaira's haunted violet gaze.

"Great," he muttered.

"What?"

"If Jonathan was alive when you came in, they'll remember that. They'll remember leaving. Which means you were the last person to see Jonathan alive. They'll just say you killed him when he was alone."

"But that's not what happened."

"But they'd think that. It's the only logical explanation. It's not like they're going to think he just dropped dead of natural causes in some painted circle. Not when this is the third time it's happened. They're going to know something's up. If you're tagged as having been there, you're screwed. I just wish you had a better alibi. Or *any* alibi, really. Because no one was in the room when Jonathan died. Except you."

And Kaira. But I didn't say it. Partly because he wouldn't believe it. Partly because I was beginning to question it myself.

"We'll need to go somewhere visible," he continued. "Let people see us to make it all plausible."

For a moment I could only sit there, staring at him in shock. How had he gone from wanting to turn me in to wanting to help me out? I wanted to be grateful, but a small part of me was suspicious.

"You'd do that? You'd lie for me?"

"For now. Until I have reason to do otherwise. You're my friend, even if you are crazy."

"Thanks. I think."

"Don't thank me. If it turns out you had a hand in this, I'm turning you in. Though, if you were guilty, you'd have probably tried to kill me by now since I'm suspicious of you."

We sat there in silence for a few long minutes, Ethan clearly wondering if he'd made the right choice in taking my side. And me, wondering what was worse: the thought that I'd made this all up, or the fear that something darker was happening. Something I couldn't explain. Something I didn't want explained.

"Come on," he said, sliding off the desk. "Let's go to the painting studio."

"I've already done the homework."

"And I don't give a shit. Alibi, remember?"

I nodded dumbly.

Part of me wanted to call Kaira, demand she tell me what she knew. If anything. The rest of me wanted to wait, to delay the inevitable. It was one thing to have Ethan thinking I was crazy. It would be another to hear the same doubt in Kaira's voice.

She'll believe you, I tried to convince myself. But if I was able to convince myself I'd seen her burst into birds, who was to say I'd made up that entire previous exchange? What if we never spoke of anything supernatural, and I was just walking in one grand delusion?

My head ached as I stood and followed Ethan down the hall to the painting studio. Every time we passed by an open door, I expected a cop to jump out and arrest me. Every time we heard conversation from a studio, my heart leaped into my chest.

And every time there was a flicker of light, the passing of a shadow, I heard a voice inside my head.

No. Not a voice. Laughter.

The falcon, drifting in and out on rays of consciousness, laughing at my plight.

It didn't take long for news of Jonathan's death to spread.

We had been in the studio for maybe thirty minutes. The only other kid in there was Tamora, who—probably at the insistence of the entire arts faculty—was painting fully clothed. And, as per usual, she didn't say a thing to us the entire time, just hummed along to the music in her headphones. The silence and her humming were driving me insane. My painting was finished and I had nothing to do but tweak small pieces, rework shading, and I wanted to scream at her to shut up or sing louder to drown out my thoughts. I kept looking into the shadows, waiting to see Kaira or the ravens or the damned falcon that didn't seem to quiet in my brain. I kept staring at my knuckles as they gripped my trembling paintbrush, wondering about the smooth, unbroken flesh on my palms. How had the cuts healed? Was it proof that I wasn't insane? Or had I imagined clutching the shattered windowsill along with everything else?

It is not right that you should bleed for her, the falcon had said. *When her blood is yours to spill.*

What the hell did he mean by that? I wasn't about to hurt Kaira. He had to mean something else. It couldn't be the thought that made my heart twist, the thought that maybe I'd slipped up, had done something terrible my brain refused to let me remember. *I had nothing to do with any of this . . . right?*

And then the door opened.

"Hi, sorry," said the security guard. I'd seen her around campus a few times, said hello in passing because everyone was generally friendly here. But tonight I felt like I was being cornered in an alley. My pulse started racing again. "Um, hello?"

She directed the last bit to Tamora, who finally caught the exchange and pulled out an earbud.

"Sorry," the guard repeated. "But . . . you guys need to head back to your dorms."

I tried to look confused. Blood continued to pump through my veins, a fire that made my heart stutter. *Don't look suspicious, don't look suspicious, she already knows, oh shit, she already knows and she's going to—*

"What's going on?" Ethan asked. He was smooth. He actually looked like this was a surprise. Maybe he'd taken an acting class or two.

"There's been another death. A faculty member. They want everyone to return to their dorms."

"Jesus," Tamora said, and exhaled. She set down her paintbrush with a thud. "Who was it?"

"I don't know. I just know they want everyone back. Sorry. Hope you were at a good stopping point."

Then, as though realizing that was a really inappropriate thing to say, she blushed and turned from the room.

We all just sat there, staring at the door. *She knows. You can't run from this. She's waiting out there to arrest you and you'll rot for a murder you never committed, and Kaira . . .*

I glanced down at my smooth hands. Tried to ignore the laughter that still echoed in the distance like a bird's cry.

Maybe that was for the best. If I was going insane, maybe I *should* be behind bars.

"They're dropping like flies, aren't they?" Tamora said.

"That's horrible," Ethan replied. He was already standing, and paused from gathering his things to glare at her. "Why would you say that?"

"Just saying what you're thinking," she said. She stretched and began putting her things away, like this was the most normal thing in the world. To have campus security come in and say someone died, to stop painting for a death. "What you wanna bet? Suicide or murder?"

"I'm not talking about this," Ethan said.

She looked to me, her gaze a lance. Cold sweat broke over my skin as she stared, head tilted slightly, like she was dissecting a painting for Freudian references.

"What about you?" she asked. "What's your bet?"

The words caught in my throat. But then I realized we were here to have an alibi. I'd play along as much as I could.

"Suicide," I muttered. I slid into my coat. "Place is too small for murder."

I could feel Ethan's glare on the back of my neck. But I was too focused on trying to keep my breathing steady, on playing it cool and acting only mildly concerned. I didn't want Tamora to read anything in my expression. Not when she's often accurately read through the layers of my paintings. When she finally looked away, I nearly crumpled to the stool in relief.

"That's my thought too," she said. She pulled on her coat, still mildly examining her painting. "Some people just can't take the stress of this place. Makes 'em crack. Surprised it was a teacher, though. Maybe they had an affair with one of the dead girls." She honestly sounded wistful. Like she wanted the gossip that it would bring.

"Tamora," Ethan said as he stepped beside me, "I say this as nicely as I can. Please shut the hell up. And never talk again. To me, or anyone else."

"Touchy, touchy," she said. She smiled at the two of us. "Maybe someone had reason to be jealous? Hot for teacher, Ethan?" She winked and turned to the door. Ethan had his hands shoved into his pockets, but his jaw was tight. "Have a good night, boys. Don't let the boogieman get you." Then she was gone.

"I never liked her," Ethan muttered to me. "But I didn't realize just how founded it was until now."

"She's scared," I said.

"Or a bitch," he responded. "I don't think they're mutually

exclusive." He sighed and shook his head, then looked at me. "You ready?"

I knew he meant more than *ready to go*. I just didn't quite know what. I nodded. I'd been ready to go the moment we stepped foot in here. I needed to talk to Kaira. I needed to know everything was going to be okay, that I wasn't insane, that I hadn't accidentally hurt someone.... *You haven't,* the voice whispered, *but you will.*

I tried to force it down to no avail.

We left the classroom in silence, the halls just as quiet as when we'd entered. When we stepped outside, into the consuming night air, the stillness gave way to a distanced sort of chaos.

The long building that housed the academic classrooms was crawling with cops and medics, the lights of ambulances and cop cars scratching over the snow in epileptic streaks. No sirens, no screams. Everything was as quiet as snowfall. No ravens in the trees and—for now, at least—no falcon, delighting in my demise. Ethan paused.

"Shit," he whispered, looking at me.

There were students out there as well. A few lingered by the cop cars, holding hands and watching it all in silence, but most hurried past. Toward their dorms and the illusion that there was safety there, that the world was normal within those walls. Toward the lie that they would wake up and in the morning everything would be okay.

But hell, maybe for them it would.

I didn't see anyone from before, but I still scanned the crowd as we neared, hoping to find a student staring at it all with a knowing look in their eyes. I needed to find someone who had seen what I'd seen. I needed to confirm I wasn't insane. I needed to find Kaira. . . .

Ethan took me by the arm and pulled me along, toward our dorm. It took all my self-control not to keep looking back, not to look too suspicious. Not to break free and run toward Kaira's dorm.

We signed ourselves in to the dorm and lingered in the foyer for a moment. The area was crowded with other guys from our dorm, and our RA, Todd, was behind the desk, fielding questions with half answers and saying on repeat, *When I know, you'll know.* There was no way in hell I could go back to my room. I didn't want to be alone with myself. I didn't want to relive tonight. So I went to the common room behind the lobby. Some guys were watching TV on the sofa while others played cards. There wasn't the same sort of fear that had lingered the last time we'd heard of a death. Maybe because this was a teacher and not a student. Maybe because we were all too used to this sort of thing to feel anything but dull resolve.

At least, they were. I was buzzing.

Ethan and I leaned against the wall and watched the TV. I couldn't focus. My brain raced with my pulse as I tried to look nonchalant. As I tried to keep building up this fragile alibi. Any moment, a cop would come in and question me. Any moment, the shadows would bleed forth ravens.

A few minutes in, Ethan's phone rang.

Oliver, he mouthed to me, then vanished down the hall to talk to his boyfriend.

I considered leaving, but I still couldn't force myself to move.

I tried focusing on the TV. Some stupid game show with people running over moats of floating pods and climbing walls and dodging swinging punching bags. It couldn't hold my attention, but the guys on the couch in front of me were into it. At least they were enjoying themselves. At least they weren't worrying about a murder being pinned on them.

This is just like when you were hit. Except it isn't you who was killed, and Jonathan isn't being brought back to life. Your sister was a sacrifice. Like Jonathan. Like the rest . . .

I ran a hand through my hair as my thoughts shot backward, as the afternoon I was hit played over in my mind. The sensation of the vehicle slamming my chest and my ribs exploding, ripping into my lungs as my legs buckled and cracked through my skin. *Deep breath. Deep breath.* But I couldn't stop seeing the blood. The blood that should have spilled when I should have hit concrete, when my body should have splayed on the road like a scarecrow.

My head throbbed at the thought. At the *feeling* of what never happened. My skull cracking on cement. Arms twisting. And my sister screaming my name.

Get ahold of yourself.

Except when I opened my eyes, the calling didn't stop.

I looked to the TV, to the sound of my name being yelled. The show contestants were screaming now. They ran down the obstacle course, trying to dodge the flames and spears that stabbed from the ground like porcupine quills. I blinked, rubbed my eyes. The carnage didn't stop. Blood spilled across the track, turned the water that other contestants swam in dark. The camera panned up, showing the audience. Only the audience wasn't sitting and watching—they were fighting each other. Flashes and explosions as guns fired, as heads exploded and stomachs ripped apart, as others beat their neighbors with sticks or swords, gouged eyes out with keys.

And then it panned back down. To my sister, standing in the middle of the arena, with a hawk perched atop her head, its claws digging rivulets into her skull. Around her, a circle of bodies, of blood. She was screaming. Screaming my name.

"I so hate this show," Ethan said, slapping me on the shoulder.

I jumped. When I glanced at him, he was staring at the screen in boredom. I looked to the TV. To the normal show of people running over low walls and dodging foam pillars.

What the hell? What the hell was that?

My heart raced in my chest. *I'm going insane. I'm literally going insane.*

"You okay, trouper?" Ethan asked.

"Yeah." I looked from him to the TV and back again. I needed to get a grip. I *needed* to talk to Kaira. "I think I just need . . . Actually, I don't know what."

"You should probably just go try to relax," Ethan said, like he wasn't consoling someone he had—a few hours ago—accused of murder. "Get some sleep. Make tea."

"Yeah," I said, glancing back to the TV. The fact that it didn't change almost made things worse. *It's just stress.* "I think I will. Good night. And thanks for, you know, not . . . not doubting me."

Ethan shrugged. "The trouble with giving everyone the

benefit of the doubt is that, eventually, you just start doubting everyone."

"What's that supposed to mean?"

He tried to grin, but it slipped the moment it passed over his lips. "That shit's fucked up. Go sleep. I'll see you at breakfast."

Then he gave me a quick hug and walked off toward his room.

I wasn't tired. The last thing I wanted was to go to my room and studiously ignore my roommate. Because, as usual, Mike would be there on his computer, chatting with his family in Canada, acting like I didn't exist. But it was better than staying here, staring at a wall because I couldn't trust myself to watch the TV or look out the window for fear of what I'd see.

And, shit. I still had pre-calc homework to finish.

I trudged up the stairs to my room. Unlike the first time, when we'd had mandatory sign-in because of a death, there wasn't any somberness in the halls. There were guys in the upstairs lobby talking and playing chess while a lone musician sat in the corner, playing a bolero on his guitar. Another group of guys were studying on the floor in the hall to my room. I stepped over their legs and said a passing hello, but they didn't really respond. I felt like a sleepwalker. Everyone else seemed unfazed by this death, but my world had shifted irreversibly. I didn't fit in here anymore. The hall felt like something out of a horror movie, even though the lights weren't flickering and the guys studying for a French quiz were far from intimidating. It was the simple fact that nothing else had changed. These guys would wake up in the morning and go through their days and not feel like the world was ending. They didn't know that gods were real, that people could be brought back from the dead.

They got to live the story they'd been told since birth.

I was a character in something completely different.

Mike didn't fail in playing his part. The moment I opened the door, I was struck by the humid scent of stale leftovers and sweat. Somehow, that helped push away the images of Kaira bursting into ravens, or my sister begging me to help her on the TV screen. Mike was Mike. The room smelled like it always did, and he was at his computer like he always was—headphones in, some rank herbal tea cooling by his laptop while he chatted away with whatever relative was still awake at this hour on one screen and drafted some essay on another. I threw my coat on the bed and sat down at my desk.

My side of the room was pretty barren—some paintings I'd done or collected, a mandatory photo of my parents and me on some vacation I barely remembered. I looked over each one. Trying to find some sort of emotional response. They were all images I'd cultivated, ones to make me remember home—however screwed up "home" was. Pictures of me and friends rafting last summer. Postcards from the few friends who stayed in touch over the years. Concert stubs and movie tickets and a boarding pass for a flight to Paris. But now, when I looked at my side, I felt like I was looking into someone else's photo album. Staring into someone else's life. Those pictures weren't of the Chris who saw his friends turn into ravens. That smiling boy by the Christmas tree with his family wasn't the same one who was killed and reborn. Those were a different life. A normal life. It wasn't mine.

On their own accord, my eyes shifted to my desk. To the only photo of my sister. Just her. Posed for a school portrait, smiling in her blue dress. I could never bring myself to frame a photo of the two of us, even though there were many. It felt like an affront to her memory. I was the reason she was dead.

I tore my eyes away from the photo. I wanted to convince myself what I'd always tried to convince myself—that that was the past, and that it couldn't touch me anymore. I was building a new life. I was honoring my sister's memory by living the best I could.

Only now, I knew that was all a lie. The past *could* reach me here. And it was reaching out with iron claws and blood.

That was a perk of boarding school, though: There was always work to be done. If for nothing more than the distraction, I grabbed my pre-calc work and opened to tonight's equations. Then I pulled my phone from my pocket and did what I'd been wanting to do all night. I texted Kaira.

Are you okay?

The words seemed so damned trite that I wanted to vomit, but I couldn't write anything else. Not if Elisa might answer. Or if someone was watching my line or whatever the cops did when you're a suspect. Because I was definitely a suspect.

Minutes ticked by. Mike shifted in his seat, then hocked a loogie and spit it into his mug. I stared at the equations and stared at the dark phone screen. Neither changed. There was no way to focus on my homework, not when my brain was preoccupied with birds and blood and Kaira's plea for help. I couldn't just sit there and wait, even if Ethan said she was safe in her room.

I couldn't let myself believe I'd imagined everything. Worse, I couldn't sit here if she was actually in trouble.

"Screw it," I muttered. I grabbed the room phone and dialed Kaira's extension.

Two rings.

"Hello?" Elisa asked in a whisper.

"Elisa," I said. I kept my voice down, but I knew Mike wasn't listening in. "Hi. It's me. Chris."

"Hey, what's up?"

"Is Kaira there?"

"Yeah. She's asleep."

I let out a breath I didn't know I was holding. Not that I thought Ethan was lying . . . I just couldn't believe anything until I knew it for myself.

"Did you need something?" she asked.

I glanced to Mike. Still occupied. But I lowered my voice anyway.

"Is she okay? I mean, did she act strange or something?"

"What do you mean?"

Thinking fast wasn't my forte. Even less so on the phone.

"I just . . . with everything going on. I know she and Jonathan were close."

"Honestly, I don't think she knows," Elisa whispered. Sadly, like she was trying to protect a small child. "She was asleep when I got in."

"When was that?"

A pause. Elisa had been in the car with us when Kaira had said she'd skip out on the movie because she had a meeting with

Jonathan. I knew Elisa was doing the mental math—had Kaira been in the room when Jonathan had died? Or after? And what was the polite way of finding out?

"I don't know. A few hours ago. She was here when I got back."

"You came right back to the room?" It was difficult to keep the panic out of my voice.

"No. Chris, what's going on?"

Elisa was the one who suspected our friends were being murdered. When the rest of us were content to hope it was all coincidence, her suspicion was raised. So trying to pull this over on her right now was feeling impossible.

"Can you just . . . Please answer the question. When did you get back to the room?"

She sighed. "I don't know. I hung out with Cassie for a bit once I got back. Wandered around. Grabbed frozen yogurt and talked. Then I came back. Some time after seven, I guess."

In theory, that would check out. It meant Kaira would still have had time to be in the classroom with Jonathan and the circle and me. Then she . . . what? Flew back to her room? It didn't make sense. How had she ended up there, when something darker had taken hold? But I would figure that out later. At least the timing worked out. At least that helped assuage the fear that I was losing my mind. Kaira had been there. Or could have been there. Right now, that had to be enough.

"Can I talk to her?"

"She's asleep."

"Please. It's important."

Another big sigh. "Fine. But don't mention anything about Jonathan. She's actually sleeping soundly right now. I don't want her having any more nightmares."

Nightmares?

Not a question to ask Elisa. And really, what were nightmares in comparison to what I'd seen tonight?

There was a rustle of movement, and then I heard Elisa trying to wake Kaira. "Kaira. Hey, sorry. It's Chris."

"Chris?" I heard Kaira ask. Then another rustle as she took the phone.

"Chris?" she asked again, her voice laced with grogginess. My heart leaped into my throat. With relief? Or fear of what she might say next?

"Hey, it's me." Another glance to Mike, who was still studiously ignoring me. "Are you okay?"

"I was sleeping." She sounded confused, her voice coming out slowly. My thoughts were spinning. *No, no. You have to remember. You can't leave me alone in this.*

"I know you were," I said, trying to keep the panic from my voice, trying not to ask a leading question. "But, I mean. Earlier. Are you okay?"

God, it was impossible to try to talk like this, knowing we were both being listened in on. It would be so much easier if this were just normal life and we could meet outside or drive around the block or something. Not that anything about this night was normal.

"Earlier?" she asked. Again, that somersault in my chest. She sounded confused. Not conspiratorial.

"Yeah. Earlier. You know. When I last saw you."

She mumbled something I couldn't catch.

"What was that?" I asked.

When she spoke again, her voice was different. Flatter. Colder.

"I'm tired, Chris. So tired. Tomorrow."

Then she hung up.

I sat there, the phone pressed to my ear while the dial tone drowned out the noises in my head. Because I think I understood what she muttered. The barest hint of a word. A breath of a plea.

Help.

CHAPTER THREE

I didn't want sleep to come.

I wanted to leap out the window, rush over to Kaira's dorm. I wanted to keep calling her, to force her awake, to make her stay with me on the phone until the sun came up. But I couldn't do any of those things, and every second that dragged by raised my anxiety another notch. Kaira needed me. She *needed* me. And that meant I wasn't going crazy. It meant I *had* seen something. It meant that even if I was a suspect, I wasn't the cause, and that was enough to make me feel less insane. Kaira had been there. Kaira had turned into ravens.

Kaira had proven that the impossible had happened. But now I could do nothing about any of it but wait.

If I leaped from the window, Mike would call security. If I snuck out while he was asleep, I'd no doubt run across a guard before I made it to Kaira's dorm. If I called her cell, she would ignore it. If I called her room phone, Elisa would answer. And if I did make it to her room, if I did get her on the phone, Elisa would ask questions. Elisa would suspect the worst. And whatever little facade we had of normal, whatever chance I had at helping Kaira through, would fly out the window the moment I was caught.

I sprawled out on the bed, facing the lines of light scratched across the ceiling, waiting for Mike's nightly routine to finish. It annoyed the shit out of me, and tonight I focused on it with every brain cell I had. Because I couldn't let myself think. I couldn't let myself wonder what was going on with Kaira, what sort of battle she was losing. *Something* was trying to steal her away from me. And if it was anything like the falcon that had haunted me since my sister's death, it wasn't something that *should* be allowed control.

After tonight, though, I didn't think Kaira had a choice in that. We'd both been living on borrowed time—something the voice inside reminded me of quite often—and now, it seemed, we were being hit up for payback. I wasn't going to give in. I wasn't going to let Kaira give in. But here I was, stuck in my room, with absolutely zero way of helping her.

I listened to Mike gargle and cough in the bathroom, before hocking yet another loogie and rinsing it down the sink. Then he came back in, in his rumpled boxers and ratty T-shirt I don't think he'd ever washed, and slid into bed without saying a word.

I clutched the sheets and listened to Mike's breathing slow and then catch as his snoring commenced. Light suddenly danced across the ceiling. At first I thought it was just snow falling against the lights outside. Then the stain of light shifted, and when I blinked, what were once streaks were wings. Another blink, and the glowing falcon stretched its wings out, burned against the ceiling.

Feathers peeled from the light as bit by bit the bird coalesced, then dripped down from the ceiling like a gleaming wraith. Every nerve in my body said, *Flee*. Or hide. I bit back the impulse to pull the sheets over my head. Like I had as a kid.

I'd been running from him since my sister had died. I'd learned how to ignore him. How to trick myself into thinking it was stress or delusions. If I tried hard enough, I could make him go away. I could make him be nothing more than an overactive imagination.

I wasn't going to run from him. Not tonight. Not anymore.

The bird didn't move like a normal falcon. It clung batlike from the ceiling, its neck craning around so a single golden eye locked on me. My skin wanted to crawl from my bones. I wanted to hide under the covers, to scream and turn the lights on and make it go away. Because that golden eye wasn't warm. It was penetrating and cold. It was the darkest part of the sun, the center of a black hole. And it had no care for human life.

"What are you?" I whispered. Mike snorted from his bed and curled over, still sound asleep.

You know what I am, the falcon spoke back, its voice reverberating in my head. It sounded masculine, and old, but I couldn't be certain—it also sounded like cut brass, like thawing ice. *You have always known. I am the one who guards your soul.*

"What do you want?"

You know that, too. I am here to take back what was once given.

"Then kill me," I whispered. Would Mike see this if he woke up? Or would he just see me talking to the ceiling? My parents had never seen it, not when I'd called out and pointed to the creature waiting in the branches, perching on the porch light. They had never seen, and I had stopped trying to make them.

The bird laughed. How can a bird laugh?

Why would I kill you? When I have done so much to protect you. You are needed, Endbringer.

I shuddered at the name; my thoughts immediately dripped with blood, his previous words ringing through my head: *Her blood is yours to spill, her blood is yours to spill.*

"Why now? What do you need me for?" But I knew. Just as I knew I was never truly alone.

Your counterpart among the Vanir has risen. The field is nearly ready for battle. It is time, Endbringer. Time to kneel before your destiny. Time to destroy the one who desires to end you. The one who wears the skin of Kaira . . .

"I won't hurt her!" I blurted out. Mike coughed and mumbled something. The bird didn't move.

But you already have, the bird said. Even with its cold, unmoving stare, I could taste the smile in his words. *You have already weakened the Shadechild. She feels for you. Desires you. She would never raise a hand against you. And that is how we have already won. That is why we chose you for this task. You have stolen her heart. Stealing her life will be simple.*

It was lying. It had to be. I hadn't stolen Kaira's heart. I barely knew her. If anything, *she* had stolen *mine.*

You were created for this, the falcon reminded me. *You were born for this. It is why I have kept you safe. It is why I have let you live.*

I shook my head. I wasn't born for anything. Especially not this. My sister hadn't died so I could *kill.*

Ask your parents, the falcon whispered. *Ask them about your birth. Two times have I saved your life. Two times am I owed your debt. And I will take it. You cannot shut me out forever. Not now, when the barriers grow thin. The battle nears. And you, my avatar. You will fight to the death.*

My heart raced and I flung back the sheets, ready to throw something at the bird to get it to shut up. But when I looked up again, it wasn't there. Just the light streaked through the darkness. Just the echo in my head, the one whispering that I was going insane.

It wasn't loud enough to drown out the falcon's laughter.

It was two when I finally decided I couldn't take it anymore. The night had stretched on and the falcon had grown silent and all that was left was the irregular cadence of Mike's snoring. I wanted to claw my skin off. I wanted to run.

I had to see Kaira.

I knew it was stupid. I knew I'd get caught. But I was going to go insane if I stayed in here.

More insane than I already was.

Before I could convince myself to stay inside, I slid from the bed and slipped on my clothes and coat. Then, boots in one hand, I tiptoed to the window and carefully propped it open. Cold air flooded in. I slid into my boots as fast as possible. Mike snorted and turned over, but otherwise there was silence. No alarms from my impending escape.

Grateful to be on the bottom floor, I crawled through the window and hopped outside, my landing muffled by the thick blanket of snow. Then, leaving a sock in the frame so it wouldn't close entirely, I slid the window shut.

I stood there and waited for a moment, my ears straining in the silence. For anything. This couldn't be so easy. Someone had to have heard me. Mike had to have woken up. But no—as I crouched there, the night air slowly sinking through my layers, I realized this *would* be that easy. I almost laughed. We spent the entire year playing by the rules, or finding our way around them. Turned out the greatest rule of all—mandatory sign-in—was just another joke.

Your time is ticking, I thought. The humor stilled in a heartbeat.

Kaira's dorm was a bit separated from mine, and as I snuck across the back of my dorm toward hers, it struck me just how far it actually was. My heart stayed lodged in my throat, and even though my fingers were numb, I was covered in sweat. Every single step felt like walking on a landmine.

The absolute silence of the night made it worse.

Not even my footsteps made a sound.

I made it to Kaira's dorm without anyone noticing. There was a moment, when I neared, that panic flared up again. *What window is hers? How do I even know?* But when I arrived, I realized there was no reason to worry.

Kaira's was the window the ravens were watching.

Where the rest of the campus was barren of birds, the fir tree outside Kaira's window was covered in crows and ravens, great black birds in all sizes. All silent. All staring at the same window. More birds crowded the windowsill, looking in.

44

My blood froze the moment I saw them.

Because, as one, they all turned their beady black gaze to me.

I considered yelling them away. I considered throwing a snowball at Kaira's window. They were just birds. Just birds.

Before I could do either of those things, they cawed.

It wasn't a normal bird sound. It was a scream, guttural and grinding and dragged from the pits of the Underworld. And the moment they cried out, they took flight.

I didn't have time to think. My body kicked into survival mode and ran.

I stumbled forward, lurching through the snow that sucked at my feet like quicksand. Birds flew past me, black shadows laced with razors, their caws endless—the screams of the damned. They slashed at my coat, left gouges in my skin. They clawed my closed eyes, pecked at my lips. I couldn't even cry out as they swarmed me, as the world turned black with their fury, as the snow bled red.

So much of my blood. So much warmth.

Light flashed. Brilliant and golden. The ravens' screams became pained as they fled, disappearing back into shadows, dissolving to night.

And there, in the snow, was a figure I'd only seen in nightmares.

He was roughly my age, glowing gold as the sun and clothed only in the falcon perched on his shoulder. Three pairs of wings spread behind him like a scarab, and a halo of daggers crowned him. The snow around him glimmered gold. Despite the brilliance, I didn't need to squint.

45

"You will not die here," the figure said. "Not when you desire to save the one you're meant to kill."

I cowered back. He was familiar, even though his voice was not. Familiar like a shadow. And that made him worse than the ravens. Worse than the threat of being caught.

He'd already caught me.

"I—" I began.

"Will bend to my will," he said. His voice was cinders and snapping sap, a harsh contrast to the falcon's simmering tones. He stepped forward. His bare feet hissed in the snow. "Your time is coming, Endbringer. The time to fight. To use your gifts. You will not squander them here."

"Who are you?" I asked. Because I knew him. Knew him like the blood in my veins. But I'd never heard his voice. Never heard his name.

"I am your other half," he said. "Your god. Your rider. And you, my vessel. You may call me Heru."

He reached out then and grazed my bloodied cheek with his hand. It burned like hell, but my body curled into his touch. Like it knew its master.

"Together, we will destroy the Vanir and nourish the Tree. But first, you must give me what I desire."

"What do you want?" I asked. My voice was so breathy. I wanted this. Wanted him. So badly.

"You. Give yourself to me, and we will make the world weep."

My pulse was fire. My skin burned. And it felt like Heaven, like sex, like every thread of me was pulling toward this presence, this light. This god.

I closed my eyes and leaned into his hand, into the touch that promised infinity.

And there, in the darkness of my mind, I saw her. Kaira. Surrounded by ravens. Her hand outstretched as she called my name.

"Her life is yours," Heru whispered, his words vibrating in my bones. "Give yourself to me. We shall kill her together. And in that victory, we both will reign eternal."

I jerked back. His spell shattered.

"No," I said. "I'll never hurt her."

He just smiled. Like he knew better. Like he knew I was destined to give in.

"We shall see," he said. "I can be very . . . persuasive."

He stood and stepped back.

"When the war comes, you will be my steed. You have no choice in this, Endbringer. You owe us your life. And the gods always take their dues."

There was another flash, a swirl of golden feathers and blades, and when I blinked again, he was gone.

He was gone, and so was I. Back in my room, back under my covers, back in my pajamas.

I bolted from the bed and looked outside. No footprints in the snow. No birds in the trees. No cuts on my body.

I stared at my arms in the pale light.

I was going insane. I was literally going insane.

But when I turned toward my bed, my heart as fierce in my chest as the thoughts in my head, my doubt dropped away.

There on my pillow was a single golden feather.

"He will take you," Mike muttered behind me. I jerked to

look at him. His eyes were closed, his head pressed into the pillow. He snored.

I shook my head, even though he wasn't watching. Even though he was fast asleep.

"I'll never hurt her," I whispered.

It was the only thing I knew to be true.

So why the hell did it feel like a lie?

CHAPTER FOUR

Morning came with a gasp at the sound of my alarm. I hadn't thought I would sleep, not after what had happened, but apparently I had. And whatever I'd been dreaming, it clearly hadn't been good. My sheets were knotted around my legs and my pillows were on the floor and my bed was matted with cold sweat. I was suddenly grateful I couldn't remember my dreams.

I turned off my alarm and closed my eyes, trying to get my heart to slow down as I tried to retrace my dream. No, I could remember something. Something about water. Water and darkness and my sister, screaming. Being pulled down into the depths by something. Something with my face . . .

"We're having an assembly."

Mike's words pulled me from my thoughts with a shiver. I couldn't tell if he sounded different from what he'd uttered last night.

"When?" I grumbled.

"Nine," he replied. "After breakfast. About that guy who died."

"Oh." Like there would have been any other reason.

And then he left, banging the door behind him.

I turned my bleary eyes back to the shadow-streaked ceiling. I didn't want to move. I didn't want to think about what was waiting on the other side of that door. Another assembly. Another life lost. Another attempt at moving forward when I knew there was no such thing. There had already been rumors the school would shut down. Jonathan's death would cement it.

I thought of the last time we'd had an assembly, when Kaira had convinced Ethan to take us off campus for sushi. When she'd run to the bathroom in a panic. Had she seen something then? Had she known what was coming for her, what the coming days would spell?

Then another thought triggered, one that vainly tried to pierce the heaviness of my mind. She would be at breakfast. We could talk after eating, before the assembly. I could figure out what the hell was going on. We would figure this out. Together.

Suddenly heartened, I slid out of bed and changed into clean clothes, skipping a shower because I hated showering in the morning and I didn't want to risk missing Kaira at breakfast. It was already eight. Breakfast had been going for thirty minutes. She was probably already there. I glanced in the mirror on the way out—I didn't look nearly as put together as I would have liked, but it would have to do. Jeans and a Henley and a bad case of five-o'clock scruff that made my sideburns and goatee look more like a beard. That wasn't what made me stare, though. My eyes were different. A bags-under-my-eyes sort of thing, yes. But that couldn't be what was making my irises look so much . . .

lighter. *It's just stress*, I thought, as though that could be any sort of explanation.

Before I could freak myself out, I stepped out the door and jogged down the hall toward the lobby.

Islington was always subdued in the mornings. The kids here didn't seem to function until after breakfast, or at least until after their first coffee, and I wasn't much different. But today felt off. Emptier. The few students walking to the cafeteria had their heads down, their conversations muted. It wasn't until I'd trudged down the front steps and gotten halfway to the cafeteria that I realized why it felt like a funeral.

The birds were still missing. The sky was heavy and gray and empty—no black shadows swirling or cawing or fighting. It was one flat silver mirror, and the dullness of it reflected on the world below. No ravens in the trees. No crows on the power lines or perched on the eaves of the buildings. Their absence was like a presence in itself. Save for the kids, nothing moved. Nothing was alive. Everything seemed caught in a pallid photograph.

Which was why I nearly yelped when something moved atop the cafeteria roof. I'd thought it was just a mound of dirty snow. Then it twitched, and golden eyes blinked. Maybe it was my imagination, but I swear the owl watched me the entire way to the front door. Even when the door closed behind me, I could still feel its gaze.

At least it wasn't the falcon. *He* had been strangely silent this morning. Normally, this was the ideal time for him to try to sneak into my thoughts. When my guard was down. When coffee hadn't helped me build the necessary walls.

The scent of coffee and burnt eggs wafted through the room, somehow comforting in the wake of everything else. This was a normalcy I could embrace. I paused by the door and looked around the room. Most of the round tables were occupied. There was noise and movement and occasionally laughter. The vibrancy was jarring after the silence outside. It seemed like an affront, almost. Like Jonathan's life wasn't worth mourning.

Or maybe we were all just too scraped out to feel anything.

I made my way through the food line, skipping the eggs for some pancakes and a banana and coffee. I had to play it cool, even if every nerve of me wanted to run over to the table and drag Kaira away to talk. That wouldn't work. Couldn't work.

Especially because a small voice inside me kept saying that I was the only one who'd seen anything strange last night. Kaira's quiet plea for help on the phone had just been in my imagination. Like everything else. There was another fear, too: that Ethan had changed his mind and turned me in, that he—always on the side of "justice" or whatever—had decided I wasn't safe. At any moment, I expected a faculty member to pull me aside. Tell me that I was a suspect, because I'd been in the room with Jonathan last. I was seen on a security camera, or some shred of my DNA had been found on his body.

That was when I heard the falcon's voice. And for once in my life, it was soothing.

Fear not, Endbringer. Your fate is not tied to the man's.

I didn't want to admit that his words were comforting.

I shook the thoughts away and focused on the room. But

something was off. My classmates weren't just talking and mingling. They were yelling.

Someone jumped from her chair to my right, punching the girl beside her before she got to her feet. Another group erupted in front of me, the whole round table flipped on its head, food and coffee flying everywhere. My eyes went wide as the fighting grew. A dancer boy in front of me was tossed onto his back, the leg of a chair immediately pressed to his neck as his breathing turned to a wheeze. A painter beside me stabbed her friend's hand with a fork, the tines piercing into the table below. I blinked, tried to force away the violence, but when I opened my eyes, it was still there. It was worse. Blood was dripping from the tables now, gushing around my feet, and above us, falcons dripped from the ceiling like curses.

Vomit rose in the back of my throat. I stepped back, about to drop my tray.

"Hey!" someone yelped. I turned. And there was Tamora, wearing a fur coat and big sunglasses on her head and completely distanced from the violence. I looked back to the cafeteria. To the normal, bustling cafeteria. "Jumpy today," she said, giving me a look that was a little too piercing for my liking. *Does she suspect something . . . ?*

I just apologized and started walking toward where we normally sat. I kept my eyes down. I didn't want a relapse.

Then I looked up upon reaching our usual round table, and my heart dropped. Everyone was there. Everyone except Kaira.

Ethan sat beside his boyfriend, Oliver, and Elisa sat a few chairs from him beside her friend—and Jane's roommate—Cassie. The space between was obviously meant for Kaira. I bit

53

down my disappointment and sat down beside Ethan. Whatever they were talking about died the moment I sat. Ethan gave me a look. Clearly they were talking about Jonathan's death.

"Morning," I said, nodding to the group. Inside, I was screaming at myself. I needed to talk to Kaira. I couldn't waste any more time here, pretending things were normal. She needed me. I needed her. I had to go. I had to go. Then I looked at Ethan, and he looked at me like he knew what I was thinking and was strongly suggesting I shouldn't.

They all gave their cordial replies, but it was Ethan who leaned over and looked me in the eyes.

"You doing okay?" he asked. "Looks like you haven't slept."

"Insomnia," I replied. Which was true enough.

He gave me another knowing look, so I switched my attention to my food.

"I'm not crazy," Cassie muttered, clearly picking up where she'd left off before I'd sat down.

"No one said you were," Elisa replied. "But it's just maybe not something to talk about."

"Like you aren't all wondering if this is some sort of conspiracy." It was more an accusation than a question, and Cassie looked at each of us in turn. I focused on my coffee. "Think about it. Two girls kill themselves and then Jonathan bites it. That looks pretty damn suspicious to me. What if he slept with them, and they, like, couldn't stand it, so they offed themselves? And then he felt guilty and did the same."

Ethan's jaw actually dropped, and Elisa stared at Cassie like the girl had sprouted a second head.

54

"I can't believe you just said that," Elisa whispered. "Jane was my friend."

"And *my* roommate," Cassie countered. She looked around, seeking support. She didn't find any. "I knew her better than anyone else. Not to be a bitch, but it's true. It doesn't make sense, but it sure as hell makes more sense than what they've fed us."

"Which was?" Oliver asked, cool and collected as ever.

"Stress. That Jane killed herself due to stress. She wasn't *stressed*. She was doing great. Hell, she'd already been accepted to her top choice. What did she have to be stressed about?"

"Was she acting strange before she died?" Ethan asked. I noticed he didn't say *killed herself* since, like me, he knew that wasn't what happened.

Cassie shook her head. "No. But that doesn't mean something didn't happen between them."

"I think you're grasping for logic in a situation that has none." Oliver's words were deep and resonant. His hand clutched Ethan's atop the table, his long fingers locked tight. "No one can know what someone is thinking, let alone why they'd take their own life. Speculation isn't helping. It just creates more harmful rumors."

Cassie didn't exactly glare at him, but her look was a mix of hurt and angry.

"It could add up. You just don't want it to," she said, and then stood and left without another word.

When Cassie was out of earshot, Elisa leaned in on her elbows. "She's not the only one thinking that," she said. "I heard some other girls on the way in. They think Jonathan got the girls pregnant, and then guilt got the better of him."

I thought of the circle on the floor, of the kids fleeing the room. I still had no idea what had gone on in there. No clue what Jonathan had been doing, or if it had been the same situation with Mandy and Jane. Maybe there was a hint of truth to it. The circle and what I'd seen looked ritualistic. Maybe he *had* been playing a darker part—maybe he'd been forcing the girls into something all along, making their deaths look like suicide. I wouldn't rule out the pregnancy thing—wasn't that always how it worked in those cults? Sleep with the leader to gain enlightenment? But I couldn't see Mandy or Jane falling for that. Not at all.

Which meant I needed to find the kids who were involved. Force Erik and Tina to talk. They'd tell me. After last night, they would have had to know that something was up.

"Speculation's not the worst of it," Oliver muttered, staring into his coffee mug.

"What do you mean?" I asked.

"Kids are already getting pulled from school."

He glanced around the table at us.

"My mom called this morning," Oliver continued. "Said she'd heard what had happened. I had to convince her not to withdraw me. Told her it was fine and I was safe and not getting caught up in anything. They think it's a cult or something."

"Who left?" I asked. My heart dropped as I glanced behind me, like maybe I'd notice a missing face in the sea of kids.

"I don't really know," he replied.

"Tina left," Elisa whispered. "I saw her on the phone with her mom last night. She was in the lobby and begging them to come get her."

56

One down. How many others from that classroom were running away?

I looked to Ethan.

"Any guys?"

Ethan shrugged, but his face was solemn. He clearly knew what I was getting at. If the kids who were there last night went home, I'd have no other alibis and no clue what was going on inside that room. No idea what they were meddling with. But that also meant there would be fewer people to point fingers at me.

I needed to find Erik before he vanished too.

"Is Kaira okay?" I asked.

Ethan shot me a glance, but Elisa actually grinned a little. Like she thought it was cute. My cheeks flushed; of course, she just thought I was crushing on her roommate.

"She's sick," Elisa said. "Wouldn't budge from bed. So I'm going to bring her some tea and a bagel after breakfast. I could bring her a note as well if you'd like." Her grin widened, and she actually found the humor to wink.

"No, thanks," I said, busying myself with the pancakes. "Just wanted to make sure."

Conversation devolved into the usual, but even the talk of classes and homework and recitals felt forced. Maybe it was just me projecting. But everyone seemed stilted, like they couldn't figure out how to make something that should have been routine seem normal. My eyes kept darting around the cafeteria, waiting for someone to point a finger. Waiting for Kaira to show up. Waiting to see a raven or crow or falcon outside the window.

57

By nine, none of those things had happened, and the two mugs of coffee I'd downed had done nothing to clear my head or rid the sluggish dread from my veins. I wanted so badly to run to Kaira's dorm and force her awake. But I would never get past the front desk. And without Elisa up there to answer the phone for Kaira, she was as good as on another planet.

When we stood up to leave for the assembly, I stayed back and put a hand on Elisa's shoulder. Ethan cast me another look, clearly warning, but Oliver ushered them both away before Ethan could tell me to keep my mouth shut.

"Are you okay?" Elisa whispered. She looked me in the eyes when she said it. There was no option of lying; she could read me like a book. It wasn't fair that actors got to learn all about body cues.

"Not really," I replied. "This whole thing . . ." I sighed, tried to hold eye contact like I normally would, because it was a sign of respect. I couldn't meet her gaze. Not now. "It's all really fucked up. I had nightmares all night."

Her eyes tightened.

"I think we've all had enough nightmares for one lifetime," she whispered. "It doesn't help when your waking life's no better."

I nodded.

"You like her, don't you?" she asked. The words cut through my daze.

"Yeah," I said. It didn't make sense; I barely knew her. But I couldn't stop thinking about her. My pulse raced every time I watched her tuck a strand of hair behind her ear while painting, or when she laughed at one of Ethan's jokes. She was a strange mix of nonchalant and poised, like she tried so hard to perfect one image of herself, she didn't notice all the stray threads poking out. And those were what ensnared me.

"I say this as her best friend," Elisa said. "She doesn't need any more pain in her life, okay? She's dealt with enough. So you better examine every one of your intentions and make sure they're pure. Because I swear, if you so much as make her sniffle, I will end you."

There was a fierceness in her voice that actually made me lean back.

My immediate reaction was to say no, of course I wasn't going to hurt her. There was a bond between Kaira and me that I couldn't understand, one that laced deeper than attraction or lust or affection. We were bound by something stronger than fate. We were bound by tragedy. By death. I couldn't inflict any worse pain on her than that.

I opened my mouth to say that she was fine, that I would never hurt her, when another thought gripped me by the throat.

You will kill her, Endbringer. Your promises are naught but lies.

Elisa's eyebrow raised as I clearly struggled with myself.

"This is the point where you say you'd never hurt her," she offered.

"I wouldn't," I choked. Why did it sound like a question?

"Right." She looked me up and down. "Convincing. Why did you want to talk to me again?"

"I just . . . I wanted to make sure she was okay."

"I told you, she's just sleeping. She's been stressed and overworked—she deserves a day to rest."

I glanced around. There was no way to say this without sounding crazy or creepy.

"Could you just . . . could you make sure? I'm worried about her. She said some things to me yesterday."

Instantly Elisa's gaze became sharper than a hawk.

"What things? When?"

Begging me to help her as ravens broke from her flesh.

"Nothing specific. I saw her after we got back from dinner. She said she was scared. Because of, you know. Everything. Then she ran off and didn't answer my texts. I'm worried."

She nodded. We both knew it wasn't enough of an explanation. Right now, though, with everything going on, it would work.

"I'll double-check," she said.

"And tell her to call me. Please. I really need to talk to her."

Elisa grinned a little.

"You're cute, you know that?"

"I—"

"Which is good, because you're also kind of stupid. You could just hang out with me during open room, you know. Kaira would just *happen* to be there, but we could be doing homework or something together."

The idea hadn't even occurred to me. It felt like a lifeboat.

"You'd do that? For me?"

She shrugged.

"I'm just inviting you to my bedroom. You're not the first cute guy to get the offer."

Despite everything, I actually laughed.

"Thanks," I said.

For the first time in the last twenty-four hours, it felt like I was getting a break. I just had to make it to the end of the day.

Despite the casual air of the cafeteria, the theater we crowded into was as somber as a funeral. Our president, Ms. Kenton, took to the stage in all black, and the room went from quiet to deathly in moments. It was eerie, watching her stand there amid the chains and swathes of tattered fabric from the Marat/Sade set. Like she was the ghost of actions past. Here to remind us that we couldn't run away forever.

She stood there in silence for a few moments. I couldn't tell if she was gathering her words or pausing for dramatic effect; no one spoke, and she had our full attention. Elisa sat at my side, her hands clutched tight in her lap. Cassie sat to her other side. Ethan and Oliver were somewhere else in the crowd.

"You all know why we are here," Ms. Kenton finally said. She surveyed the room, and for a moment it almost felt like an accusation. "We are here because last night we lost another member of our family. Mr. Jonathan Almblad, beloved teacher of folklore and myth, has passed away."

She began pacing back and forth. The fabric hanging around her swayed like a ghost.

"I have already begun hearing the tales and rumors of his death. And in a school this small, such rumors can be devastating. We are not here to aggrandize death; we know the pressures facing you are real, and we have made every effort to ease them, and for you to take comfort in our care. We know there is speculation that Mr. Almblad's death is linked to the passing of your classmates. Let me be the first to say that we have found no connection between these deaths. And, in the manner of full disclosure, it has been relayed to us that Mr. Almblad died of a heart attack in his office."

My heart shot to my throat.

She was lying.

I tried seeking out Ethan in the crowd, but I couldn't see him in the shadows. Elisa caught my glance, her lips poised in a question, and I brought my attention back to Ms. Kenton.

"That is what I have been told to tell you." She stopped walking. "But that is not the truth, and you know it. There is a murderer within the walls of this school. And we know who he is."

Her eyes locked on me.

"Christopher Wright," she called, her words ringing out like executioner's blows. "We know you were there when Jonathan died. We know you had a hand in his murder. And for that, you face death. Grab him."

Hands clamped on my wrists. Elisa stared at me, her nails digging into my forearm, and a dancer boy I didn't know restrained my other wrist. Someone behind me clamped their hands on my shoulders. My heart hammered in my chest as their nails dug into my skin. This couldn't be real. This couldn't be real. This couldn't be—

"You were born in bloodshed," Ms. Kenton said. She walked toward me, stepping over the heads of the kids in front of me, her legs stretching as she ascended the rows of seats. In her hand, she gripped an ornate dagger. "And you will end in bloodshed."

"No, please," I begged. More hands clamped over my lips. My throat. Lifted my chin, exposing my neck.

Ms. Kenton's face loomed over me, her head silhouetted in the spotlights like a halo. But it was her eyes that glowed the brightest. Golden. Hawklike.

"Blood is your power, Endbringer. Your curse and your gift. We will make the world run gold with blood."

She pressed the tip of the dagger to my throat. Metal bit into flesh. I tried to squirm, to break free. *This isn't real. This can't be real. I'm hallucinating.*

"How sure of that are you, Endbringer?" she whispered, her voice hot in my ear. "When reality is yours to bend."

I didn't close my eyes. Couldn't. I saw her smile as she slid the blade into my throat, sliced through my trachea, cut off my breath and blood. I felt warmth spill down my neck, spread over my chest. But I didn't die. Didn't feel the pain. I couldn't breathe around the blade. And I couldn't die with the falcon in my blood.

"The world is yours," she said. "Make it weep." Then she jerked the blade to the side, ripped apart my flesh.

I twitched, flung back.

She was gone. Only Elisa's hand remained on my arm, and when I looked over, my breath ragged, she was staring at me. Her eyes were wide with confusion. Sweat dripped down my skin, and my pulse was a chaotic, fluttering thing.

Ms. Kenton was still on the stage, still pacing back and forth, talking about community. She wasn't staring at me like she knew a deadly secret. No one but Elisa was looking. I hadn't called out.

I hadn't yelled. Sweat continued to drip down my skin. What the *fuck* was happening to me?

"I'm afraid," Ms. Kenton continued, "in light of recent events, that we are unable to cancel the school day. I wish I could give you the time needed to mourn, but we simply have no more time to spare. We are canceling the morning classes, but your schedules will have to resume after lunch. Those of you who had Jonathan as an adviser are asked to visit the counselor's office today to be reassigned. Jonathan's classes will continue with a substitute: our dear English professor, Mrs. Walsh, will be taking over."

She sighed. I kept waiting for her to shift, for her sad demeanor to twist into something malevolent. I kept waiting for her to attack, for the rafters to drip blood. *What the hell is going on with me?* I thought.

"Death is a terrible force, dear students. Do not for one moment believe that our continuation of classes is meant to be a disservice. Jonathan will be greatly missed. We will hold a vigil tonight for those interested in paying their last respects. Please remember that we are here for you when you need us. At any time."

There were a few closing remarks, but I couldn't pay attention. Not through the fear that this was all an illusion. Not through the terror that coursed through me: I was going insane. I was going insane. And there was no way to tell if what I'd heard was truth. I was too busy trying to sort out the facts from my hallucination. I knew that Ms. Kenton was lying: Jonathan hadn't died in his office like she had said. He had died in a classroom in a circle of ink, just like the two girls. Maybe it had been a heart attack, but the location was still off. That meant she was covering something. She knew what was going on. Or she was afraid of us knowing. *Unless that was a hallucination as well . . .*

When the assembly was finally over, I booked it from the hall and out into the cold morning air. I gulped it down. I paced back and forth in front of the theater, telling myself it would all be okay. I would talk to Kaira, and it would all be okay.

Ethan wandered away from Oliver a few moments later, his hands sunk deep into the pockets of his pea coat, a guarded look on his face.

"Why did she lie?" I asked Ethan the moment he was near. I had to focus on that; otherwise I'd start wondering what was wrong with my brain.

"Shut up," he whispered. He glanced around, but no one was paying us any attention. The few kids who lingered outside were in small groups, talking or heading out to wherever. The morning was free, and only Ethan and I knew something was amiss. At least beyond the obvious.

Ethan started walking away from the main campus, toward the lake. I followed at his side. When we were safely out of earshot, he started speaking.

"I don't know what's going on anymore."

His words were flat. It was an understatement and we both knew it, but hearing him say it gave me a spark of hope.

"What do you mean?" I asked.

Ethan seemed to consider my question for a moment. Like he didn't fully understand what he meant himself. "I mean yes, she was lying. Maybe not about the heart attack, but definitely about him being in the office. But what does that tell you?"

"That she's covering something up."

"Maybe. It also means no one came forward. If any of those students you saw fleeing reported something, she's keeping it under wraps."

"Or they didn't say anything at all."

"Either way, you might be in the clear. If they reported you, you'd already be in for questioning. And I doubt they'd wait to speak up."

I couldn't imagine I would be that lucky.

"It also means . . ." He sighed.

"What?"

"It also means I trust you."

I stopped walking.

"Why? What changed your mind?"

He shrugged and looked into the woods. The trees were stark and empty, snow lying thick and undisturbed on the ground. I wanted to say it looked beautiful. Instead, it just felt cold and barren.

When he finally answered, his words seemed to get eaten up by the emptiness.

"If they had said the truth in the assembly, that Jonathan died exactly like the others, I might think you had something to do with it. But they're hiding the truth." He shook his head like he was trying to ignore his own thoughts. "I don't know what's real anymore, Chris. Jonathan died just like the others: no marks, no note, no reason. I don't think that's something you could pull off. Whatever this is, it's—"

"Supernatural."

He glared at me. "I was going to say 'unnatural,' but yeah. I guess that works too. Something is wrong. Maybe they're keeping things a secret because they're covering it up or because they don't honestly have a clue. In any case, I don't think you killed him. Or the others. And I also believe you about Kaira."

My heart skipped over.

"What? You believe me?"

"Not about all of it," he muttered. "But something's going on. She didn't respond to my texts. At all. And when I went by her dorm to get her for breakfast, she flat out refused to see me."

"And that makes you suspicious?"

Me telling him about Kaira being taken over by ravens didn't ring an alarm, but her not responding to texts did? Even though I was mildly hopeful, it also felt a bit like betrayal. He would always believe her over me. *And that's why you need to get her to tell him what happened.*

"Kaira isn't like that. She doesn't just push people out. I've nursed her back to health before. I've been there for her through . . . everything. Something about this just seems wrong."

"You think she was there last night?"

"Maybe. I don't buy your story. But there's too much here for it to be a coincidence. She was healthy yesterday." He kicked a pile of snow.

"We need to talk to her," I said.

"I know. But I don't think even my charms could get us past the RA."

There was always Elisa. There was always dropping by the

room during open hours. But that wasn't until the evening.

"We could sneak in," I offered.

"In the middle of the day? While classes are out?"

"What else? We have to try, Ethan. I'm going to go insane if I just sit around, wondering if she's okay. Especially because we both know she's not."

"I know, I know . . ."

My gut twisted with a different thought.

"Ethan . . . what if you're right? And this is unnatural? What if she's next?"

He stopped fidgeting and looked at me. His eyes were wide.

"You think she . . ."

"We don't know what the others felt beforehand. But she's acting sick. Distanced. And she was there last night."

"Shit," he whispered. When he turned, he didn't just walk back to campus. He ran.

CHAPTER FIVE

Somehow we both managed to make it to Kaira's dorm without falling on our asses. We gathered ourselves outside the door and walked in slowly. I knew that if we were going to pull this off, we had to act normal. *Ethan* had to act normal. But that didn't mean my pulse wasn't racing, that the urge to run through the dorm and pound on Kaira's dorm wasn't strong. I held back. Kept my hands in my pockets, my face smooth.

I let Ethan do all the talking.

"You know I'm not supposed to let you two up there," Maria said from behind the front desk.

"I know, I know," Ethan told the RA. "And I wouldn't normally ask. But I'm really worried about her. She isn't returning my calls. And she skipped breakfast."

Maria quirked an eyebrow. She was always flawless—perfect makeup, perfect hair. Even today, in all black, she looked like she was auditioning as a fifties pinup.

"Well, let me see if she's up for company."

She picked up the phone and dialed. I exchanged a glance with Ethan. He didn't know why I was so nervous. He hadn't seen all the birds outside her window last night.

He didn't have gods saying he was going to kill her.

I watched Maria's expression intently. She bit her lower lip, and after a few moments hung up the phone.

"She's not answering," she said.

Obviously.

"We should check on her," Ethan ventured.

"No, *I* should," she said. Then she looked us over and gave a little half smile. "Still, I know she'd probably be happier to see you than me. Just don't tell anyone I let you do this. It's probably against protocol."

Ethan nodded gravely and I said nothing as Maria got out from behind the desk and headed toward the stairs.

It took a lot of self-control not to run up the stairs in front of her. My body was electric as we walked down the hall. This was slow, too slow. Kaira needed me. Kaira needed . . . *Kaira probably needs you far away from her, lunatic.*

I pushed down the thoughts when we arrived at Kaira's door. There were a few magazine cutouts, and the floor sparkled with the remnants of glitter still stuck in the carpet. I wasn't focusing on that. I was focusing on the heat of my breath, on the unnatural silence that seemed to creep down the hall like a fog.

Maria knocked out a rhythm and waited. No response. Which meant Elisa wasn't in and Kaira . . . *She's just asleep. She's okay.* I couldn't block out the image from the night before—*had it happened? Had I seen that?*—of a thousand birds crowding her window. Watching. Protecting. Protecting her from me. Or whatever it was that wanted to take control of me.

Another knock, this time followed with, "Kaira, are you in?" in a slightly worried tone.

Still no answer. The blood in my ears pounded.

Maria opened the door.

The shades were drawn, and even though I heard the familiar clicking of the ancient radiator, the room was as cold as ice. Quiet as the woods in the snow. And everywhere I looked, crouching in the shadows like specters, were ravens.

Again, as one, their eyes turned toward us the moment we opened the door. Turned toward me. And in the back of my mind I felt something awaken: a ripple of searing hatred, a growl that curled in my lungs like the scream of a hawk.

But the birds didn't move to attack. They didn't shift from the desks and counters, from Elisa's bed that shined like a beetle's back, every surface glistening and oily and black.

"Kaira?" Maria ventured again. Her voice seemed to echo in the room. Still, the birds didn't move. My skin crawled.

I wanted to warn Maria away. It wasn't safe in here. The birds would attack if we—

Maria walked in, completely oblivious to the birds that sat like sentinels all around Kaira, like the room had grown a second skin. The birds seemed oblivious to her, as well. She pulled back a curtain, letting in a thin billow of gray light. The moment the room lightened, the birds dissolved in billows of smoke.

I shook my head. *Get it together, Chris. Get it together.*

Then I saw Kaira, and all thoughts of the ghostly birds vanished.

71

She was curled up in her bed, the sheets wrapped around her like a cocoon. Her face was half covered by the sheets, but I could see her eyes—dark and shaded, but not with makeup. She looked pallid, like her skull was pressing closer to her skin. Maria made a worried noise in her throat and stepped over to the bedside while Ethan and I hovered a few steps away. My breath returned, but that didn't mean I felt relaxed. She was sick. Beyond sick. And at any moment, I expected the girl to break apart into birds.

Kaira was here. Whole. What did that mean for my story?

"Kaira?" Maria whispered. "Kaira, baby? Are you okay?"

Kaira grumbled. Maria put a hand on Kaira's forehead.

"She's freezing," she whispered. She glanced back to us. "I think we need to take her to the nurse."

Ethan and I exchanged a glance. We needed to talk to Kaira. Which meant we needed Maria out of the room. I wanted to scream in frustration. Kaira was there. *Right there.* And I couldn't ask her what I needed to ask her. I couldn't confirm anything about last night. I didn't care if it was against the rules or something; I stepped over to Kaira's side.

"Kaira," I whispered. "Can you hear me?"

She mumbled and shifted over, her eyes fluttering open for a second. At least her eyes weren't purple.

"Chris?" she whispered. Scared. Like she was calling out for help. Then she groaned and pulled the sheets tighter around her, effectively covering her face.

I reached out to touch her shoulder before I could stop myself.

My vision burst white, then black, and I was standing in the darkness. Standing in a pool of light. Shadows writhed against the perimeter. Shadows that twisted and fluttered with glistening feathers, with claws that slashed, with glassy eyes. Millions of ravens, pressing against the light. Trying to break in. To kill me. To take us.

Kaira was before me. Her dark skin looked bleached out, her limp hair entwined with feathers. Around us, inked into the ground like smeared blood, was a ring. The only thing keeping the birds at bay. The only thing keeping us in.

"Chris," Kaira whispered, her eyes the flat white of terror. *"Don't let her take me."*

And there, behind her, just outside the circle and glowing like a wraith, was the ghost of a girl. Her hair was long and black, her skin porcelain and covered in a cloak of raven feathers. Her eyes were the same violet as Kaira's had been last night.

"Chris!" Kaira flung out a desperate hand, but as I reached back, the vision shattered, pierced by a pain on my shoulder that nearly made me scream out.

I blinked, and I was back in her room. Back at her bedside. With only the lingering pain of the falcon's claws on my shoulder. With only the echo of his promise, that I would be the one to destroy her.

"Come on, boys," Maria said. Her words broke the final bonds of whatever spell I'd been under. Reality snapped back into focus. She took my arm, gently, but clearly not willing to let go. What was that? What did it mean? "We should go. I'll call the nurse."

She started to draw me away. I didn't budge.

73

"Come on, Chris," Ethan said. "She's clearly not in a place to talk."

He wasn't looking at me, though. He couldn't take his eyes off Kaira. It was clear from that expression that he was just as worried as I. And that he knew there was more to this than a cold. Even without the visions, the room didn't feel right. He *had* to feel it. Something terrible was happening, and Kaira was at the center of it all.

Maria guided me away from the bed, toward the door. I didn't want to go with her. I couldn't just let Kaira lie there. But what could I do? Even if I stayed, how could I help? The answer was simple: I couldn't. Whatever this was, it was beyond me. It was beyond any of us.

But that didn't mean I was going to stop trying.

Numb, I let Maria take us back down to the lobby, where she called for the nurse to come and check on Kaira. It was clear Maria was dismissing us, but I didn't want to go. I lingered there, watching her lips move but not actually hearing her speak. All I could think of were the screams of ravens. Their eyes on me as I entered the room, as I tried to spy on Kaira. All I could sense was the taste of my blood as their talons slashed me apart. . . .

"Come on." Ethan nudged me. "We have to find Erik about that sketch."

His words jolted me back to action.

If I found out what Jonathan had been doing, I could figure out how to undo it. I knew it was all connected—the birds, the deaths, the bloody circles, and the nightmares. They'd been playing with something. Forces that even I knew they shouldn't have been. If I wanted to stop them, I needed to figure out what we were dealing with.

I needed to figure out how to destroy the god or hallucination or whatever the fuck it was trying to take over my mind. Otherwise, how could I rescue Kaira from the same thing?

"She's not sick," I said when we were outside. "You know it."

He glanced at me. There was a lot of weight in that expression, but I couldn't figure out which way it was falling.

"I don't know what I believe right now," Ethan said.

He looked away and continued walking toward Erik's dorm. I expected him to say more, but the silence stretched between us. I wasn't going to break it, not if it meant losing his tentative trust. He led us through the lobby and down a hall. He knocked at a door the same as all the rest. Instantly my palms went cold with sweat. What the hell was I supposed to ask? *Hey Erik, what sort of strange ritual did you do last night, because I'm pretty certain it killed Jonathan, and now my friend is acting strange and has a terrible illness.*

A guy I recognized from last semester's poetry class answered the door. Nick. But I wasn't paying him any attention. I was looking behind him.

"Shit," I whispered.

He looked to me, clearly confused.

"Um. Hi?"

"Sorry," Ethan said. But his voice had just as much disappointment as mine. Because half of the room behind Nick was empty. Or, mostly empty—there were spare socks and a few small boxes and a stack of bowls on the empty bed. Like someone had left in a rush. "I take it Erik's not in?" Ethan continued.

Nick shook his head, clearly still wondering what we wanted and why we were both upset over not finding it.

"He left first thing this morning. Said his parents told him to come home." He shrugged. "Can't say I blame him. Shit's fucked up."

I closed my eyes. Tina was already gone. Erik had left. The other students who'd gone home had probably been those involved. *They* had seen something terrible happen in that classroom. *They* knew that there was something out there, something supernatural, worth running from.

If I was smart, I'd have left as well. But there was no way I would leave Kaira's side.

I would save her if it was the last thing I did.

"Did he leave a contact number or anything?" Ethan asked.

This was why I needed Ethan around. His brain worked when mine went into shutdown mode.

"Yeah," Nick said, pulling his phone from his pocket. "I have his cell. What do you need it for? I dunno if he wants me giving it out."

"Class," Ethan said smoothly. "We were going to be doing a project together. Was just dropping by to grab his notes, but if he already left . . . Well, don't want to be adrift."

Nick looked between the two of us. My stomach churned at the way he seemed to study me. Like he knew I was involved in something. Like this was suspicious enough to raise questions.

Stop. Being. Paranoid.

Whatever Nick saw, it wasn't enough to deny Ethan Erik's number. Ethan thanked him and led me away before I could ask

76

any questions. Probably because Ethan could tell I wanted to, and knew it was a horrible idea. We left and made our way to Ethan's room.

The place was warm and cozy in a way mine never was. Glowing fairy lights draped over the photo-laden shelves, and the air smelled like cinnamon and cloves. A harsh contrast to the stark white walls and scent of old socks from living with Mike. Instead, Ethan's room reminded me of the teahouse Kaira had taken me to, T'Chai Nanni. My heart twisted just at the thought of her.

"You want to do the honors?" Ethan asked, flopping down on his bed. He shoved a few throw pillows aside and patted the bed next to him, his cell phone in hand. I sat down but couldn't even pretend to make myself comfortable.

I took the phone and dialed Erik's number.

It rang twice before he answered.

"Who is this?" His voice was gruff. Like he'd been crying. Or running hard.

"Erik?"

"Who is this?" he repeated.

I looked to Ethan, wondering if I should lie. I barely knew Erik. I mean, I'd seen him around, had him in my math class. But we weren't friends.

"Chris. From school."

The phone went dead.

"The hell?" I asked, looking at the phone. "He hung up."

"Try again?"

I was already redialing. It barely even rang when Erik picked up.

"Listen, I don't want to talk," he said. "Leave me the fuck alone."

Then he hung up again.

I dropped the phone onto the bed and leaned back against the pillows.

"He won't talk."

"So he's hiding something," Ethan said.

"Probably."

I closed my eyes and tried to remember anyone else who had been in the room last night. Anyone who could point a finger, or at least tell me I wasn't crazy. The only one I could think of, the only one still on campus, was the one person who was the furthest away. Kaira. She felt like the only person who could save me. Which was ironic, since it was becoming more and more apparent that I needed to save her from myself.

"What do we do now?" I asked, looking over to Ethan.

He shrugged.

"We move forward, I guess. Maybe the worst of it's over."

It isn't, Endbringer. Not for you. That, I can promise you.

I didn't look toward the voice. Toward the wall. Toward the streaks of gold cast by Ethan's lights.

I didn't need to. I could feel the falcon there, his gaze trained on my throat.

You will suffer, he said. *Until you let us in. Until you beg for it to stop. For you, the worst is only just beginning.*

CHAPTER SIX

There was no way in Hell I could pretend the rest of the day would be normal.

Ethan and I spent an hour or so lying on his bed, listening to music and pretending the previous conversations we'd had never had happened. Finally, when he sat up to go finish some photo work and asked how I'd spend my day, I realized that he and I were never going to be on the same page. He thought something strange was happening. I *knew* it. I knew it in the pit of my bones in a way he never would, no matter how hard I tried to convince him. He couldn't see the falcon that lingered in every streak of light. He didn't see the ravens guarding Kaira like a coven of steadfast witches. He didn't feel the clock ticking down with guillotine hands.

His neck wasn't on the chopping block.

Still, he was looking at me like he expected an answer. Needed one. Something to continue to convince him that I wasn't a suspect. Or a threat.

"I think I'm just going to work on my essay before lunch," I lied. I felt terrible, but not because I was lying. I felt terrible because the lie itself was easy.

"Sounds thrilling," he said.

"Russian lit usually is," I replied.

And gods, it felt forced. We both knew it. We both knew this was a dialogue we shouldn't be having, because there were more important things to talk about. The absence of what we should have been saying was like a weight between us, a void that threatened to drag us in. I knew, though, that there was nothing to say. My truths would sound like insanity to him. So I had to keep my mouth shut, and he had to continue to pretend that everything was back to normal—between us, with Kaira, and with the school.

I knew the way he looked at me.

I'd seen it on my parents, after my sister Bri died and I tried—just once—to blame myself for it, to say it was because I had been allowed to live. After, when they refused to talk about it, they would stare at me just as Ethan was now. Like they knew I had a secret, but they would rather pretend I didn't than find out what it was. And they were angry with me for it.

He opened the door and I stepped out into the hall.

It took a few steps for me to realize he wasn't following me. I paused and turned. *What did he forget now?*

Ethan was slumped in the doorway. A handful of pencils jutted from his neck, thin lines of blood dribbling to the floor, his mouth stuffed with paper, a notebook open in one hand. Even from here I could see the black and red circles splashed across the pages.

80

I stumbled forward. His chest was still moving. I could save him. I could . . .

Something caught my foot and I fell. It was another classmate, some guy I had only seen in passing. Or, it was part of him.

I held down the vomit and looked up at Ethan.

The shining god Heru stood in my way.

Even though I knew he was the same height as me, he filled the hallway; his wings spread out to brush the walls, and his halo of daggers circled lazily behind him. Those blue eyes pierced me sharper than the pencils gouged in Ethan's throat.

"Why are you scared, Endbringer?" he asked. "Do you not understand your destiny?"

He smiled, and even that was brilliant. Even that was terrifying.

"What is this?" I asked. I had to move past him. I had to save Ethan. *This can't be real. This can't be real!* "What have you done?"

The guy—the god, the *creature*—knelt in front of me.

"Oh Chris," he said, his voice deceptively soft. "You still believe I am the demon in all this? I didn't give you your name, your title. This isn't my doing. This isn't my will alone. This, all this, is yours."

He gestured with his hand, and my gaze obediently followed. We were no longer in the hall. Instead, a field stretched out around us, a great black tower piercing the clouds in the distance, its base as wide as the horizon. Something about it called to me, like a pulse, like a duty, but that wasn't what made my breath catch in my throat.

It was the bodies.

They scattered across the field like ants, limbs broken, the ground marshy and red. Some carried weapons, but it was clear that not all were warriors. There were children piled against one another, and figures clearly caught while fleeing. My stomach turned at the sight, but I didn't vomit. My hands clutched at the blood-sodden soil. Everything up to my wrists was smeared with red.

"This is what you were born to do," Heru said, at my side. He stood proudly, surveying it all like it was his kingdom. And maybe it was. "Life and death are your playthings, Endbringer. This world is yours, ripe and ready to be plucked. So many offerings to be made. So much power to harvest."

"I wouldn't—" I began, but he interrupted.

"You would," he said. "And you already have."

"Chris?" came a voice.

"No," I sobbed. The pain that struck was harsher than a lance, and it stabbed from the darkest shadow of my heart.

I turned my head.

And there she was. Bri. Standing atop a body. Not just any body.

Kaira.

"No!" I cried out. I forced myself up and ran over, tripping and stepping on bodies whose faces I didn't want to see but did—classmates, teachers, friends. They piled atop one another, a mound of my madness, and at the top was Kaira. The pinnacle of what had happened.

Of what I had done.

"Chris," Bri said. She stared at me sadly, her short dark hair limp and twined with seaweed, her eyes as pale as moons. More kelp tangled around her wrists and ankles. Like chains.

"Bri!" I called out. I couldn't get close enough. Every time I moved, every step I took, the mound grew higher. Every action I made inspired more bodies. More loss.

"It hurts," she cried. Despite the pain in her voice, she didn't move. She was as still as a little porcelain doll. "Chris, it hurts so bad. Help me."

"Bri, I'm—"

"You could save her, you know," Heru said. He stood by my side once more; I didn't spare him a glance. I could see the light.

"I'm trying," I replied.

"No," he said. "You're not. You're just pretending you are."

That made me stop. My heart hammered in my lungs, and there was a desperation in my chest I hadn't felt since Bri had gotten sucked out into the tide. The desperation was heat. A flame.

"How dare you—"

"If you wanted to save her, you would stop running. You would embrace the gifts I am trying to give you."

"This?" I yelled, gesturing to the bodies. "All this death? How is that a gift?"

"Because the more you sacrifice to the Tree," he said, his voice quiet with reverence, "the more the Tree will return. You are the Endbringer. After all that came before has been lost, the world is rich with possibility."

He looked up to the top of the mound. Was it my imagination, or were there tears in his eyes?

"What are you talking about?" I asked.

"You hold more power than you know," he whispered. "It is your birthright. This death and destruction you see—it is not so dark as all that. It is the fire that cleanses and fertilizes new growth. Yours is the gift to start over. To create the world anew. You bring the end. And the end brings a new age. Some do not desire this. Some would change the plans of gods."

A single body rolled down the pile, flopping limply at my feet. I knew without even looking that it was Kaira.

"Kill her," he whispered. "Use the gifts I give you so freely. And then, in the wake of our victory, even the doors to death will be yours to open and shut." He leaned in, his lips brushing my ear and sending fire through my veins. "Kill the girl, and I will personally bring you back your sister. Refuse, and I will ensure dear Brianna is cast to the farthest reaches of Hell, where even in your mortal death, you will fail to find her."

I looked down at Kaira's body. To her fluttering breath, her hair tangled over her softly moving lips, an arm over her brow. Like she was sleeping. Just fitfully sleeping.

And I saw the bruises on her neck. The handprints that burned with memory on my palms. There was another glow then, and not from the god at my side. It was golden and warm, streaming between my fingers. A different sort of fire.

"What have I done?" I whispered.

"Nothing yet," Heru replied. "But you will. And you will delight in it."

CHAPTER SEVEN

"Um."

I jolted.

Ethan stood in his doorway, looking at me with one perfectly cocked eyebrow.

I was kneeling on the floor, my hands clenched against the hall carpet.

And I had been giggling.

The mirth cut short, and with it came a shot of adrenaline, a fear that pushed me to standing before I could think. What had he seen? What had he heard? What had I actually done?

"You okay there?"

I barely heard him over my pulse, over the frantic line of thought echoing in my head.

"I—"

But I didn't have an answer. My words trailed off, and we stood like that, staring at each other, until the door at the far end opened and another student walked in and Ethan kicked back into gear. He shook his head and walked forward, toward the exit, clearly expecting me to follow. I did.

"Are you getting enough sleep?" he asked once we'd left the dorm.

"Not really," I said. Which was the truth, save for the fact that I didn't tell him why. He definitely didn't need to know I'd snuck out to see Kaira.

Which, now that I thought of it . . . Maybe the ravens really *were* protecting her from me.

Because that was the scariest thought of all—the relief I had felt after what Heru had promised. The *rightness*. There was something in that power that made everything else insignificant. The fear. The isolation. The guilt.

With that much power, I could rewrite everything. . . .

"Earth to Chris," Ethan said, tapping me on the temple. I snapped back to reality. What had he been saying? Clearly the look I gave him asked the question for me. "I said you should go get some sleep. Maybe see the nurse."

His thoughts must have gone to the exact same place mine did: Kaira was in the nurse's office. His look of concern turned to suspicion.

A small part of me flared in anger at that, that he would be so quick to assume I was faking sick to see her. But then again, wasn't it a founded belief?

"I think I'll just take a nap," I lied. The plan I'd hatched from before was still valid. I wasn't going to let Heru or the falcon get in the way of me saving Kaira. I wasn't going to start believing they told the truth. They couldn't bring Bri back. No one could. "Don't think I can make it through the class day."

He nodded, still looking at me suspiciously.

"Well then," he said. He leaned in and gave me an awkward hug before stepping back. "Take care of yourself."

I agreed and watched him wander off toward the art building. The second time he turned to look at me, I headed toward my room.

I was lucky: Mike wasn't in. Probably meant he was out practicing, since he never seemed to hang out with friends. As usual, the place smelled like old clothes and stale food, thanks to his side of the room, but my disgust at it was muted. I was still shaking from what I'd seen. From Heru.

This whole shit about the Aesir and the Vanir was foreign. But it rang a bell. I'd been a huge nerd in middle school, and had lived in books of mythology and fantasy. I didn't head to the library, though—I opened my computer and typed in the words that had been ricocheting in my head like cursed shrapnel.

The next few hours were spent poring through various wikis and articles and stories on Norse mythology. The Aesir, I'd already known of. They were the gods that had infiltrated pop culture: Thor and Odin and Loki and the rest. The Vanir were the second tribe, but I couldn't find out much beyond that. As for Heru . . . he made the least amount of sense. Heru was an Egyptian deity. Most commonly known as Horus.

I sat back in my chair. Looked up at the ceiling. My head throbbed, and nothing made any more sense than it had earlier. Is this what Jonathan had been playing with? Trying to invoke the old gods? For what, though? And how did that relate to something that had happened to me nearly ten years ago?

Maybe he'd been similar. Maybe Jonathan had made a bargain with the gods, or been spared from death. Maybe he was trying to serve them, like Heru wanted of me.

But for what? For what?

I sighed and stood, my limbs shaking with the fear of what I was about to do. I pulled on my coat and boots and headed toward the nurse's office. The trek across campus was silent. I kept waiting for someone to come out and demand to know why I wasn't in class—I'd already missed lunch, and surely that was enough to raise suspicion. It didn't happen. That almost made things worse.

"I figured you'd come here," Ethan said.

He sat on a bench outside the nurse's lobby, legs crossed and a book facedown on his lap. A bouquet of flowers sat beside him. He definitely didn't look happy to see me.

"What are you doing here?" I asked.

I definitely wasn't feeling happy that he was there either.

"Same thing you are," he replied. He yawned and stretched himself to standing. "But I have a better chance of achieving it."

"You were waiting for me?"

He shrugged and grabbed the flowers.

"You're predictable. And underprepared. Besides, I wanted to see her too. I figured I might as well wait around until you showed—there's no way in hell they'd let you in to see her on your own."

I knew, though, that wasn't the only reason he'd waited.

Maybe it was paranoia, but I figured it was because he didn't want me alone with Kaira. Whatever I learned in there, whatever she and I said, he wanted to be in on. He wanted to be proven right. Or wrong. Just like me.

Ethan walked over to the door and held it open.

"Afternoon, boys," the nurse said. She looked up from her computer and gave us a warm smile. It was one of those smiles that said that—even in the worst of situations—everything would end up okay.

God, I wished I could believe that everything would be okay.

"Hey Bettie," Ethan said, giving her his biggest smile. "How you feeling?"

She laughed. "I believe I'm supposed to be asking you two that."

Damn it, Ethan was good.

"We're just dandy," he replied, somehow pulling off the word. He separated a single flower—a rose—from the bouquet, and held it out to her. "And I thought, on a dreary day like this, you could use a little brightness."

Her grin widened and a slight blush rose to her cheeks as she took the flower. I could tell from her smile that she was on to our game.

"Thank you, dear. I'm touched. Who are the rest for?"

"Oh, these? Well, we were hoping we could see Kaira."

She looked between him and me.

"You know that the point of being in the nurse's office is to get a little alone time for recovery, right?"

"But flowers!" Ethan chirped. His grin widened. "Everyone

knows that flowers aid recovery time by boosting the patient's overall mood."

She chuckled.

"I don't believe I've ever heard of that study."

"Oh, it's scientifically proven, let me assure you."

She shook her head. Maybe she was trying to convince herself that she should turn us away, but the smile told me Ethan had already won. He was right—there was no way I could have pulled this off on my own. Which just made me a little angrier . . . *Where the hell is that coming from?*

"Well, far be it from me to stand in the way of science and recovery," she said, still holding the rose. "Sign in, please."

We did so, and maybe it was my imagination, but Ethan seemed indignant to hand me the pen. I was practically shaking with adrenaline, and my signature came out as a jumble. Bettie didn't seem to notice. She slid back the clipboard and stood, leading us down the hall.

"Now, I don't want you two disturbing her," she whispered, pausing outside an open door. I could just see the footboard of a bed from this angle. "She needs her rest. But I'll give you a minute to sit with her."

Then, patting Ethan on the shoulder, she continued on down the hall. Humming.

Ethan stepped into the room, flowers held before him like he was using them as a shield.

The room was warm and dim, everything oak and burgundy—the antithesis of Kaira's cold, shadowed dorm. Despite the illusion of healing, there was a sickness in the air that I didn't think I was alone in feeling. A coldness that seeped up through the floorboards. The whisper of dark feathers at the room's edges.

I might not have been able to see them, but I knew the ravens were there. Watching her. Watching me watch her.

Ethan let out a sigh, which released the constriction in my own chest. Kaira didn't wake up when he stepped in and placed the flowers on her nightstand, or when he knelt and put a hand on her forehead.

"She's still cold," he whispered to me. Kaira's breath rose and fell smoothly. She almost looked peaceful, if not for the darkness still ringing her eyes.

A dozen different emotions seemed to play over Ethan's face while he knelt there, his eyes intent on her. Concern, yes, but also hints of fear. As though my story had sunk into his marrow, and no matter how much he wanted to convince himself I was just crazy, part of him believed me. He was waiting for Kaira to transform into something supernatural and terrible. Or, now that we were faced with her—clearly fine, clearly not supernatural at all—he was scared of what I'd do next. He was wondering if I'd killed Jonathan.

I stood in the doorway, torn between wanting to run away and wanting to rush to her side, force her awake. Now that I was here, facing the inevitable truth, I wanted the answer a whole hell of a lot less. *Who are you in there? And what have you done with the girl whose skin you're wearing?*

"Are you just going to stand there?" Ethan asked, and I started back to reality.

"Sorry," I replied. I wasn't certain what I was sorry for.

91

I shuffled over to her bedside, but I couldn't reach out and take her hand. I couldn't bring myself to touch her. Every blink, and I saw the damn hallucination. Kaira, her bruised neck imprinted on my palms; the hallways drenched in blood.

I couldn't tell which of us was the dangerous one in here. Maybe we both were. Maybe that was the problem.

You're being ridiculous, I thought. Then I sat down beside her on the bed and took her hand. Her skin was cool and her fingers twitched gently under my touch, not quite curling around mine but not shying away, either. Like any normal sick or sleeping person. I could count on my hands the number of times we'd actually touched. Why was it that every time, it seemed like a doomed experience?

"What are you thinking?" Ethan whispered.

"That this can't be real." Everything was too quiet. My pulse too calm. I knew what I'd seen last night. I knew I wasn't insane. But in this silent room, that knowledge was distant. This was reality. And a girl breaking into birds didn't fit into a quiet nurse's office at the edge of the woods.

He didn't answer. Not for a while.

"This can't go on," he finally said.

"What do you mean?"

He gestured to Kaira then turned the motion to brushing her hair from her face. "She's just sick, Chris. She's overworked and overburdened, and it burned her out. I don't want . . ."

"What?"

He sighed and then looked to me for a brief moment before his eyes flicked back to her.

"I don't want you scaring her," he whispered. "When she wakes up, I don't want her worrying about what you thought you saw. She's already been through more than enough. She doesn't need to worry about magic, too."

"I was right," I muttered. "You didn't just want to see her. You wanted to chaperone."

"I never said that," he replied. A little too late. A little too forced.

"You didn't have to. You think I'm a threat. I thought you said you believed me."

"I think you're confused and that something strange is going on, yes. But I think she doesn't need any more confusion." He sighed again. "Think of what she's been through. What she's going to go through when she wakes up. I know this girl: She's a martyr. If she thinks she's even remotely responsible for what happened . . ."

"All right, boys," Bettie said. My heart jumped into my throat. *How much had she heard?* "Your minute's up."

She stepped inside, and her body language was enough to let me know she wasn't going to budge. Even if we hadn't gotten any of our answers.

Well, I'd gotten *one* answer. To a question I hadn't realized I was asking. Ethan wasn't on my side. He didn't believe me. He might not have turned me in, and he might have believed that I wasn't responsible. But he still thought he knew what was best for Kaira. He still thought he had to protect her from my overactive imagination.

For a split second, I felt like I was balancing on a scale. One part of me wanted to tip into siding with him, into thinking he was right, that I was crazy and he needed to keep me away from her. The hallucinations, Heru's promise of killing her . . . But then I looked at her, saw the shadows haunting her eyes. If I gave up now, she was as good as dead.

"Thanks for letting us see her," Ethan said. He managed to keep his voice cool and even. I didn't think I could even if I wanted to.

I debated staying back, demanding a moment. But I knew it was stupid. I needed to make sure I could come back here. Getting banned from the nurse's office wouldn't help anyone.

"Yeah." I picked up Kaira's hand and kissed the back of her knuckles.

She stirred. My heart stopped.

"Chris?" she whispered. Her fingers tightened.

"I'm here," I said back. "It's okay. I'm here."

"Don't leave me," she whispered, barely loud enough for me to hear. And it didn't sound like a sick girl asking for company. It sounded like a girl who was scared. Just like the girl who had pleaded for me to save her last night.

"I won't," I whispered back. I kissed her knuckles again. Ethan cleared his throat, but again, *screw him.* "I promise."

"Please," she said. Then her fingers tightened and her body stiffened and she let go, rolling over and pulling the covers tighter.

I wanted her to open her eyes. I wanted her to say more than a plea. But that was enough. She needed me. And I wasn't the only one who had heard it.

No one moved for a moment. No one spoke. I couldn't tell if they were shocked she had spoken, or shocked I'd had the nerve to kiss her hand.

"Well, looks like she'll be better soon," Bettie said. She put a hand on my shoulder. "But she needs her rest. She's had a long week."

Grudgingly, I got to my feet and let her lead us out of the room. Ethan didn't look at me the entire way.

"Can I come back tomorrow?" I asked as we walked down the hall. While it was still fresh in Bettie's mind—Kaira had reached out for me, and I had been there.

"We'll see how she's doing," Bettie replied.

It wasn't a yes, but it was good enough.

Ethan stayed silent when we left the nurse's office. I walked a few feet before looking back. He stood by the door, looking up to the sky like he was hoping for some sort of divine answer, his hands shoved into his pockets and whatever friendship we'd cultivated shoved into the past.

He might have pissed me off in there, but it wasn't my nature to hold a grudge. Life was far too short. My sister's death had taught me that.

"What?" I asked. I didn't backtrack. This was my version of meeting halfway.

He shrugged. Then he trudged the few feet between us. It felt like a minor victory, and that was just stupid. This shouldn't be a battle between him and me. So why was I angry? Why did part of me *want* it to be?

"You still don't believe me. . . ."

"I can't," he said. He shook his head. "I can't believe any of this." When he looked at me, I felt suddenly, terribly alone. "You need to stay away from her, Chris. None of this happened before you. Just . . . I don't want her getting hurt."

"I wouldn't hurt her."

"But this fantasy of yours would."

His words were so blunt, they cut off the ones that had begun to grow in my head.

It's not a fantasy, I wanted to say.

"Go get some rest," Ethan continued. "For real this time."

Then he turned and walked away.

That was when the other words came back into focus. The words I wanted so badly to force away.

You're doomed to hurt her, Endbringer. Worse than you will ever realize.

CHAPTER EIGHT

Islington was surrounded by forests, and the woods were dotted with tiny cabins used during the summer months for camp. All of them were locked, but that meant nothing to a school of teenagers. Locks were just another challenge of living out in the Michigan wilds. Locks gave the illusion of privacy. Right now, that was exactly what I needed. I couldn't go to my room, on the very good chance that my antisocial roommate would be in. I couldn't go to a study room or to a studio. I needed to be alone. Truly alone.

I tried to make my gait look natural, like I was meandering, when in truth I wanted to run full out. I followed one of the many paved paths that had been cleared of snow, feet shuffling along, hands clenched tight in my pockets. The woods were silent. No birds. No hiss of falling snow. I passed one couple walking the other direction, but we didn't make eye contact or even acknowledge each other. They held hands and kept their heads down, and something in me panged at the sight. The memory of holding Kaira's hand, of how right it felt. How warm. My fingers clenched tighter against my palms.

I wasn't going to hurt her.

I was going to save her.

No matter what Heru said. Or promised he'd do. Or promised I'd do. If he thought using my sister as bait would work, he was wrong.

Bri was already dead and gone; even if she *were* a spirit, she would never ask me to bring her back. Not at the cost of another's life. And I wasn't an idiot—I'd read enough stories to know that you didn't try to bring back the dead. It never went well for anyone involved. I had to save the girl who was still alive. The one I could still try to forge a life with.

After a while, I veered off the main path and made a fresh trail through the snow. My feet sunk slowly through it, every step labored, but I was too distracted to care about the slush that spilled into my boots. I zigzagged through the woods so my destination wouldn't be clear from the path. Then, once the trees shut everything away, I beelined toward a cabin.

The exterior was traditional and wood and covered in mementos of summer's past: faded dream catchers and paintings and names graffitied on the siding. The windows were boarded shut and the door appeared locked. But I'd been here before. On the nights I needed to escape, when I needed to stare at a wall and think without worrying about others coming in and asking how I was, what was I doing, did I need anything? I shuffled around to the back windows and pulled off a piece of plywood. The inner window was open.

I shoved myself up and over the sill, slipping into the dark interior. Thin streams of gray light filtered through cracks in the window boards, but the room was otherwise black and empty. Perfect. I never thought I'd be so happy to see a place devoid of light before.

There were a few bunk beds along the walls and a couple of desks by the window I'd jumped through. I sat down on one of the desks, my fingers fumbling toward a lantern there. I didn't turn it on. There was a pack of cigarettes beside it, along with a lighter. I thumbed through the remaining cigarettes—there were three fewer than last time I was here, but that was fine. It's why I left them. There was a sort of mutual respect among the rule-breakers, here. I knew there would be a handle of whiskey under the mattress on the top left bunk, and condoms and porn in the top desk drawer by the entrance. I was sure there were other gifts and common items I hadn't discovered yet. Probably some left in recent days.

But I wasn't here for booze or sex. I pulled a cigarette from the pack and placed it between my lips, the filter cold and tasting like ash. I didn't grab the lighter.

Heru kept promising me powers. Powers that could raze the world.

I'd seen Kaira break apart into ravens and fly off into the night. *She'd* found power. Even if it had taken her over. Even if it was keeping her captive.

If I was going to save her from something supernatural, I needed to fight fire with fire. If I wanted to fight against Heru, against whatever was holding Kaira down, I needed to be on the same level.

And the power that I'd felt in that earlier vision—terrifying though it was—seemed like just the thing.

Heru thought he could control me. He thought I'd bend to his will. He didn't know what he was dealing with.

I reached into my pocket and pulled out my knife. My power was blood? Well then, let's see what sort of power I could get from giving up some of my own.

It was a small cut—just a nick on the tip of my thumb—and the moment I did it, I realized how stupid this was. I was cutting myself in a dark cabin in the middle of the woods. I was trying to do magic. Not, like, sideshow magic. Real, literal magic.

It was insane.

Then again, so was hearing gods speak and watching ravens take away your classmate. Maybe this was sane, in the light of all that. *The light.*

I didn't know what I was doing, only that now that the urge was there, something else was taking over. I brought my thumb to the end of the cigarette, smeared it with blood. I could feel every fiber that scratched against my cut flesh. I could feel my blood sucked out into the tobacco, into the paper. Humming filled my ears—the sound of my pulse, the sound of the silent woods. And the sound of something else. The sound of *power*. It vibrated like a low cello string, thrumming against my spine.

I cupped my bleeding hand around the cigarette, imagined a light, a power, curling against my palm. A haze of heat. A spark. A flame.

I inhaled.

And there, in the dark, my blood blazed red, the tip of the cigarette flaring into life with a hiss.

Smoke filled my lungs, heady and strong.

The cigarette fell from my lips, rolled along the floor, but I was too busy laughing to watch it, to see the embers flashing off and fading in the cold.

My laughter filled the cabin. I toppled from the desk, clutched my knees to my chest as I rocked back and forth on the floor. The floor so cold, I couldn't feel it. I could only feel the heat in my chest. The tears flowing down my cheeks. The laughter that scratched against my throat—too loud, too loud, but not loud enough to drown out my thoughts.

I wasn't going insane.

I wasn't going insane.

I had power.

The fire. The blood. The smoking cigarette. This was real.

And that meant the rest of it was real too.

The gods were after me and Kaira. And if I wasn't careful, they would make me kill her.

CHAPTER NINE

I didn't know how long I'd stayed in that cabin. I didn't know how many times I'd cut myself, over and over again, until I'd gone through the entire pack of cigarettes and my hand was bloody and numb from cold.

But there weren't any cuts.

Every time I used the power, my skin healed new and fresh. Only the blood and char of tobacco remained.

I was high as a kite. The power . . . the *power*.

It was like nothing I'd ever experienced before—stronger than any drug, than any hormonal rush. I felt myself grow addicted to it. As I sat there, legs crossed, leaning against a bunk bed, I felt the need to try again. The cigarettes were gone. I traced the edge of the pack with my thumb. Considered other things I could burn. I had more skin I could try. More blood I could shed.

Life and death are your playthings. . . . There were other fires I could play with. I knew, somewhere, I could find a dead moth, a broken bird, more blood. . . .

"No."

The word fell from my lips before I could force myself to action. No, that wasn't right. I wasn't playing with this power. I was training. To save Kaira.

I didn't need to play God. I needed to protect her from them.

Angrily, I pushed myself up to standing. I wasn't doing her any good in here, lighting cigarettes and staring into the dark and getting stoned on magic.

But how are you going to actually save her?

The thought came up unbidden, stopping me in my tracks. I stared out at the fading gray sky, night slowly seeping into the woods. Lighting fires was one thing, but how was I going to use this against a . . . what? Against Heru, sure. But I had no idea what was keeping Kaira down. I had no idea how to target the god or whatever that was keeping her captive.

I had a power. And that power seemed pretty useless.

"It's something," I muttered. "It's a start."

Yes, came another voice. I shuddered at the words of the falcon, at the shift of light through the trees—a flare I swore was in my head. *It is a start. You have opened the door. To me. To us. Use it, Endbringer. Use it, and let us in.*

"Never," I whispered to the night. To the shadows.

I pulled myself up and out of the cabin, not bothering to replace the board. There was a small urge in the back of my brain to set the whole thing on fire, to burn the whole place down.

I didn't. Of course I didn't. But the fact that I wanted to scared me deeper than I could admit.

I thought I was fighting against them. I thought I was finding an answer. Instead, the anger, the hatred . . . it showed that I was doing the exact opposite. Those weren't my feelings. I knew they weren't my feelings. But as I hustled through the woods, barely noticing that my prior tracks had been wiped clean, the anger seemed like the most real thing in my life.

"Chris?"

Oliver's voice cut through the silence and the fury of my thoughts. For a moment, I thought maybe I'd made it up—another hallucination, just one more tick in the "crazy" box. But then I saw his shadow approaching me from farther down the path. I bit back my anger and the thoughts from the cabin, tried to shift back into normal human interaction mode. Which, it turned out, was damn near impossible.

"What are you doing out here?" he asked when he neared.

"Thinking," I said. "You?"

He nodded.

"Same."

He sighed, and that was enough to tell me everything I needed to know.

"Ethan talked to you, didn't he?" Try as I might, I couldn't keep the bitterness out of my voice. He noticed. In the light of one of the streetlamps, his face suddenly became guarded.

"Yeah."

"What did he tell you?"

If he had hesitated, I would have thought he was lying. But he shrugged and turned and started walking with me, immediately starting in with, "That Kaira's really sick, and he's worried about her. And you."

"Why me?"

Another shrug. Maybe he *was* hiding something. Maybe he just shrugged a lot. I don't think we'd ever really hung out, the two of us. And this wasn't a normal circumstance.

"He said you're taking it really hard," Oliver said. "That you're . . ."

"What? I'm what?"

"Imagining things," he said.

The words were small punches to the gut.

"Did he say what?"

"No. Just that you felt responsible for Kaira." He looked over at me. "He's sorry, by the way."

"For what?"

"Treating you like the enemy."

"Then why isn't he saying it?"

"Because it's Ethan. He's proud as fuck. He loves her, you know. And it scares him to see her hurt. Hell, he's even been lashing out at me."

That came as a surprise. They were always lovey in person. His swearing was a surprise as well—Oliver was always straight-laced, as my mom would admiringly say. Dressed well, was always polite. Maybe that was just his public persona. Maybe, like the rest of us, he was living more than one life.

"Sorry to hear that," I muttered. "And I'm not imagining things." *And I have a pack of burnt cigarettes to prove it.*

"I know you aren't imagining things. He gets like this when he's overworked."

The woods around us were heavy and darkening, but for some reason, with him there, I was able to momentarily forget all the strange shit that had been happening. He was like this six-foot-tall pillar of stability. It was like, whatever the storm was, he'd weather it. And by being in his presence, you'd weather it too.

I hadn't realized how much I needed that feeling.

I let my hands unclench in my pockets.

"I heard she's better," he said.

"Not really," I replied. *She's probably worse.*

We walked in silence for a while. The lights of campus split through the tree branches, leaving long lines on the snow.

"It's not you," Oliver said eventually. "He's really freaking out. He cares too much."

"What a curse."

He stopped walking and looked at me. "Actually, it can be. It sounds cliché, I know, but it's actually pretty debilitating at times. Severe anxiety, panic attacks. I've tried to convince him to take something, but he's too stubborn to even do St. John's Wort. But when he starts worrying about someone, it's like this. This downward spiral where he feels responsible for everything, and suddenly everyone else becomes an enemy, because he's drowning and they're dry."

I didn't tell him that his boyfriend thought I was insane, that he thought I had a hand in Jonathan's death.

Oliver wasn't the enemy.

Wait, what was I talking about? *No one* was the enemy. No one, save for the falcon and that bastard god.

"Everyone has their issues," I said, my words more clipped than I'd intended. *Mine involve staving off possession.*

"This isn't the time to push people away."

"I appreciate you trying to convince me not to be angry at your boyfriend. Really. But I'm not the one pointing fingers here."

He didn't refute me.

"What did you see the other night?" he asked instead.

"What do you mean?"

"I'm not an idiot. Ethan's been acting strange ever since you guys went up on the roof. He's not telling me something. I know him; if I push for answers, he'll clam up."

"It's nothing."

"It's not nothing."

I couldn't tell him the truth; I wasn't naive enough to think he'd believe me when Ethan would not, especially when Ethan had been there to see at least part of the strange things that had happened. Not even with a magic trick up my sleeve; I didn't think cutting myself would yield very good results in front of him. But I also knew that expression. He wasn't going to let this drop. Not until he thought I'd told him something Ethan hadn't. Not until he thought he was in the loop. He didn't realize this wasn't a loop he wanted in on. It was safer to be in the dark. And far, far away.

"Cassie was right," I admitted. "It was ritualistic. The deaths. Jonathan was involved somehow, and last night . . . when I came back last night, I caught the tail end of what they were doing. Kaira was there, yelling at them to stop. She ran out when I got there, wouldn't answer her phone calls. And then she woke up sick the morning after. Ethan's worried about her. So am I. Because whatever was going on in there was dark."

"You think she was caught up in it?"

I shook my head. The lie was difficult to spin. Too much or too little information, and he'd stop believing me. We were nearing the lake, where fishermen's huts glowed in tiny spots of quiet warmth, their lights streaking across the snow. Like rays. Or feathers. I looked over at Oliver, forced down the hum in the back of my head. *Not now, not now.*

"She wasn't involved. Not like the others," I managed. "I think she found out about it and was trying to stop it."

"But what is *it*?"

"I don't know."

He gave me a look.

"Honestly, I don't."

It was then I realized he hadn't stopped studying me.

"You don't think it's over." It wasn't a question: His words were almost a promise.

Now it was my turn to study.

"What do you mean?"

"I know that tone. You're afraid. If it was over, you wouldn't be worried. But you think it's going to happen again. Another murder."

I also think Kaira's possessed, and I'm about to be, but yes. That too.

I nodded.

He sighed.

"Fuck."

"Yeah." I let my reply linger, then started walking again. "I don't know what to do. And Ethan seems to think I'm crazy for believing there's still danger. He's worried that if I bring it up to her . . ."

"I told you—he has a strong protective streak."

"Yeah, but it's not helping anyone here. I need to know what Kaira saw in there. To make sure it doesn't happen again."

"Maybe he's right, though? Maybe it's not the best time to ask her? I know you think she's strong, but Kaira can be as fragile as the rest of us. I don't mean to take sides, but maybe it's best to just hold off on digging deeper until she's better."

I should have known Oliver would team with his boyfriend. But I'd hoped he'd at least see my side of things.

Kill him.

The words echoed in my ears.

"What did you say?" he asked.

I opened my mouth to say I didn't say anything.

But I couldn't speak. Had I said that out loud? Why would—

Kill him. Before he is a threat.

I looked over and saw Oliver, impaled on the tree, blood dripping down his wounds like sap. My hands were coated in his blood. Blink, and I saw myself laughing, tracing crimson circles at his feet. Offering him as another sacrifice to the gods. My gods.

His blood will be your power, Endbringer. Embrace it. Use it. Kill the Shadechild; bring back your sister.

I stumbled back, panic constricting my throat. And when I blinked, Oliver stood there, unharmed. Waiting for my reply.

I didn't answer him. I looked around, my heart still racing. Tree limbs curved like daggers. Blink, and bodies hung in the branches. Some impaled, others twisting from nooses. I dropped to my knees. Squeezed my hands to my head and shut my eyes, tried to shut out the carnage, but I couldn't force out the smell of blood, the sound of birds feasting. The sound of Heru laughing.

"Chris, are you okay?" Oliver asked, his voice a thousand leagues away.

When I opened my eyes again, the bodies were still there in the trees. Their blood dripped rivers, and carrion birds spiraled in the sun. And the bodies, their eyes. They all stared at me. Just like the crows outside Kaira's window.

But these didn't fill me with fear. My heart was racing, yes.

With anticipation. With excitement.

"No," I muttered. Squeezed my head harder. I couldn't force away the screams, the laughter—my laughter, my madness, my *power*. Heat built between my fingertips. Heat, and light.

"Chris—"

Oliver's voice was far away. I looked at him, where he stood, his arms bound behind his back and vultures pecking at his innards. He was still talking. How was he still talking?

"No!" I cried. Tears formed. They didn't wash away his image. The vultures picking at flesh. The blood ringing his bound body.

I screamed.

And there, walking through the carrion, was Kaira. But not Kaira. She wore her cloak of black feathers. Her eyes glowed violet.

Ravens tousled in her hair. She walked through the dead and dying, and she was smiling. Somewhere in the back of my chest, I felt a growl form, a hatred that burned brighter than any I'd ever known. And a single word, a single motive.

Kill.

I shook my head, tried to force down the anger, her otherworldly visage, but there was no escape in the darkness. I felt her neck in my hands, ravens bursting from her mouth like black tongues. I felt my blade in her chest, piercing shadows and feathers and ancient bones. I felt her blood in my veins. The falcon's claws in my heart.

I will kill her. I will kill them all.

"Chris," she said. Her hand on my shoulder.

My vision exploded. I was no longer in the woods. A field spread around me, bodies lying like broken chess pieces. Piled against each other in drooping towers. The scent of decay clung to my nostrils, churned bile in my throat, and when I brought my hand to cover my mouth, I saw that it, too, was covered in blood. Blood, like the crimson that flowed in streams, that turned the ground to marsh. I gagged, looked away, tried to find some patch of land not covered in carnage. Smoke curled in the distance. Towers burned. And farther, staining the horizon black, was a great tree. The World Tree. Yggdrasil, its trunk stretching up between the realms of gods and man. The moment I saw it, I felt the pull. The desire. The need.

To serve. To kill. To feed.

"Chris," Kaira said again. I turned to her, a sword somehow in my bloodied hands.

Kaira was yards away. She stood proudly, bloodstained,

commanding a chariot drawn by ravens. And I, I floated above the flooded ground, glowing and golden, with three pairs of wings sprouting from my back and a halo of daggers behind my skull.

May our battle nourish the Tree on which our worlds turn.

She said.

I said.

And we charged. And the world froze.

I closed my eyes against the impact.

This isn't real. This isn't real.

The blow never came. Slowly, I opened my eyes. My fingers dug into the snow. Clean snow. Oliver stood there, his hand on my shoulder. Not Kaira's hand after all.

What the hell was that?

What the hell is happening to me?

And then, his voice: *You have opened the door, Endbringer. You will let me in. Or I will make you suffer.*

"Are you okay?" Oliver asked. His voice sounded too loud. I shuddered. No, I wasn't okay. How the hell was I going to be okay?

How was I going to save Kaira, when I couldn't even keep my own shit in check?

I looked to the ice. To the fishermen's huts all quaint and pastoral with their warm interiors and shadowed faces. The quiet lake. The quiet woods. Everything too quiet. Too beautiful and quiet. Why didn't they realize? The world was going to end. And I was going to bring it about.

I let Oliver pull me up to standing. "I'm fine. Sorry, just . . ." But there was no lie to make sense of what I'd done. What I'd seen. "I should get some sleep."

He didn't say anything for a moment. He studied me, watching, waiting to see if I would let on more. Waiting to see if I could give a logical explanation for what was clearly insanity. If I had hoped to gain him as an ally, to get him to convince Ethan I wasn't insane, I'd just destroyed that chance.

Maybe that was for the best. Maybe I shouldn't let them close.

I wanted to be safe.

I wasn't safe.

Finally, though, Oliver nodded and began walking. He didn't ask me to say more. I couldn't tell if I found that comforting or enraging. Why didn't he see that something was wrong? Why didn't he sense that this was bigger than murders or suicides, that the world as we knew it was crashing down?

Why was I the only one sane enough to see it?

When we reached the campus again, he paused and turned to me, dropping his voice to a whisper.

"Do you think she's the next target?" he asked.

Kaira's image flashed through my mind, but not the scene with her covered in ravens. It was the two of us, me with my hands around her throat. A smile on my lips. I pushed it away. I would *not* hurt her. No matter what Heru thought, no matter what he showed me. I would never hurt her. Never.

"I hope not," I replied.

He nodded, like that was enough. I wished that could be enough.

We walked back toward the dorms together. Oliver was in the other guys' dorm, and when we reached the entry to mine, he lingered there, hands in his pockets and his eyes darting around to everywhere but me.

"Don't hold it against him, yeah?" he asked. "Ethan's under a lot of stress. Losing people is really hard on him, you know? He's scared for Kaira, and that makes him act out."

I nodded. Losing people was hard on everyone, so why did Oliver make it sound like Ethan had a special reason?

Maybe I didn't know anything about my friends. But they didn't know anything about me, either.

"Try to get some sleep," he added. Then he stepped forward and gave me a hug.

"Her death will be sweet," he whispered into my ear, hugging me tighter.

I jolted back.

"What?"

"What?" he replied.

"What did you say?"

"Nothing." His expression changed. Into one very similar to the way Ethan had been looking at me since last night.

Then I saw the falcon, perched on a streetlamp behind his shoulder, glowing with a light of its own.

"Right. Sorry. Good night."

I didn't give him or the bird a second look. It was all I could do not to run inside.

Her death will be sweet.

It wasn't the words that scared me. It was the effect they had on me.

Deep in the pit of that flame in my chest, I felt excited.

CHAPTER TEN

Clouded dreams.

Golden

Feathers

Branch and Bone.

The gods created you for this.

I sit in the gnarled branches of the World Tree while falcons
swirl above, rocs
and thunderbirds, great wings flashing light
lightning.
Clouds part like palms, streams of light and blood
an offering of gold.
"You cannot run from us."
He says.
They say.
Heru floats above the boughs, his wings unfurled and glowing, rays
of light caught by the clouds, daggers swirling
an aura of iron.

115

"You were made for war. For victory.
Their end is your beginning."
And I turn from the branches of brazen birds
to see the field. Bodies strewn like snowflakes, blades
broken, cities carved. Carrion
birds feasting.
"I don't want this."
But my words falter. Fail.
I *do* want this.
I was made for this.
I want nothing less.
As ravens fall, as owls weep, the golden boy extends
his hands, the heavens
open, breathe light unto the field. Bodies glisten
like gold. Beautiful in their decay.
"The Tree must have
its sacrifice. The world must offer itself
to be given itself. Yggdrasil created you
for this. Created her
for this. Us
for this. It demands our piety.
Our offering. Only then
will its branches blossom. And in
those buds, our ambrosia
will flow."
Honey drips from the heavens, from branches
far above. Honey, thick and sweet.
Thick and sweet and red

as blood.

It falls to the bodies, coats them
in tar. Falls on one body. With a cloak of raven feathers
and hair as dark as the banished night.

"Kaira."

And I am beside her, my hands reaching
for a heart that will not beat, a hand
that will not clench. Her cloak
splays like wings, shredded and bent. The ravens
ring her, broken, beakless, a zero circle.

"You were born of blood," Heru says
his golden light a heat I can't escape.

"Too young to remember . . ."

And his hand is on the back of my neck, presses up. In. Through
my skull, clutching my brain, and there is light
such light
as the world breaks and my skull cracks
and I am there, before a woman. Who is my mother.
Is not the mother I know.

She lies in her blood on the hospital table
and my father is held back, doctors screaming his name
as he screams hers.

But I am there. The child that killed her, held
in a doctor's arms. Bloody, silent, my lips
sticky with her blood.

No.

No.

"No—"

"The child of the Aesir is born in blood
and through that blood he wields his power."
I turn to scream, to kill the god
but he is gone, the room is gone, and the black sea
leaks against the shore. White sand
dark waves
dark hair. Her body
twisted like the brambles we plucked
berries from, her eyes as white as shells, their mysteries
hollowed and cold.
"Your sacrifices are many."
But it is not his voice. It is hers. My sister's. Whispered
in my ear, an echo
of memory.
"I never meant for you to die."
It sounds like a lie. My thoughts falter. My heart
sings battle.
Death is mine.
Life is mine.
A god does not weep for his domain.
Her body doesn't answer. Her lips part
only with the pounding waves.
When I turn, the shore is lined with bodies, my sacrifices
to myself, to the Tree, to the god
I was born to be.
Kaira.
My mother.
My sister.

My friends.
My tributes.

"When my dawn rises, even gods will bend knee."
I say. He says through me.
As my wings spread, as our thoughts
become one.

Even gods will kneel.

CHAPTER ELEVEN

Mike shoved me awake the next morning.

It took a few moments for my head to clear, for the dreams of blood and screaming to fade into the pale light of day. My sheets were knotted around me, disgustingly moist with cold sweat.

"You okay?" he asked gruffly. It might have been the first time he'd ever asked me that.

I shook my head, or nodded it. I wasn't certain what sort of motor control I had.

"You were screaming."

"Sorry."

He looked me over, partially like he was making sure I was actually okay, and partially like he was pissed because I'd done something to force this interaction. Then he sighed exaggeratedly and turned and headed out the door.

I looked at my alarm clock. Breakfast was nearly over. My stomach rumbled, but I couldn't force myself out of bed. Couldn't keep my eyes open. A migraine pressed in from the corners of my vision, ashes coating the inside of my mouth. I winced, rolled over, and pulled the covers over my head. In light of everything that was happening, who the fuck cared if I got out of bed today?

My dream latched to my awareness like a tick, sucking my energy and my ability to move forward. It wasn't the promises of bloodshed that filled my veins with ice water. It wasn't Heru's insistence that I would cause the end.

It was the scene in the hospital. The scene that felt ripped straight from memory, and not hallucination.

It couldn't have been real. The woman I'd seen in the hospital bed wasn't the woman I'd grown up with. The dream woman had been blond, and my mom was a brunette. The woman on the table had willowy, long limbs, like a sylph from a Greek tragedy. My mother was short, muscular, more interested in rock climbing and crunching numbers than paying attention to me.

It was a dream. There wasn't an ounce of truth to it.

But I couldn't convince myself of that. Because the idea that she—Lauren Wright, the woman who raised me—wasn't my biological mother made too many other things make sense. Like the fact that Bri had always looked so much more like her than I did. The fact that she favored Bri, and treated me like I was a pest.

The fact that my father hadn't treated me any better.

You're the reason we're going through this.

My father had said that on more than one occasion.

As though I was the cause of his and Mom's fighting. As though he blamed me for more than my sister's death.

There was no way the dream was real, though. No way I'd

been lied to all my life. They wouldn't have held that from me. Right?

There was also no way in Hell I'd ever be able to ask either of them for the truth.

Other dreams clattered in my head like the blades of war, snippets of memory from last night, or other nights—I couldn't hold them apart. My sister, swinging in the tree behind our house by a noose made of seaweed. Kaira, surrounded by falcons that pecked and clawed at her bloody flesh. And the field, littered with bodies, the sword in my hands dripping crimson. The taste of Kaira's breath on my tongue.

Her death will be sweet. Sweet. Sweet as our ambrosia.

I pressed the pillow tight around my head, wished it would stuff out the dreams. But even as sleep edged back in, I couldn't escape the eyes of the falcon. They burned into the corners of my brain. Waiting for me to be weak. Waiting for me to give in.

I focused on my breath. On the blood pumping in my veins. And then I focused on my fingers, on the blood pulsing beneath my skin. I focused on the power.

My breathing slowed. My pulse calmed.

And there, in between heartbeats, I felt the heat build, a slow burn, until the pillow was as warm as an oven against my head.

I kept it there. I kept the heat going. It made me feel real. It made me feel alive.

I didn't get out of bed until well after breakfast. I knew I needed to eat something, so I forced myself from bed and downed a double dose of aspirin. Then, changing into the closest clothes

I could find, I left. Today I was going to save Kaira. One way or another.

Sun filtered through the clouds, and I winced against the glare of light off fresh snow, at the sounds of kids yelling and laughing and throwing snowballs with the first taste of sun. I didn't look at them. I didn't trust what I'd see. Even then, with every few blinks I'd see flecks of blood on the ground, or a spray of raven feathers like some forgotten offering. Then I'd blink, and the hallucinations would go away. Usually.

I stepped into the Dark Note Café and ordered some cheese bread and a froyo shake, fumbling my money over without looking at the guy behind the register.

"You okay, bud?" he asked. I glanced up briefly. Rocker hair, all black, a few chain necklaces. Ike.

"I'm fine," I lied.

"Good, good," Ike replied, handing me my change. No blood on this, thankfully. He said something I didn't catch, then turned and started getting my shake ready. There wasn't anyone in line with me: no one to avoid eye contact with, no one to feign conversation. I kept my eyes down anyway.

I went to an empty seat in the corner by the windows after Ike handed the shake over. My mother would have killed me if she saw me using this as my only meal.

Would she? Would she even give two shits? I couldn't imagine what she'd say if I told her, point-blank, that I knew she wasn't my real mother.

Especially because I still wasn't certain that was correct.

I didn't look outside. I kept my head bowed and tried to sip my shake, tried to force down the ache in my head. Closed my eyes.

Took a drink.

I nearly spit it out.

The shake was darker than it should have been. It tasted like iron. Like blood.

It's all in your head.

But I couldn't convince myself of that, because even after squeezing my eyes shut and then looking back at the shake, it didn't change. It didn't lighten in color. The iron tang in the back of my throat didn't fade.

It was blood. I was drinking blood.

The worst part was the taste.

The taste. I actually enjoyed the taste.

I pushed the shake away. I didn't want to drink more. I didn't want to want to drink more.

Fuck, maybe I am going insane.

I tried to force myself to calm down like I had barely an hour ago, but calm wouldn't come. My breath became ragged. I felt trapped.

Do not fight what you are, Endbringer, Heru whispered inside my head, his breath on the back of my neck. *Blood is your power.*

The window in front of me cracked with a bang. My head jerked up at the spray of blood on the pane, a kid's body slumping to the ground outside while, beyond, hawks and ravens circled and screamed like the kids fighting below. Dozens of students, screaming and killing each other in the snow.

It's all in your head. It's all in your head.

Maybe I was speaking it aloud. I squeezed my eyes shut. *It will go away. Just like before. Just keep breathing.*

But then there was another crack, and this time the glass shattered in, and when I opened my eyes, I was surrounded by ravens. Ravens screaming. Screaming in Kaira's voice.

I batted them away even as they tore at my flesh, ripped through my clothes, beaks seeking blood, eyes, tender skin. The chair fell to the floor and tangled in my feet. I went down, still thrashing, my crash buffered by blood. By bodies.

I can make this madness end, Chris, Heru promised, his voice cutting through the ravens. *I can make all the pain go away.*

And it *was* pain, worse than I'd ever known. My flesh sliced to ribbons, my blood choking my lungs, and still the ravens came, clawing and screaming, and through them I saw Kaira's gaze, her face not sad—triumphant.

I couldn't stop the scream that pierced my lips. A muffled scream. A hawk piercing through the ravens, prying its way down my throat. Its feathers were burning tar, were sandpaper. It scratched down my neck, my throat, became a sun in my chest. A heat that burned through me, a light that forced the ravens away. A light that forced Kaira away.

Blink.

Together, gods and men shall bend knee.

And the bodies around me were my friends. My offerings to the Tree. To my own immorality. I stood, blood dripping slowly from my hands, down my golden blade. There was no more screaming. Only the silence of the dead.

This was what it felt like to be powerful.

This was how it felt to be loved. Revered.

This was how it felt to be a god.

"Yo, you okay?"

I turned, and Ike was there, holding my cheese bread in front of him. My chair was toppled on the clean floor. The window was whole. Only Ike looked broken. Lines of blood streaked the corners of his eyes. Tears for what I would do. For what he *wanted* me to do.

"Let my death serve the Tree," he said, his words flat as bell tones. "Let my death serve Creation."

My heart beat like a hammer in my chest, a burn that threatened to incinerate me.

Ike didn't call out when I pushed past him.

But I could hear him laughing.

I didn't know where to run. The moment I stepped outside, though, I realized the vision had stopped. There were a few kids walking to class or practice or whatever, but the snow was pure white—no stains of blood, no splatters of brains. I paused and tried to catch my breath. Ike didn't come out from the café and no one approached to ask why I was clearly having a panic attack. My breath was ragged and short and the world was spinning and my mouth still tasted blood.

My hands, buried deep in my jacket, still burned hot with the memory of power.

Then I saw him.

He walked slowly down the path, straight toward me, the snow around him glowing and melting at the rays of his brilliance. His wings were spread wide, and his bloody halo circled slowly. He was a sun in a landscape of gray. He was impossible to turn from. And even I, knowing his true nature, couldn't look away. I felt the pull. My hands burned. His power. *Our* power. I took a few steps forward, a tug in my chest pulling us closer. He smiled.

"You see?" he asked when he neared.

His warmth . . . it sank through my clothes. It eased the fear in my heart. In his light, there was no fear, no pain. No ravens or shadows. There was only light. Only power.

"This is what I will give you," he said. He was only a foot away, and now my heart was hammering with a different sort of emotion. He smelled like lightning, like danger. I wanted to touch him. Wanted him to touch me. I wanted that power to flood through me, for the spark to connect. My chest was fire, my breath short. The heat was intoxicating. I wanted it to burn me alive. "Embrace me," he said.

He reached out, placed one golden hand against my cheek. A small moan rumbled in the back of my throat as my own limbs reacted, the jolt of his power, his beauty, filling me, compelling me. My hands sought out the sides of his face, his skin smooth and burning, like gold warmed in the sun, his jaw as strong as the current that surged through me. I leaned in, breathed in his scent. His energy. His wings folding around us in a cocoon of light.

Our lips touched.

"Um, dude?"

I jolted back.

My hands were still cupping Ethan's face. Ethan, who was

standing stock-still, his eyebrows nocked in confusion and his lips tight.

"Shit," I said, dropping back. I looked around. Heru was nowhere to be seen.

Why did that fill me with sadness?

What had I almost done?

"Umm . . ." Ethan said again. He was looking at me like I was crazy. "What the hell was that?"

"I—"

I couldn't finish the sentence. I couldn't think of anything to say.

"Why did you just kiss me?" Ethan asked. His voice was remarkably calm. Like maybe I wasn't the first straight guy to kiss him out of nowhere.

"I don't—" I started backing up. Panic built in my veins. Heru was after me. Heru was winning.

"Don't tell me you're on something," he said. He stepped forward. "Or that you're suddenly going to yell 'no homo' or whatever."

I shook my head.

"It's not that. I didn't mean . . . I didn't know . . ." I stopped, and I looked at him. Really looked at him. Was it really Ethan standing there in the snow? Or was it Heru in disguise? How could I tell what was real and what was fake? Now that the visions were more than just blood. They were more than the future.

The visions were now.

"Ethan," I said. "I think I'm in trouble."

He looked concerned.

"What do you mean?"

I shook my head. I couldn't answer. I couldn't make him believe me.

Instead, I slipped a hand into my pocket and nicked my thumb on the blade of my pocketknife.

Ethan didn't register surprise when I held my other hand palm up before me, when I channeled that blood into something more potent. My palm burned hot, glowed orange and gold. And then, in a curl, a wisp, a single tendril of flame appeared above my hand, dancing over my flesh like a demon.

"Something's happening to me," I whispered. The flame between us was the most terrible of secrets. If others saw, I didn't care. I couldn't hide anymore. What did it matter, the illusion of safety?

They will all die in the end.

The thought came from nowhere and snapped me from concentration. The flame winked out.

For the longest moment we stood there in silence, staring at the cold space where the flame had been.

"Shit, man," Ethan finally said. He drew his eyes from my palm to my face. His lip quirked into a smile. "You are in trouble if you think that's enough to fight me off."

I stepped back, just as Ethan's body curled apart, golden feathers exploding from his skin and rays of light piercing his flesh. I didn't stay to watch.

I turned and ran.

I had to find Kaira. *I can't. I can't. Forgive me. I can't do this.*

Behind me, I heard the screams of the falcon. And before me, Islington was covered in ravens.

Ravens lined every surface, cut circles in the air. They cawed from power lines and benches, rooftops and trees. They perched on the bodies of my classmates—some kids fighting, others prone and bloody. They screamed. The birds. And the kids. The ghost of my sister, appearing on benches and in trees. Always sad. Always accusing. Always begging me to bring her back.

I beat the birds away as I ran toward the nurse's office. Toward Kaira. Blindly. Unable to look up, to let my eyes be vulnerable to sharp beaks and sharper talons. I knew I was screaming. I knew that Heru was never far behind.

He would never be far behind.

I had let him in.

I had played with his power.

And that power would never be enough to save Kaira.

But I had to try.

I had to try.

The ravens didn't stop at the entrance. Shadows bled them into the room, dripping feathers like tar, an oil on the surface of everything. Lights flickered, or maybe it was just their wings, a strobe of shadows. Bettie was behind the desk, ravens in her hair, ravens at her lips. She moaned something, a harsh rasp, but I didn't stop to save her. She was already gone. And I had to save Kaira. I had to find Kaira. She was the only way out of this.

I rushed down the hall, the walls a living mass of black, fluttering wings, the ceiling a warren of charred heads with blind eyes and dripping beaks. The floor a crush of feathers and frail bones.

I followed the cold.

I rushed in, and there she was, lying in her bed, and the door slammed behind me. No ravens in here. Nothing out of place. Just Kaira in her bed, her eyes closed, and a terrible chill in the air.

But it wasn't silent.

Birds pounded on the door. The locked door. How did I lock the door? Birds calling my name, demanding I open up. Birds stealing Bettie's tongue.

Kaira didn't wake when I sat down on her bed. She didn't move when I put a hand to her icy forehead, when I patted her cheek. She was cold. Cold and gaunt like the dead, her eyes great shadows, her hair a spiderweb.

"Kaira, please," I whispered. I opened to the power, tried to give her some of my warmth. Tried to keep myself from burning her alive.

Please save me from this. Please help me. Please make it stop.

Because I knew—I hoped—that if she woke up, she'd help me fight the monsters. She'd send the ravens away. We could live normally; all this could be over. This could be okay.

"This will never be okay."

The birds outside still pounded, but the words were a bell, a clarity in the storm. I looked up at the god, who held the falcon in his glowing hands.

"Don't you see, Chris?" the god and bird said as one. "This will never be over. She is not your savior. Just as you are not hers. These are not your roles. She is the one who is causing all this. All your pain. If not for her, you would not be here. Your sister would not have died. This girl . . . she is your enemy. She is the pain behind your madness. Only we can make it stop. Only *she* can make it stop."

131

"How?" I whispered, staring at her, angry that the words could escape my lips. I wasn't listening to them. *I'm not giving in.*

"Kill her," the voices said. And I felt him now, behind me. His arms wrapped over mine, hands sunk into my hands. A warmth. A glow. A guiding.

My hands moved up to Kaira's neck. Her pulse was a caged raven, wild and violent and frighteningly delicate. One squeeze. One crush.

"And this will be over," he whispered in my ear. "All of this. Over."

I closed my eyes. I forced out her image. It didn't help. Her throat begged as the boy demanded.

"End this," he said. "Kill her, and the nightmares will cease. Embrace me, and you will know Heaven. Such a little thing, her life. Take it. It is yours."

When I opened my eyes, Kaira blurred around the edges, her body crystalline and glowing. But no, those were my tears. Falling to her skin. Turning to ice on her flesh. My fingers tightened. My fingers glowed.

"Bring her home," Heru said, but now it was my sister's voice, and her hands were on my shoulders. Telling me it was okay. Not her voice. Heru's. Was there a difference? Were they the same?

It didn't matter. It didn't matter. This had to end. For both of us.

"I'm sorry," I whispered. To myself. To the birds storming against the door.

I closed my eyes and tightened my grip.

KAIRA

CHAPTER TWELVE

Wake up, Kaira. Wake up. Her voice. My voice.

It inked through the darkness like silver, a swirl. It lifted me, steadied me. So why did I feel like I was drowning?

Wake up, Shadechild, she begged.

She had begged so much. To wake up. To let her speak. But I wouldn't. I wouldn't let her control me. I wouldn't let myself be someone other than myself.

I am you. And you must wake up.

The darkness grew thicker. Darker. And I was scared; my heart fluttered weakly, and the darkness closed in. I felt it press against my lungs, curled closer than Munin, closer than coffins. It contracted, a serpent, a snake, a dragon around my throat. *The Midgard Serpent guards the Tree, a dragon coiled beneath the sea.*

I couldn't breathe. Not underwater. Not in the darkness.

I had never been afraid of the dark. The shadows were my home. *Our* home. So why were these shadows so terrifying? Why did I suddenly fear the end?

Wake up!

And the darkness wasn't black; the silver not stars, but blood. A constellation of red sparks. Of ravens falling from the trees. The Tree. They fell in droves, in heavy clouds, the sounds of their broken caws barely overpowering their thuds when they hit.

Kaira, wake up! Do not let him win before it has begun.

She stood before me, wearing my skin, but though she stood within reach, she was eons away. She tried to reach. To force me to wake. But I would not be led. I would not be forced. I swirled in the stars, in the darkness. Hot blood like rain fell on my face.

Maybe this was my end.

Maybe this was what I had been waiting for.

So why did I hear crying?

His crying.

His.

"Chris."

My eyes blinked open, heavy-lidded, and there he was, leaning over me. His skin glowed gold. Angelic. Why was that terrifying?

Why was he crying?

Why couldn't I breathe?

My eyes did a slow scan, down from his closed, weeping eyes, to his arms. His arms stretched to the hands clasping my throat. His muscles contracted, straining—but not with pressure, not with force. He wasn't pressing tight into my neck, though I couldn't force in air. He strained against himself.

"I can't," he whispered. "I can't."

136

His grip didn't loosen.

Chris.

I tried to speak. Found only a gasp.

Then he opened his eyes. They locked on mine, and there it was, that spark, that gravity, that jolt from his chest to mine.

His golden eyes.

He blinked and pushed himself away, leaped off the bed. My lungs expanded on their own, a labored breath in, the rattling bones of the dead.

"Kaira," he said. Or asked. Blood thrummed in my ears, and I could barely hear him over the noise. My ragged pulse. My angry pulse. "It's you."

Like I would be anyone else.

Then he shuddered and clenched his hands to the sides of his head. His nails dug in, red half-moons pooling blood. Every muscle in his face contorted, his eyes shut so tight, I thought his eyeballs would rupture. What the hell was going on? Why was he here, in my room, covered in tears?

I tried to reach out, to get him to stop hurting himself, but I couldn't move. My limbs were limp, way too weak. Pain looped around my neck. I tried to push myself up to sitting, and the world swam with shadows.

"No," he whispered. To himself? To me, for trying to ask him what the hell was going on? Someone was pounding outside the door, calling his name. Saying he couldn't be in here.

Wait, this wasn't my room. Where was *here*?

"I won't do it," he said. His fingers clenched deeper. Blood dripped down his cheeks, and I couldn't move to make him stop.

I couldn't yell at him. Not even when his fingertips glowed gold, when the skin beneath charred and cracked.

His eyes snapped open and landed directly on me. My chest constricted.

"I'll never hurt you."

I'd never heard him sound so afraid. So unsure. And so determined.

Before I could ask what he meant, before I could even connect that he'd just been trying to strangle me in my sleep, he scrambled to his feet and slammed out the door.

The nurse, Bettie, stood there, confused, looking between him and me.

"Let him go," Freyja said from the shadows.

Let him go? Where? Where would he go?

Then it clicked.

I knew that fear. I knew that face.

I'd worn it the night I'd stared into the mirror, my mother's scissors slicing into my wrists.

Energy pulsed through my limbs. I couldn't let him hurt himself. I had no idea what was going on, but I knew that: I couldn't let Chris be hurt.

Before I could let Freyja or the nurse stop me, I pushed myself from the bed and ran down the hall. My head was fuzzy. The hall twisted as I ran. Chris raced in front of me. Fast. So fast. His coat trailing like wings. Freyja screamed in my head, telling me not to follow. *Let him go. Let him end it. Let this battle end now.*

If she wanted me to stay back, I would run forward. It was the only thing I knew for certain. I would never do what she wanted me to.

I ran faster.

Chris darted out of the nurse's office. I stumbled after him, vaguely aware that I was wearing pajamas. Vaguely aware that they weren't mine.

What was mine, anyway? What was mine beyond this fear, this need that clawed and cawed in the depths of my chest? The need to save him. The need to let him go. One of those emotions was mine. I didn't know which. Maybe they both were—maybe that was the problem. But I knew which need I'd act on.

So I ran, unable to do more than croak out his name. I didn't feel the cold air that slipped through my pajamas when I burst out the front door, barely noticed the ice that stuck to my bare feet. Chris dodged past a few kids wandering from the Dark Note, and they did little more than mutter. Until they saw me. Me in my pajamas and no shoes, and then they gasped. Beyond that it was silent, the air unnaturally calm and still, like we were all waiting for the storm to break. There was only the blood in my ears and my feet slapping icy pavement.

The ground felt warm. Maybe I was bleeding. Or maybe I was so cold, the rest of the world was a furnace.

I certainly didn't feel the wind whipping my face, the flecks of snow that had begun to fall.

I focused solely on Chris. Because my thoughts were a congealing whirl, my mind still stuck in that cosmic blackness, the slow swirl of constellations. If I let my gaze slip, if I let myself look at the corners of my vision, I would see her. Freyja. Standing naked in the snow, sometimes wearing my skin, sometimes her own. I knew the look she wore. I knew the disapproval. But as I ran across campus, Chris always a few steps ahead, I realized I didn't care.

She might be a god, but Chris was my friend. He was mortal, with a very mortal, very tender heart. I wouldn't let him snuff that out.

Why are you saving the one you need to kill? Why, when he was trying to kill you?

Because of his eyes. That look. That gravity.

That loneliness. I knew it. I knew it better than anything else.

We ran to the edge of the campus, him never slowing down, not even when I managed to yell his name—but how could he hear it over the ravens that cawed behind me? They burst from the trees at my footsteps, swirled above and around me in a cloud, never ceasing, never silencing. They screamed out not his name, but mine—they begged me to stop. Demanded it. The birds didn't vanish when we entered the woods. Freyja didn't cease her apparition at the corners of my vision, her face pained.

"You must kill him anyway," she called. "Let this end."

I couldn't. I wouldn't.

I followed closely at his heels. And there was someone else there, flickering in and out. Not Freyja. A girl. Her hair was short and dark and dripping wet, and she watched the both of us with eyes like moons and tears dripping diamonds.

Was she just in my head? Like Freyja? Like Munin?

Were they all in my head?

"Chris!" I yelled again. My word broke through the ravens,

but he only ran faster. And that was when I heard him. Yelling, *No, no, I won't hurt them. I won't hurt them.*

"He lies," Freyja said, flickering beside me, like Peter Pan's shadow, untethered and unceasing. "He will kill you."

I pushed her voice away. Pushed her *down*. I don't know how I did it, but I'd spent my entire life suppressing things. Maybe I was just used to it. Or maybe she was tired of fighting me.

We reached the lake too quickly. He didn't stop running, and I didn't stop following, even though the warm snow reached up my calves, nearly swallowed my knees. How was he faster? How was he so far ahead?

It was deep winter, the lake studded with ice houses and pickup trucks, yet the moment his feet touched the ice, I felt a rake of fear in my chest. I knew what he was going to do. I tried to run faster. Tried calling his name again.

Chris ran faster. Glowed brighter.

Then he stopped, just skidded to a halt in the middle of the ice, far from the huts, far from the shore. Far from me. I watched him stoop as I ran, watched him carve a small circle in the snow with a bloody knife, a ring of red, of roses. *Ashes, ashes . . .*

No. No, no, no.

I tried to run, but my legs slowed. Like they were stuck in molasses. Like they were no longer mine. And I felt her then, in my mind, clawing through my veins. Her words commanding me to stop. *Let him go. It will be easier then. Let him go.*

He turned to face me. Or maybe not me. Something flickered before him, just outside the circle. Something glowing and gold, a lace of wings and light. A bird. A boy. To the other side, the dripping girl, screaming silently, her hands outstretched, unable to pass the bloody circle.

I slowed. I forced Freyja down. Tried. She resisted, pushed harder, telling me this was the way it should go.

"You want me," Chris said. Not a question. Not to me. He stared defiantly at the figure that was and was not there, and it was then I knew who his anger and loneliness were trained at. The glowing, winged god. The figure that made my cold blood boil. "Then fucking have me."

The ice was thick. There were trucks parked on it farther away.

So why did I hear the crack? Why did the whole world shift?

Chris brought the knife to his wrist. He didn't slice. He stabbed.

I screamed out, but even I couldn't hear it over the rush. Chris flared with heat, with power. It poured into and from him, a light. A burn. He seared like the sun, and with it, a roar. A howl.

Thunder like gods calling.

Ice cracking.

The lake beneath me shifted. I fell to my knees, and then there was silence. Silence and darkness.

When I looked up, there was no sobbing girl. No circle of blood in the snow. No glowing figure.

No Chris.

Just a hole in the ice, the water beneath as black and surging as hell.

"You can't save him," Freyja said beside me, staring on with dispassion. "You should not try. Let him die. It will be easier for you both."

142

I wanted to scream at her, because what the hell did she know? I couldn't push myself to my feet. My legs had gone numb. Gelatinous. But I scratched my way forward, pulling through thick snow, even as—at the edges of my senses—I heard people calling out. Fishermen? Coming toward me. Toward us. Freyja kept pace at my side, her whispers of *he is lost, he is lost* spurring me forward.

Why did she sound so sad?

I forced my way forward, my tears staining the snow black.

Toward the hole.

Toward Chris.

Toward Hell.

When I neared, I nearly collapsed from the effort.

"He is gone, Kaira," Freyja said. She crouched beside the hole, beside me, both of us staring down into the sloshing black, the shatter of tiny ice crystals, swirling like sinking boats. Sinking stars. "His soul. He is gone."

He wasn't gone.

Not so long as I was there to find him.

I looked from the water to Freyja. I felt the sadness in her voice. Like she, too, felt the loss. And maybe she did. Maybe even the gods felt pain.

"Then you're helping me find him. Or dying with me."

The last things I felt as I slipped into the warm water were her hands on my back. The slow unfurling of carrion wings.

Then the water swallowed us whole.

CHRIS

CHAPTER THIRTEEN

Dreaming.

Must be dreaming. Screaming.
His hands
on my heart.
Tumbling
in darkness, sinking
light lifting. Not
lifting, falling
deeper.

"I won't
let you hurt her."
I will save her. God,
let this save her.
My words
choke

on water
not water. Something

heavier. Oilier. Deeper. No ocean
runs this deep. No lake
spans this far. Fathoms stretch
and he grips my heart as I grip
his throat, Kaira's throat. No. *His* throat.
Heru.
I must do this. I must
die. I must end this.
Him.
I must end him.

"I won't hurt her—"

We sink deeper. His light
fades. My light. My lungs.
Her hand,
reaching
down, a reaper—wings
of shadow. Fingers touch

"I won't—"

slip.
Fingers
slip. Sink.

fade

I won't . . .

You will.

KAIRA

CHAPTER FOURTEEN

Hell hath no fury.

They say that, don't they? Something about hell, and a scorned woman?

But that was not true at all. Because hell was silent. Hell hath no fury.

At least not here.

Maybe I just wasn't feeling scorned enough. Though Freyja definitely was.

I didn't need to ask where we were. I could feel it. Just like when you closed your eyes and walked into your childhood bedroom. I knew this place in the hollows of my bones. And now that I was here, I knew it had always been here. Always calling. Always waiting.

But still, I asked the question.

"Where are we?" Even my words felt heavy.

Freyja stood beside me, looking at the darkness like she *had* come to her childhood bedroom. And maybe she had.

"The Underworld," she whispered.

Just the way she said it made me know there was a capital U.

"Right," I replied. I stared around, tried to make shapes out through the darkness. But there was just shadow, just the cold, damp earth beneath my bare feet. The air was heavy and cool and wet, cavernous. Maybe it was my imagination, but I could feel the weight of the worlds resting above me, just as I could feel the yawning expanse of this place. Of course this was the Underworld. This afternoon I'd woken up in the nurse's office with a boy's hands on my neck. Where else would I have gone after that?

I looked to Freyja. She leaned against something— something wide and smooth that seemed to stretch from the floor up into the emptiness—and she watched me with those cold, violet eyes. I wished she would put on clothes; looking at her made me feel self-conscious.

It was then that I realized: This was the first time in ages I wasn't fighting her off. Wasn't trying to keep control over my own thoughts. Right now, I actually felt like myself. The "me" from before I killed myself, from before Munin's words of warning. I felt mortal and normal, and that made me want to laugh. Because I was in the Underworld, and that meant I was dead.

I'd spent the last few days fighting Freyja off, and the last however long in some strange half-consciousness, grappling with her, trying to keep her from fully taking control. I knew I'd invited her in. I'd jumped into that classroom circle and let myself open to her, if only to take down Jonathan and that . . . thing . . . that was controlling him.

The thoughts made my head swim. What had happened to Jonathan? The god made of owl feathers? And why did I keep thinking of Chris, when his mere mental image made my heart race? Even that, though, slid from my senses.

None of it mattered if I was dead.

The Underworld was a lot chillier than all those right-wingers had led me to expect. Where was the fire and brimstone? Because, I mean—I'd committed suicide to kill my ex. It wasn't like I expected to go to Heaven.

"It's not Hell," she said, looking at me. Her violet eyes were paler than usual. She looked tired. Could gods even get tired? "At least, not entirely. There are many levels to the Underworld. Infinite, really. You have a lot to learn."

"Why are we here?" If I was dead, okay—that wasn't the strangest thing I'd encountered. Something continued to claw at the back of my mind. A reason. A need.

"Because *you* dragged us here," she said coldly. "To save that worthless boy."

Memory hit me like a frigid wave. Chris, running toward the lake. Stopping. Stabbing his wrist. And then . . . a brilliant light. A hole in the ice, the water within as thick and warm as blood as it sucked him down. As it sucked *me* down. How had I forgotten about that?

I looked around, my heart suddenly hammering in my chest because, holy shit, I needed to find him. To *talk* to him. Chris had tried to kill me. I should have hated him for that. Instead, I was worried.

I was staring at a goddess who had tried to control me. I'd seen the glowing presence Chris was running from. We were both fighting our demons.

"Where is he?"

He'd been there. Just out of reach, beneath the waves. Our fingers had touched, and then he'd slipped away, and we'd both slipped into congealing darkness.

"The boy is not here because he tried to kill himself. You tried to save him. Those intentions lead to different places."

"So I'm dead?"

"Not quite. Not yet."

"Helpful."

She shrugged. I didn't think that was a motion gods would do. Every other time I'd seen her, she'd been apocalyptically powerful. Killing Brad. Taking down the force behind Jonathan. Now she just looked like a naked teenager, the same age as me.

"What happened to Jonathan?" I asked.

"Dead." She looked down when she said it, but not out of remorse. Like she was pointing.

"And . . . whatever it was controlling him?"

"Banished," she said, just as short. She looked at me. "And then you decided to throw away that victory by coming here. To save a boy I've told you time and again you will have to kill."

"I'm not killing anyone," I said.

"You already have."

But even though she mentioned what was normally a trigger, I wasn't paying attention to her, not really. If this was the Underworld, my body was somewhere else. I'd read enough to know that only souls could travel through the lands of the dead. So what was happening to my body? Was it still underwater? Slowly drowning?

"Your soul is here," she said. She sighed. She sounded perturbed. Gods could feel perturbed? "And so am I. Stuck."

Apparently gods could be passive-aggressive, too. I think I preferred just hearing from Munin. The raven at least was forthright. Most of the time. Freyja was just starting to sound spoiled.

"How long do I have?"

"Time doesn't exist—" she began, but I cut her off.

"Until I'm actually dead. Are you saying we could just stay here forever?"

"Forever is a measurement of time." Her voice fell flat. She stared at me like I was an idiot, as if suddenly realizing what it would mean to be stuck with me for eternity. Whatever "eternity" meant, that was.

I growled in exasperation and started pacing. The shadows never changed. Whatever lay beyond the two of us was completely obscured.

"Fuck," I grunted. "Okay. Fine. I came here to save Chris. So how do we do that? Where'd he get sent?"

"To where the suicides go."

My heart sank. My mom was pagan, so I'd never grown up with the hellfire speeches so many of my friends had endured. But that didn't mean I hadn't read Dante or heard the lectures from others. There was always a special place in Hell for the people who'd taken their own lives. Which I thought was complete and utter bullshit, because that never took into account the multitude of reasons someone would try to kill themselves, most of which had nothing to do with sin or selfishness.

"I don't believe in that," I said.

"What you believe does not matter here. It's not your death we're dealing with, but his. Which means we must follow his rules."

"What do you mean? You mean Hell *changes*?"

"The Underworld is infinite. Heaven and Hell exist here, in all their forms. Just as many gods exist here, in all *their* forms. What you call them is not so important. What you *believe* is what changes your experience. Since you have decided to follow this boy into death, you are following in the trail of his beliefs."

I stopped my pacing to look at her. We weren't *following* anyone. We were standing around, talking about Chris, when he was in danger.

"I need to save him."

"You cannot."

"What do you mean, *cannot*? Like, it's impossible? Or you just don't want to help?"

"Both." She said it so matter-of-factly, so without remorse, that I wanted to punch her. I balled up my fists, but I didn't leap. She might not be acting all godlike right now, but that didn't change what she was.

We were in the Underworld, and that meant I needed her help.

It also meant I needed to show her that she still needed mine.

"I'm going to save him," I said. "And you're going to help."

She just stared at me, her violet eyes empty.

"He tried to kill you, Shadechild. Just as you will do to him. Let him die down here. Let this go. And we can both return to Midgard. We will have won."

"Won *what?*" I asked. "You keep talking about a war that doesn't exist."

"Not yet," she said, "but it will."

She pushed herself away from whatever she was leaning on and walked over to me. When she neared, she dropped her voice to a whisper.

"There is so much you do not know, Shadechild. About your destiny. About his. It would be better if you let him die down here. For yourself, and for him, and for everyone you love."

"I don't believe in destiny," I said.

"And yet your entire life has been carved by it." She said it not to me, but to the shadows behind my ear. As if she were speaking to a mirror. "You cannot escape what you were made for, Kaira," she said. "No matter how hard or how fast you run, it will always find you."

My heart seemed to stutter at the fact that she said *made for* and not *born*, but I had bigger things to worry about.

"I'm not leaving without Chris."

"Then you are damning yourself to killing him in the mortal plane, or dying by his hand."

"It's better than letting him die down here by his. I have to try."

Something crossed over her face then—an emotion I didn't think I'd ever seen. Not in her. She looked lost.

"He was trying to kill you," she whispered.

159

"I don't believe that," I replied. "Otherwise he wouldn't have taken off. He's being hunted. By another one of *you*."

I actually did punch her then. Well, pushed her, really, but the action jolted her from whatever downward spiral she was in. Her eyes focused, and she glared at me.

"The Aesir and Vanir are at war," she hissed. "We are nothing alike."

"You're gods," I replied. "That's close enough."

"I am not a god," she said. She stepped back. "And neither is the godchild of the Aesir."

"I don't give a shit what you are. I don't care about this war. I care about finding Chris. You're going to help me, or we both die down here."

She crossed her arms and stared at me.

"Perhaps that would be for the best."

The shadows behind her rippled then, folding in on themselves like paper, and a moment later the great raven Munin appeared from the darkness, flapping down to land on her shoulder.

"You should not be here," he said. His voice was grating and oceanic, something older than time itself.

"*She* refuses to return." Freyja really did sound like an insolent teenager then. Talking to her father.

The raven looked at me, its pale eyes dim moons in the dark.

"You must return to the mortal world. You must lead us to victory."

I shook my head.

"I'm not leaving. Not without Chris."

I didn't know where this resolve was coming from. I barely knew Chris, and Freyja had a point—I *had* regained consciousness with his hands around my neck. But it also wasn't about him. I was tired of playing by their rules. I was tired of being a pawn. Saving Chris was my choice—something neither of them wanted to do—and that alone made fighting for it worth it.

Silence stretched between us. I felt it in my chest, a sort of weighing, like Munin was studying my resolve. I steeled myself. I wasn't leaving the Underworld without Chris. I wasn't going to be some vessel for someone else. This was my body. My life. My soul. My decision.

If they thought they could take that from me, they didn't realize what it meant to grow up with a pagan feminist for a mother.

Finally, after what could have been an eternity, Munin cocked his head to the side and spoke.

"You will find the boy. Then you will return to the mortal world. And there, you will live out your roles."

He didn't leave right away, and I could tell by the way Freyja's brow furrowed that he was speaking to her. Telepathically or something, because of course that was a thing. Before I could ask what the hell they were discussing, he flew off. The shadows seemed to swallow him whole, until only the white of his eye showed, until that too was eaten by shadow.

Freyja glared at me.

"I hope he is worth it to you," she said. "And I hope, for your sake, he isn't too far gone."

I didn't bother to ask what she was talking about.

I was starting to realize that when it came to the gods, ignorance was better than bliss.

Freyja and I walked in silence for a while, me just a step behind her. After a few dozen feet, the cavernous space sank in on itself, and I was able to make out walls around us. The air grew heavier, wetter, and every breath made me think I was inhaling air that hadn't seen human lungs in millennia. If ever. Farther on, I realized that the empty hall echoed with the sound of dripping water. Black stalactites stretched from the ceiling, some smooth and obsidian, others caked with crystals. *Stalactites stick tight to the ceiling, and stalagmites? Well, they might just reach up there some day.*

Gods, how was that tour guide's quote still stuck in my head?

Really, I thought I was taking this all quite well, or maybe I'd just left my doubt in my body, underwater. I was here in the Underworld with the goddess or godchild or whatever who'd been trying to take over my body. And right now, we weren't struggling or fighting. She was helping me rescue a guy I sort of knew and sort of liked.

The last thought nearly stopped me in my tracks. It wasn't the first time I'd thought it, of course, but it was the first time it really had weight. I mean, I'd gone to the Underworld for him. That *had* to be more than a passing crush.

Hormones didn't make teens that stupid, did they?

Munin and Freyja said he was my enemy, but something in my gut said otherwise. Something said that if I had him back in my life, if we worked this out, we would be unstoppable. Maybe that was why they didn't want me to save him. Maybe they were afraid that, if I had someone else in my life going through the same shit, I wouldn't put up with theirs.

"So where are we going?" I asked. My voice echoed down the hall. We'd already been walking for . . . what? A minute? A few seconds? I thought back to when we got here, but I couldn't place it. Maybe she was right about time not existing here.

She looked to me.

"And would you please put on clothes?" I asked.

She looked down.

I didn't think she rolled her eyes, but she may as well have.

The next blink, and she was wearing clothes. I expected something, I don't know, regal or whatever. A dress or silk shift or the like. But she wore tight leather pants and a loose gray tunic, a belt studded with daggers draped across her hips.

"Better?" she asked.

I nodded.

"I already told you where we are going," she said. "To find your lover."

"He's not my lover."

"Yet you love him."

That stopped me. A crush was one thing. But *love*?

"I don't love him."

The words came out on their own, a habit I wasn't ready to kick. I loved my parents. I loved Ethan. I wouldn't love a boy. At least not a straight one.

Freyja spread her arms. "We stand in the Underworld to rescue your enemy, and you cannot even tell me it is out of love?"

163

My mouth dropped open.

I thought of Chris. Of his stupid little smile and the way he kept eye contact when talking. Of the way his fingers held his paintbrush, and his hand danced over his canvas when he lost himself to his work.

I thought of his fear, of the agitation in his eyes when he'd told me about his sister. About when he was hit by a car and brought back in exchange for her life. About living forever with that guilt.

My heart twisted with the memory. Standing in the snow together so close, he could have kissed me, the cold air turned away by the gravity between us. That moment when I thought that maybe I wasn't so alone. That maybe someone else would be able to know me—all of me, even the shit I wanted to hide from—and not run away screaming.

Or end up dead in a circle of their own blood.

Was that love? I didn't think so. There weren't any fireworks, and I didn't want to jump his bones.

But I also couldn't stand the thought of being away from him. Of losing him. I wanted to be near him, wanted to watch his brows furrow while he worked. Wanted to hear him talk about art and movies, wanted to feel his heat as we walked side by side. Our hands linked and held in the pocket of his jacket . . .

"You are smiling," Freyja said.

I quickly stopped myself.

"You are in love," she continued, stepping closer. "Even if you do not see it. And that love will destroy you."

164

I pushed past her. I had no clue where we were going, but the tunnel only went one way.

"What do you know about love?" I asked. The words sounded cliché even before I said them.

"More than you," she replied. "Pray it stays that way."

CHAPTER FIFTEEN

I had a thousand questions I wanted to ask. And, as usual, I couldn't find a way to voice a single one. So we walked deeper into the land of the dead, the outer world silent and my inner world on fire. *Even though I walk through the valley of the shadow of death, I will fear no evil; for you are with me.* I had no idea where I'd heard that line—probably a movie—but I'd always liked it. Something about the visual of a shaded valley in the mountains. I didn't know, but I'd always found it comforting.

And fitting. Though I didn't think the original verse was about walking *with* evil.

I couldn't find a single scrap of fear in my body as we walked through the dark. Freyja was there in front of me. She was the one I'd been running from my whole life, and now here we were, in the land of the dead, and I no longer had to run. What was it they said about keeping friends close and enemies closer? I was walking with the shadow of my death. What was there to fear?

166

Instead, I only felt confusion. A thousand amplifying questions, and a single resonating need: to find Chris.

"You still haven't told me what's going on," I said. The tunnel we were in kept twisting deeper down, but beyond that, nothing was changing. Save for my ability to stay quiet.

"You're in the Underworld. We are finding the boy you're supposed to kill. I thought that was obvious. Even if pointless."

So gods could be testy, too. Good to know.

I stopped.

"But *why*? Why the hell do I have to kill him? Why was I saved for all this?"

She didn't pause, and she didn't answer, which meant I had no choice but to jog to catch up. I didn't let the question drop, though.

"What was that thing I saw on the lake? The golden thing. You called it—"

"An Aesir," she said. Her words were tight. "There are two realms of gods, Kaira: the Upperworld and the Underworld. The higher gods—the Aesir—live in the boughs of the Yggdrasil, the World Tree, luxuriating in sunlight and bliss and beauty for all eternity. The lower gods—the Vanir—live in the Roots. Where we toil away to ensure the Tree lives. For if it fades, we fade. We are the caretakers of Yggdrasil and, by extension, the Aesir."

"I never read that," I muttered.

"You wouldn't. Humans know about gods because we want them to. That also means we can withhold information."

I glanced at her. In this eerie nonlight, she truly did look otherworldly, like I could pass a hand through her and feel nothing but smoke. I'd never thought of gods like that. That they'd been the ones telling mankind the myths. We were the recipients. And we only got what they wanted us to have.

Seeing as my interactions with Freyja were tense at best, I could see why mankind didn't know much.

"But you're not a god?" I asked.

"No." For a while, she said nothing more, and I thought that was the end of it. Then her eyes flicked over to me, and I saw something in her expression that looked both angry and sad. "Gods are created, or simply part of Creation. I was born. For you."

For some reason, I didn't want to press the subject.

"And the Aesir? What's the war?"

"That is complicated and not for me to say. Munin will tell you when it is time."

I wanted to stop walking again—it seemed like my only tactic or upper hand down here—but I knew she wouldn't stop for me.

"Bullshit," I replied. "Munin told you to help me get Chris. You tell me I have to kill Chris. Which is it?"

She sighed. Again, she made a face that made me think she wouldn't answer.

"Letting your lover die down here would be the best for him, Shadechild. It would be the kind thing to do." Her words dripped with sadness, like she actually gave a crap about Chris's well-being. "That is why I begged you to let him go. But that is not what the gods want. They demand a war. And so, Chris cannot die down here. Neither can you."

There was a memory, a vision . . . me, on a battlefield,

168

surrounded by the dead. And Chris, standing opposite me, his body glowing, wings curled from his back like an angel of death.

Is that what we were? Angels and demons? Fighting the eternal, clichéd war?

Freyja laughed.

"Not quite," she said.

Right. I forgot she could read my thoughts. I tried to make my brain silent. But honestly, I was horrible at it. Big reason why I preferred painting over meditation—only one of those made my thoughts cease, and it didn't have to do with chanting.

We continued walking, the air getting deeper and heavier, the walls smooth and occasionally encrusted with diamonds or amethysts. I reached out and touched the gems. They glowed brilliantly under my touch.

"It's all real, isn't it?" I whispered.

"What?"

"Everything."

She shrugged. Answer enough. We kept walking while I tried to keep my brain still. I had to find Chris. I had to bring him back. If only things in life were that easy. And in death, I suppose.

"Much of what you have read or been told is a lie," she said after a while. "Or a truth that humans twisted over the years. But the root is there: The gods are real. The gods are hungry. And you are the one they chose to supply them with what they desire."

My gut twisted.

"What's that?"

"What you've already given," she replied. She made sure to

pause and look at me. Her smile was probably the first godlike expression she'd worn since coming down here: It was at once detached and cruel, impossible to understand and terrifying in its nuances. I could have tried painting it a thousand times and never once captured every meaning.

"The gods demand blood," she said, and it was then an old dream filtered into my brain. A man in a cloak. Jonathan. With the ravens Hugin and Munin on his shoulders—Odin's messengers. "The gods have always demanded blood. To speak with divinity, you must pay in pain."

I shuddered when she finished quoting my dream, like my body was trying to flush her words from my system. But I was still left feeling tainted.

"What do you mean?" I asked.

"Why else would the gods demand war, Shadechild? The Tree must be nourished. And since mankind has moved away from making sacrifices, you will do it for them. Our war with the Aesir will make the mortal world rich with blood, and Yggdrasil will flourish."

"I'm not killing anyone," I said for what felt like the millionth time. And, like all times, it felt futile.

"You already have. You swore yourself to me and to this task the moment you asked for your ex-lover's death. Brad died at your hands, and in his blood, you became ours." Her expression became stoic, but I could tell she was hiding something. "We aren't here to save Chris, Shadechild. We are here to bring him back to Midgard, so you may sacrifice him properly. The World Tree demands it."

Then she turned down a side tunnel I hadn't seen before, vanishing into the shadows.

I didn't follow right away. I stared at the space she had left, at the hole she had punched through my heart.

This wasn't a rescue mission after all. We were just here to gather the pigs for the slaughter.

No.

No, I wasn't going to let them use me. Just as I wasn't going to let them use Chris.

Maybe Freyja was right: Maybe humans had gotten their myths wrong over the years. But if there was one thing I'd learned in my studies, it was that gods thought they were omnipotent. They were proud. Cocky.

And they could be fooled.

I locked the thought deep down inside, where I'd hidden Brad and the thousand terrible things I'd experienced in my life. It was the one note of light in the darkness, the one balm against all that pain. It was stronger. *I* was stronger.

And if she thought she could control me, she—and the rest of this fucked-up Underworld—had another think coming.

The tunnel she'd vanished into wasn't a tunnel at all, but an opening to a view that made me stop in my tracks, all thoughts of anger or revenge vanishing in an instant. The Underworld was vast and quiet and glittering like a galaxy. I could only stare and blink at the edge of everything, trying to take it all in. Trying to make it make sense.

I couldn't tell if there was a ceiling or a floor—the shadows were too thick, the darkness too deep—and above and below me was nothing but space. But the space wasn't empty. Even through the darkness I could see them. I could *feel* them. The pulse I'd felt since entering here amplified by a thousand. It shimmered over my skin like electricity, tugged at my veins, dared my heart to come closer, *closer*. I knew its power. I felt its need. Just as I knew the Underworld in the marrow of my bones, I knew what waited before and around me. And yet, my lips still formed the question.

"Are those . . . ?"

"Yes," she replied, her own voice tinged with the barest hint of awe. And spite. "The roots of the World Tree itself. Behold, the pillars of Creation."

We stood there for a moment, looking out into the darkness. The roots were impossibly large, twisting and twining down through the cavern like shadowed cursive. Some were as thick as skyscrapers or houses; others so wide, I couldn't see anything past them. One spiraled down toward us, various tubers jutting from the bent-angled shape, looking for all the world like some Tim Burton creation. I reached up, went on tiptoes. The pull was too strong. I had to touch it. I had to *feel*. I stretched up, and it felt like the root stretched back down.

My fingers touched treeflesh. I barely had time to register that it was warm, pulsing.

Blood leaked across my vision—blood and starlight—and everything was swirling, swirling and sparkling like fireflies on a lake, a lake of blood, a lake of power, and there at the lake's edge was a wolf, and under the lake roiled a dragon, and in the stars the gods waited and wept as the worlds spun and glittered, as oceans churned galaxies to life, as waves curled those galaxies back under, as the Tree stretched and groaned in its growth and branches fell and roots stretched. A lake of worlds and blood and starlight spiraled at its base and—in the distance—other Trees with tangled roots, and at the heart of that web, a spark, a fire, a serpent lined with teeth, and in those roots, in the shadow of feathers and shattered bones, I heard a heartbeat. Her heartbeat.

My heartbeat.

Pain flashed as something smacked against my wrist. The vision shattered, and suddenly I was back. Back and cold and covered in sweat, my breath panting and my eyes dripping tears.

Freyja's grip was tight on my wrist. She stared at me for a long, long time.

"You would do well not to touch the face of God without permission," she whispered.

Then she let go of my hand and turned. I glanced up, my heart racing. The root still dangled there, just within reach.

What the hell was that? But I couldn't ask, because part of me knew I couldn't know. There were some things mortals just weren't meant to understand. The longer I was down here, the more I believed it.

Thankfully, Freyja didn't let me stand around and wonder. She walked forward, off the ledge, and for the briefest moment I thought she was stepping to her death. Then I realized there was a staircase jutting out from the earth, slabs of stone stretching from the cliffside and leading down into darkness.

"I thought Yggdrasil was a metaphor," I muttered as I followed her down. Because if there really was a big tree stretching between the realms, why didn't it exist in the real world? I mean, my world.

"It exists," she replied. "Though most do not see it. The Tree is what holds the cosmos together. The axis on which our realms spin."

"It's so beautiful," I whispered. And I didn't even mean the vision. The farther down we went, the more accustomed I grew to the light, the more I noticed the details: the crystals that studded a few roots, as though the sap had turned to amethysts. Or the pulse that hummed like music in my veins and ears, telling me this was perfect, that everything was okay. My fingers itched to paint this—to create a landscape of twisting shadows and silver-leafed stars. *I wonder if I'll ever actually paint again.*

"Beauty is a weapon," Freyja said, pulling me from my thoughts. "Do not be lulled by it."

"Is it dangerous here?"

"Of course. It is dangerous everywhere."

"But you were born here," I said.

"And you were born on earth. Did you feel safe there?"

A hundred other memories should have surfaced—walking home alone at night, watching school shootings on the news, or the thousands of angry, violent protests against abortions or gay rights or anything remotely liberal—but the thought that cemented itself in the front of my mind was Brad. His beauty had been a weapon, and he had used it to cut me deep. I hadn't felt safe since then. At least, not around guys. Save, perhaps, for Chris.

"Exactly," Freyja said, confirming that she could read my thoughts.

But I couldn't see what could be dangerous down here. I mean, sure, the Underworld was always seen as treacherous, but this place was quiet. Just the sound of our muted footsteps on stone, even our words somehow swallowed up in the darkness like we were covered by blankets. It was too quiet. Too slow. Chris was trapped somewhere, being tortured—because wasn't that what Hell was? Eternal torture? And the longer we slowly meandered, the longer he suffered.

"Where are we going?" I asked.

"Down."

"No shit."

She glanced back at me; I couldn't tell through the shadows if she was grinning or pissed.

"Your lover sent himself to the deepest bowels of the Underworld," she said, before turning and continuing on. "A place I have never been, and a place from which few ever return. So I do not know where we are going, precisely. I do not know what we will find. I only know that we must go down. Down to the places where the damned are kept. From there, it is anyone's guess."

"And after I bring him back. After I save him. What's this war? You know, the one I refuse to be part of?"

"There has always been a war, Shadechild," she whispered, her pale eyes fixed on mine. "Between Heaven and Hell, the

Aesir and Vanir, the light and the dark. And the human world has ever been the battleground and the prize."

She sighed, ran her hand along the earthen wall. Crystals glimmered into light at her touch, tracing constellations that raced out into the night. More roots twined through the earth, one as large as my torso twisting into and out of the wall like an obsidian worm, its skin smooth and giving off a heat I could feel even from here.

"The mortal world is the crux on which our entire existence, this entire cosmic system, rests. Perhaps it would be best for you to see, to understand. To know why you must fight. To know why there must be blood."

She knelt then, facing the wall, and pulled a thin dagger from the belt at her waist. I heard her mutter something, a prayer, perhaps. The hum I'd grown used to changed pitch, became almost a murmur, and maybe it was a trick of the light or maybe it was truth, but I swear the root in front of her moved. Toward her. Like a cat arching its back to be pet.

Freyja reached out, still whispering her prayer, and sliced a slight, thin line against the root.

There was no denying it this time: The root twisted slightly, and rather than amber, sap poured out, a glimmering, bluish-purple light filtering through the slash.

"Come," Freyja said, holding her hand out to me. I took it. Why was my hand shaking? Why did this feel like some strange form of Communion?

She guided me down to kneeling. The slash was at eye level. Had it been that height, or had the Tree moved to accommodate?

"It is time you understood your role in all this," she said. "As it has been before, it shall be again."

I barely heard her over the pulse in my veins, the pulse in the Tree. My hands reached out on their own, pressed against the root, as my neck craned closer and I peered inside the core of the universe.

CHAPTER SIXTEEN

I floated above a field. It spread before me, but I was not part of it. I floated above. Behind. And even though I could smell the air, the lightning waiting in the clouds, I knew it was a memory. Not mine. One I had been born with and had been born to forget.

The air was heavy with anticipated rain, the clouds gray and thick and churning, but the rain wouldn't come. Just as the fields below—once filled with wheat and cattle—would fail to yield food. The knowledge was deep—it seared through the core of me: The world was dying.

I turned, or perhaps the world turned, and I saw the Tree. I could only see the trunk of it, and barely a glimpse at that. It rose from the earth like a monument, as wide as the horizon and stretching farther into the heavens than the eye could see, its roots digging deeper than the earth ever went. I saw the Tree. And I wept.

I could feel its pain. I could feel the hunger. It echoed in my own stomach, twisted itself through my heart. I felt it call out. It didn't demand blood. It begged for blood. For sacrifice.

It begged to be seen so it might do its work.

"Without worship or sacrifice, the Tree withers," came Freyja's voice. I didn't see her, but I felt her there, beside me, a shade of ice. "To sacrifice willingly is the greatest power. But it can be offered. It can be taken. The races of old knew this—they offered their captives, their priests, their maidens. They gave the greatest gift back to the Creator: their own lives, so others might live. But as time seeps forward, many forget the power of sacrifice. The debt they owe to Creation. Humans believed that life was simply theirs to live, a gift freely given. They forgot that all things come with a cost, and those who refuse to pay not only suffer but damn the rest.

"Without worship, Yggdrasil dies. And as the Tree dies, so too do the worlds it supports. That is why the War was created, why the godchildren are born. We are made to remind humanity of their mortality, of their rightful place: kneeling, reverent. Fearful. We are made to take what should have been given."

Shadows swirled in the field, lightning flashed through the clouds, and between one heartbeat and the next, the scene was no longer empty.

A boy stood in the field, naked as the moon, hair as dark as midnight, while a dark-skinned girl with glowing hair and luminescent wings floated in the sky.

"May our sacrifice nourish the Tree," they said as one. His voice, cold diamonds; hers, a brilliant lotus.

The girl floated down, her feet just barely alighting on the starved grass.

A circle burned itself into the ground between them. They each held out a hand.

"To the Tree, we give our lives," they said. "May this be the first of the blood given. May all blood spilled nourish Yggdrasil. May the gods feast, and the Great God thrive."

Then they cut their palms, spilling their blood into the earth. Two armies appeared on the horizons the moment they did so. There was a shudder. A vibration ringing low in the air like a gong. A hunger. A thirst. The first taste of blood. The need for more.

The Tree accepted the offering. And the Tree would accept many more.

I blinked, and the godchildren were locked in battle, and around them the armies crashed and bled, their cries a hymn, their blood a blessing.

This world had seen bloodshed so many times. But rarely had it experienced war like this. A war dedicated to serving the gods. A war waged only to make the ground rich with offered blood.

I wanted to feel disgusted. I wanted to think this was wrong. So many people dying. So much blood. So much agony.

But all I felt was the elation of the power, the flood of ecstasy that dripped through the soil; the roots of the World Tree soaking it up hungrily. I felt the Tree pulse with pleasure, felt it grow stronger.

Day tripped into night, and night flashed to day, and weeks

passed in a matter of moments. Soon, there were only the god-children, standing amid the dead, locked in their eternal battle. They were wounded, panting, the girl wielding a sword with bloodied hands while the boy fought back with a spear carved from the Tree itself. I watched them battle, and felt the fear rise in my chest. The boy was faltering—I could see it in his missed swings, in the way the girl's blows came a little too close to his body.

And then she struck.

In movies, deaths are beautiful. Scripted and choreographed and artistically rendered.

This was nothing like the movies.

She hacked into his shoulder, her blade becoming lodged in his bones. He screamed as he dropped the spear, as she pulled out the blade with a terrible wrench, blood and bone grinding against the glowing steel. She struck again, this time low, cutting into his calves. He fell to the ground with another scream. His blood was red and smoked with shadows.

Around them, a new circle formed. This of his blood as he fell to the ground and convulsed, the red liquid oozing against the saturated ground, curling around his body in an arc, carving a trail through the fledgling blades of grass.

The girl stood over him. She raised her sword high.

"To the Tree do I offer this sacrifice. May the Aesir forever reign in Heaven."

"To the Tree," the boy choked.

Then she stabbed down, straight through his heart, and he said no more.

I expected something more. Something beautiful. Perhaps for his body to dissolve into the ground, or vines to pull him under, or for shadows to seep in and swallow him whole. None of that happened.

"For the Aesir," the girl whispered.

"For the Aesir," Freyja muttered bitterly. I blinked, and was back in the cavern, kneeling at her side. My skin was covered in goose bumps, and tears ran down my cheeks. Why had I been crying?

"Always for the Aesir," she continued. "Every battle has been won by them, and so the Underworld grows restless. The battle is made by the Tree to nourish the Tree, but we—the servants—have our own desires. The gods of the Underworld wish to rise up, to live amid the sunlight in the branches of Yggdrasil. The victor of the war is worshipped by mankind, to live eternal in the hearts of men, under whatever guise they choose. The Vanir have lain outside the memory of men for too long. They want victory for more selfish reasons. But in the end, our desires are unimportant. Just as your desires are unimportant. We must all set aside our personal wants for the needs of the Tree."

"It's just a tree . . . ," I began, but she shook her head.

"The Tree is God."

"But I thought . . . I mean, you're sort of a god. And Munin, and the Allfather . . ."

She continued shaking her head, and stood.

"There are many gods. But there is only one God. And that is the Tree. There are many worlds and many World Trees, but the sap of God flows through them all."

So much for God being a man with a beard. Or a woman, for that matter.

"How vain, humanity is, to believe that a being that has existed for eternity—that *is* eternity—would wear their face."

"Says the goddess-thing who looks human," I replied.

She shrugged and held out her hand. For some reason, I took it, let her help me to standing.

"I was made in your image," she said. She looked right at me—right through me—when she said it. "And—again—I am not a goddess."

"Right," I replied. I sighed and stared around at the cavern. "So it's all for this. To feed the Tree."

"It's why you were born. And why I was born. And why your lover was born. All to wage this war. All to serve the Tree."

I'd spent my life running away. First, from the fact that I couldn't remember my past. Then from a past I didn't want to remember.

Now it felt like all my running had led straight to this: a brick wall at the end of the road and no way to turn back. I might have been moved by the vision, but now that it was fading, I was just getting pissed.

"Don't take it personally," she said. She started walking again. It was only then that I realized the root had healed itself.

How could I take it personally when everything about this was impersonal? Nothing in my life mattered. Nothing I'd done had mattered. Nothing I wanted to do mattered. I was just, what? A piece of machinery? Living fertilizer?

"Does it ever piss you off that your only role in life is to kill and die?" I asked.

I hadn't meant to say it, really. And when she didn't respond, I thought maybe I hadn't. Then, a few steps later, she said without stopping, "Every day." She looked over her shoulder then. "You're not the only one who gave up their hopes of a future for the Tree."

"And you just go along with it," I muttered.

"I have no choice," she replied. "I am made of the Tree, and I will die for the Tree. Those who win the battle live for eternity. The other isn't even granted rebirth. Focus on that."

Like hell. I wasn't going to live forever if it meant giving up what made me human.

Maybe I was just a cog. Maybe I wasn't the first mortal to go through this. But maybe they'd never dealt with someone like me before.

I may have spent my life running, but I'd also spent it learning how to survive. How to make life *my own*. And there was no way anyone would take that from me. Not Brad. Not Freyja. And not some fucking Tree.

CHAPTER SEVENTEEN

We didn't speak as we continued on. The path dipped and twisted, tunneling and then opening, passing under tangles of roots or brilliant skyscapes of crystals and gems. Eventually the path led to what seemed to be one enormous root, which we hopped on top of and began treading slowly down. I wanted to be running. We should have been running. Chris needed me.

But what was I going to do once I'd saved him? What would happen when we were back in the mortal world, back at Islington? Back with Ethan and Oliver and Elisa and *holy shit, I hadn't even thought about them. How are they doing? Are they worried?* Elisa couldn't stand sleeping in our room when I was away. Said it gave her nightmares. And I'd woken up in the nurse's office. How long had I been out, and how many nightmares had haunted Elisa in my absence?

Funny that I wondered that, seeing as it felt like I was living one.

I tried not to think about Chris, but of course he was all I could focus on. Just the thought of him made me feel warm, even surrounded by the heavy, cold air. The curve of his smile when he thought I wasn't looking at him. His hair shifting colors from auburn to maple in the thin Michigan light. I could *feel* him. Still. Even here, in the depths of the Underworld, I could feel him out there. Needing me. And in some strange way, I knew I needed him. And not just because of some cosmic war I still refused to play into.

Chris wasn't my savior, but he *was* the first spark of warmth I'd felt for as long as I could remember. Even dating Brad—at the height of my stupid infatuation with him—had seemed wrong. Like I was playing the wrong part in a play. Chris was like a complementary color. He didn't mirror me, but when I was around him, I felt more myself. More comfortable *being* myself.

"Beauty is a weapon," she said again. "Do not think for a moment that your love for him is true. He was crafted to compel you, just as you were created to draw him. It is part of the battle. It is a sacrifice that makes the Tree sing."

"What the hell do you know of sacrifice?" I hissed, suddenly jarred back to the cold reality. "All you've done is kill and take. Is that why you want me to kill him? Because you're jealous? Because you just want my life?"

She was on me before I knew she'd turned around. One moment, she was ahead. The next, her hand was on my chest, pressing me to a root. Her eyes blazed, and it was not my imagination—the rest of the world dimmed around her, the jewels of the Tree blinking out to fuel her anger.

"You know nothing of what I've sacrificed for you. You think you are the only one to know loneliness. To know loss." Her voice cracked. She didn't look away, though, even though tears formed in her eyes. "You know nothing of me, Shadechild. I have lost more than—"

She cut herself off, her eyes going wide with fear. I opened my mouth, but her hand was pressed over it in an instant, silencing my question.

Then I heard it. Like wind through the branches, or a rusted gate opening far away, the noise sending chills up my spine.

"Shit," she whispered. I almost laughed, if not for the fear that paralyzed me—*shit* didn't seem like a curse word she should know. I forced her hand off my lips. She didn't resist. She was too busy staring wildly into the shadows.

"What is it?" I whispered.

"That beautiful danger I spoke of. Be quiet." Then she yanked me forward and began to run, dragging me in her wake.

The keening screech grew, and it wasn't a single note but a cacophony of pitches, a hundred voices screaming. I was suddenly acutely aware that I was in a foreign land, with no clue where I was going, no clue what I could be up against, and no way to defend myself. Not that I'd know how, even if I had the opportunity. The only thing protecting me was a creature that wanted to use my body to kill a boy I thought I was falling for. Which didn't sound like much protection at all.

No matter how fast we ran, every step we took seemed to bring the screaming closer. The dread that iced through my veins gave me speed, but even that didn't seem to be enough. I was reminded of those dreams, when I'd woken up screaming

187

and covered in sweat, because I had been pursued. Woken the moment the talons had clutched my heart.

There wouldn't be any waking when this monster caught me.

I covered my ears as I ran. But still, the screaming sliced through, and the scenery didn't change, and I felt, with this terrible sense of certainty, that I was going to die down here. My mind conjured a thousand different horror stories, nightmares that leaked into the landscape like ink, covering the darkness with promises of pain and destruction. The noise grew. Freyja ran faster.

Then it stopped.

We stopped too.

"They are here," she said.

She actually sounded afraid.

"Who?" I asked.

I didn't need to ask.

The lights around us began to blink, like the moon through a murder of crows. But there wasn't anything fluttering around in the silence. Nothing moved. No breeze or wind, just the blinking of lights.

Blinking.

Not like gems. Like eyes.

Then the roots began to shift.

Shadows peeled from treeflesh, unfolding into monstrous shapes that stretched themselves out into figures my brain couldn't comprehend. Bats. Or vultures. Or women made of shadow and tar. They stretched silently from the roots, their eyes glinting violet, their teeth and talons glittering razors.

"Run!" Freyja yelled. Daggers materialized in her hands in a swirl of shadow.

The creatures launched themselves toward us. There were hundreds of them. Thousands. Women with cicada wings and raven silhouettes, and they leaped from the tree roots, screaming like the damned. My legs froze in place. Their faces were too long, their mouths too stretched. Their limbs oiled and inked and elongated, wings in dozens of shapes, all of them horrible. But I couldn't run from them. I couldn't move a damn muscle. The harpies swooped, screamed, and I swore they were calling my name. . . .

"Damn it, Kaira!"

Freyja turned and shoved me. Hard. I stumbled away, but the momentum was the shock I needed; I kept running. And I didn't look back.

I heard her. Heard her screaming and fighting, the sound of her daggers clanging against claws, the rip of flesh, but it was muffled under the harpies' cries. Muffled under the screams of them following me.

My breath burned in my lungs and I ran faster, stumbling deeper into the darkness, the light not growing. I prayed that the end would be near, that I'd wake up and this would all be a dream. But I didn't wake up, and blood thundered louder in my ears as my breath ripped through my throat. This wasn't a dream. Definitely wasn't a dream. I was definitely going to die.

They swarmed me. Of course they swarmed me. I had nowhere to go but forward, and in no time they were there, blocking my way, their great slick wings moving slowly, like lungs breathing sickness, their bodies somehow beautiful and grotesque, like a figure painter had taken her exquisite work and stretched it, stained it. Coated it with coal and nightmare.

A creature landed in front of me. I bit back a scream. Where were the ravens now, to protect me?

"Such warmth," the harpy hissed. Her words scratched from her lips like sandpaper. "Give us your warmth. Let us hold it."

"Let us taste it," came another.

"Such sweet warmth."

I held my fists up. Like I could fight. Like I could possibly fend them off. I couldn't hear Freyja anymore. Was she too far away, or was she dead?

"Pretty girl," the first harpy said. She stepped toward me. Her feet were talons. Vulture claws. Her calves scaled and coated with muck. "So pretty. You will make us pretty."

"Get away from me," I said. Because there was nothing else to say, and even as the words left my lips, I knew it was pathetic. The harpies didn't laugh or smile. They didn't register the fear in my voice. The one before me took another step forward. She reached out, her clawed fingers inches from my shoulder.

She smelled sour, like rotten milk. Bile rose up in the back of my throat.

"Let us wear you," she said. "Let us wear your warmth."

Then I realized why my stomach twisted at the sight of her. Her face wasn't her own—the skin was stretched tight, stitched into place. And it was decaying.

Sharp pain pierced my shoulder. I screamed and tried to dodge away from the harpy whose talons had dug into my skin.

190

Another scream, this coming from the harpy. She lunged.

I shoved my shoulder into her, tried to sidestep. But I wasn't a fighter. I wasn't trained in self-defense. She grabbed me, wrenched my arm even as another swooped toward me. I ducked low. Pushed against flesh, tried to move past her. I had to keep running. Had to make it . . . *Where?*

It didn't matter. The answer, or the question.

I made it three steps. Then a hand caught the back of my shirt, scratched against my spine. My motion twisted. I tripped. Fell sideways.

And with a terrible rush of fear to my throat, I realized I hadn't fallen onto the root. I'd fallen off.

Even the darkness couldn't swallow my screams.

CHRIS

CHAPTER EIGHTEEN

Screaming.

So much screaming. Whose voice?

My mother, screaming, covered in blood. A baby wailing. Bri. Bri screaming my name, her words bound in blood. And Kaira. Calling out to me. Afraid. Kaira.

Kaira.

My eyes fluttered open, and I thought . . . I thought it had just been a dream. It had to have been a dream. It couldn't be my reality.

The dark room, the circle of light pooled against the dirt floor. A hospital bed, half in and half out of the shadow leaking against the edges. The empty hospital bed. But I knew it was the same. The same one I was birthed on.

I could taste the tang of her blood on the air.

I forced myself to standing. Where was I? What had I been doing?

My thoughts swam with my head and I swayed to the side,

or maybe the room tilted. Though the bed didn't move and the shadows stayed solid. I looked to the darkness. Tried to find a wall out there. Rooms had walls. And I was in a room. A room with walls.

And then I heard her scream again.

My body moved slowly—turning to face the bed, feet shuffling not forward but away. Away from the woman on the bed, her face twisted in pain and her hands clutched to the bed, to my father's hand. Her knuckles as white as the blanks of her eyes that turned to the ceiling. Seeking. What? God? Release?

Both?

My father knelt there. He leaned in, held her hand tighter even as blood spilled from her gown and down the bed, the gurney. Dripping to the floor. Red molasses river.

"There is no God here."

My dad's words.

No, mine. My jaw working against itself.

He held her hand tighter and the air was cold, so cold. Her blood pooled and crystalized. Spread like two arms around the circle of light. I turned. My mother screamed again. I couldn't watch this. Couldn't see . . .

She was there. In front of me. The circle of light, the bleeding bed. I turned again. And she was there, screaming. Only my dad now stood above her, holding a blade to her belly. A machete.

"He must live," my dad said. A voice deeper than darkness. A falcon. "He must be born in blood."

I closed my eyes, but I could see through my eyelids. Covered my eyes. Could see through my hands. The blood, circling me, caught in the center of light. And the blade piercing her stomach as light pierced the sky and she screamed. I screamed.

But why was I screaming?

The sand was warm beneath my knees, our sand castle nearly built. She'd drawn a circle around us. To keep the monsters out, she said. Because monsters couldn't cross our moat without the password.

The password was *Pink Cheetah*.

"I'm going to find a shell for the roof," Bri said. She stood and dusted the sand from her knees. The sky was gray. So was the horizon. But the water beckoned and I nodded and told her not to go far, because I had to build the drawbridge from the driftwood we'd found. Just in case the monsters got past the moat. Sometimes even passwords weren't enough. Even I knew that.

"Should our moat have a Loch Ness Monster?" I asked.

She didn't answer.

I looked up. There was only gray. I pushed myself to standing.

"Bri?"

I walked forward. But I couldn't get over the moat. The moat was wide and filled. With something dark.

Then she called my name.

"Bri!" I screamed to her. She screamed back.

And I tried to run, but the moat stretched out, and the dark waters churned and bubbled and steamed. And something swam through it, wiggling against the surface. Scales rippled through the water and I wanted to run away. Back to the castle. Where it was safe. Then Bri screamed again, and I knew I couldn't just stay there.

One toe into the water. The warm water.

A snake tail snapped out and wrapped around and pulled me under before I could blink or gasp or step back, and I was down, down. But I wasn't drowning. Even with the dragon's tail around me, I could breathe in the blackness. Bri couldn't. She was in front of me, fighting a dragon the size of the moon, its claws wrapped around her tiny body like she was a doll. Bubbles popped from her lips as she screamed. My name. And I screamed back, but I couldn't reach her. The dragon no longer held me, but I couldn't swim, couldn't move in the thick water that pulled me down. Down. Away from her. Until she was a white dot in the sky. A star.

The dark sky, so cold. A thousand tiny stars spread across it, a blanket of gems.

"You came," she whispered.

I looked down, wondering why Kaira was surprised. Of course I came. I would follow her to the ends of the earth and farther. She stood in the starlight, and I'd never seen her more beautiful. Her eyes locked on to mine, her smile a curve, her dark skin glowing with a light of its own. She stepped forward. She wore a long coat, as white as the snow at her feet, and her streaked hair was pulled back behind her, falling over her back in multicolored threads. Her earrings were dangling white circles. Like outlines of the missing moon.

She stepped forward, and I stepped toward her. The space between us closed, folded in like hands coming to prayer, and I swore the night air grew still. Like even the woods around us had been waiting for this moment. Were holding their breath.

"Kaira, I—"

Her finger pressed to my lips, silencing me. Then she leaned forward and replaced her finger with her mouth.

I melted.

Her lips were cold, frosted from the night, but when she pulled me close, she was warm, and her tongue danced over mine, and I felt my heart race against my ribs. This was what I had wanted. Had dreamed of. Had thought I could never have.

Her.

I had wanted her. And now she was drawing my arms around her waist and leaning in to me. She pressed so perfectly against me. Like that was where we were meant to be.

"I love you," she whispered, leaning back to look into my eyes. Her eyes glinted in the moonlight. My heart flipped again.

"I love you too," I said, and it was the truest thing I'd ever felt.

I leaned in, pressed my lips to hers once more, and the warmth in my chest blossomed, became a sun that lit the night with heat and gold. The pressure between us built, and I pulled her closer, the love in my heart turning to desire. To need.

"Chris," she muttered against my lips. I bit her lower lip in response. Her moan filled my veins. I bit harder, tasted the iron of her drip against my tongue. She gasped, arched her back, her hands against my chest. Her hands tightened.

The heat grew brighter. I wanted her. Needed her. I covered her mouth with mine again, my teeth bathed in red.

One arm gripped her waist, our hips pressed tight. The other hand trailed up, slid under her hair and around the fragile curve of her neck. I grasped the base of her skull, pulled her tighter to me, until our teeth clashed and bit and it hurt, but oh, did it feel like Heaven. So much heat in Heaven. So much golden light. I closed my eyes against it, the circles of her earrings burned into my eyelids. The circles. The circles.

"I want you," I whispered into the golden light, into the shadowed circle. "I want you more than life itself."

She struggled. Her breath hot in my lungs, her heart a trapped rabbit. Her ribs snapping against my chest.

And then the light faded. And her pulse fell as she dropped from my hands to the ground.

As my love dropped lifelessly to the ground.

As reality fell through my senses.

"No. No, no, please."

I collapsed to my knees. No, I couldn't have done this. Wouldn't have done this. I wouldn't have hurt her.

You were born in blood. This is your power.

"Kaira!" I screamed.

"All this blood on your hands," my sister whispered. "All these deaths."

I turned to her, but she wasn't there. Just the hospital bed at the edge of the circle of light. The empty hospital bed. But I knew it was the same . . . I knew . . .

"Come on, honey," my dad said, holding my mother's hand. "Come on, you can fight through this."

The screaming. The blood. And my sister yelled at my weakness as my mother yelled for mercy.

"Fight!" my dad yelled. As blood encircled the room, as the screaming grew louder.

I curled in on myself, clutched my hands to my ears.

There is no God here. . . .

KAIRA

CHAPTER NINETEEN

I woke to cold.

For a moment I thought I'd truly woken up, that it had all been a nightmare—though how far back that nightmare went, I wasn't certain. Snow flecked the ground in front of me. Was I outside? Had I fallen asleep in the woods? It was quiet. So quiet. Save for the distant sound of dripping.

Then I pressed myself to sitting. Or tried to. My back screamed out, and I bit back my own cry. I reached around, feeling the tattered cloth, the matted blood. And I remembered.

Immediately I jerked my head up, looking toward the sky and surroundings for any sign of the harpies. But there was nothing. Just a net of tree roots above and the snow-covered ground. A hole in the roots that looked like a space I might have broken through. No harpies. No danger, save for my leaking blood.

No Freyja.

I couldn't help the cry of pain as I forced myself to standing. Every joint ached, and the snow below me was soaked crimson, a splatter that made me wonder how I was still alive. *How far did I fall?* But the thought was as numb as my bare feet. All I could think of was getting out of here. Getting Freyja. Getting Chris.

Before it was too late.

What if she was dead? What if it was already too late?

What would happen if I slowly starved down here?

My hand still clutching the slash on my back, I hobbled and looked around. I wasn't entirely certain I was on solid ground; the snow sloped away on both sides, a gentle rise. Had I landed on another root? Was this whole place just a labyrinth of roots and stones and demons?

"It is what you make of it," came a voice.

I spun around—wincing at the movement—and there, standing beside my bloodstain, was a man that had definitely not been there before. I stepped back. Not that there was anywhere to go—the roots and vines formed a dome around us, as thick at the top as they were at the sides. Keeping danger out. And me in.

The man's skin was white. Paler than even Freyja's, his veins a cobweb of blue beneath his flesh. He wore nothing but a tattered robe, a shapeless, colorless blanket as ragged as he was. Even his beard seemed threadbare, like it was made of wisps of spider silk and frayed string. Despite all of that, his eyes were sharp and clear. When they looked into mine, my heart skipped over. I knew it was cliché, but those eyes seemed to look right into my soul.

"Who are you?" My words didn't chatter; they were more of a groan. Even speaking hurt.

"You have lost something," he said. He took a step forward,

his bare foot landing in the bloody snow. He didn't seem to notice.

I opened my mouth to say I'd lost many things—my mind included—but I couldn't get the words out; a sharp pain lanced up my spine, bringing me to my knees. Fresh blood coated the hand I shoved into the snow to keep myself from falling face-first. More blood dripped from my lips. The harpy's slash burned, but not just at the cut; I could feel the toxic poison of her claws pumping through my veins. Coating my heart.

The clarity was cold.

I was going to die down here.

"Perhaps," he said. He knelt before me. "But not, I believe, in this place."

He reached out and placed a finger under my chin, gently coaxed me to look at him. If I could have spoken or moved or cried out, I would have. His touch was freezing. And the line across his neck, though well stitched, explained why he looked like a corpse.

He *was* one.

"I am Mimir," he whispered.

The name stirred something at the edges of recognition, but I couldn't place it. He helped me to my feet.

"Where—" It was the only word I could force out before the pain hit and rendered me speechless again. I stumbled. If not for his hand on my arm, I would have fallen once more. For a dead guy, he was strong. He didn't even shift when my weight fell on him.

"Shh," he said. "You've lost a great deal of blood. And there is much more to lose, I'm afraid. Yes. A great deal to lose."

I looked at him. It didn't sound like a threat and he wasn't even looking at me, but it still made my hackles rise. Not that I could have fought him off. I had no weapon and no strength, and the girl who was supposed to be my fighting half was probably dead beneath a pile of half-bird monsters.

Mimir chuckled. It sounded like rocks falling down an icy slope.

"Your shadow is still out there," he said. "The creatures of this world have no interest in killing her. No, it was you they were after. And they cannot find or harm you here."

Where is here? I wanted to ask. The only sound that came out was a groan.

He guided me toward a root that spiraled from the sky, a curlicue that glittered like black ice. Had it been there before? The dripping sound grew louder as we neared. Every step was agony, and I wanted to scream at him to help me.

"I'm surprised you haven't figured that out yet. I thought you so bright. . . ."

Apparently Freyja wasn't the only god who could be sarcastic.

"Oh, I am no god," Mimir said. "Just an old man with an older burden."

An oblong, concave stone rested within the curl of the root, like a bowl. Water dripped from somewhere above, a slow, steady rhythm that filled the basin to the brim. But despite the ripples and constant stream of water, it didn't overflow. The bowl was barely an inch deep. And yet it seemed fathomless, deeper than any well. . . .

That was when his name clicked, my brain thick with poison. Mimir's Well, the place Odin went for wisdom. The place Odin lost his eye.

I looked to Mimir, who didn't look very much like a sage muttering prophecy. And then back to the stone, which didn't look like a well at all. This was the place the gods had ventured to learn all the secrets of the world. And yet here I was, a mortal girl, and Mimir was acting like showing me this was nothing.

I could drink from that and know everything in creation. *Everything.* Maybe even how to get out of this war without spilling any blood. My back throbbed again. I didn't care about answers: None of those would matter if I died. I opened my mouth, but the only thing that came out was a trickle of blood.

Mimir chuckled again. "You will not die here, Kaira, despite the poison in your veins. My well holds the knowledge of all things. To a god, perhaps, it would show what will be. But you are a mortal child; such knowledge is not for you. Not when you have free will."

I couldn't hold myself up any longer. The snow at our feet was red slush, and my legs were sticky with congealing blood. It was starting to feel warm.

I knew enough to know that was a bad thing.

I need . . .

"Waters heal," he said. He waved a hand over the stone bowl, and ripples passed under his fingertips, the water peeling *up* to touch his skin. Droplets collected on his fingers. "Wells have always been used to heal the wounded." He held a bead of water before me. "Drink, and you will heal. Drink, and you will know.

For I think that is why you fell here, of all places. You need to understand your other half. You need to know the truth of your soul."

I knew enough about gods and myth to know that there was always a price. One usually too high or horrific for mortals to pay. My vision and thoughts swam. Mimir was the only force holding me up, and now my legs were burning. So was my chest. So were my veins.

Odin gave his eye to look into your well. I knew that. I could almost see the Allfather kneeling here, offering his sight so he could truly see. . . .Wait, was he there? Were the roots moving, or was it my imagination?

Mimir smiled. His lips almost mirrored the curve of his scar.

"The Allfather desired a great deal of knowledge. He sought me. This situation is quite different."

I slouched against him. This would have a price. This would have a terrible price. My vision shadowed at the edges, and with every blink, it was harder to open my eyes. I opened my lips and felt blood dribble out.

What do you want? I wanted to ask.

"I wish for you to understand," he replied. "You need your shadow as much as she needs you. And unless you work together, we all are doomed."

I coughed. My blood splashed into the bowl, twisting in the waters like a crimson shroud. Mimir leaned forward, examining the shapes my blood made in the swirl. Dimly, I thought he would be upset, that I'd somehow ruined the magic.

Instead, he made a clicking noise in the back of his throat and muttered, *"Interesting,"* to himself. What was interesting? My life was leaking out with every beat of my poisoned heart. And for some reason, that wasn't as frightening as it should have been.

"You will die soon if you do not drink," he said. His voice sounded far away. As though he were speaking from the bottom of a very deep well. "And I cannot force the waters upon you."

Water, warm water . . . I closed my eyes, and I was in my dorm, the hot darkness of my shower, the steam of water cascading down my back. The walls bristling with raven wings. *Munin? Munin, where have you been in all this?*

Something smacked my cheek. My eyes fluttered open.

Mimir's palm was streaked with red.

"Drink, Shadechild," he commanded. "Drink, and heal. And understand."

He used his bloodstained hand to lift my arm—the other held my entire weight—and guided it to the water. The clear water. Hadn't I bled into there?

The water was warm. But then, everything was warm. Hadn't I been shivering? How was the snow so warm? The water burning? It sizzled like static against my skin, but it felt good. Divine.

With Mimir's help, I brought my shaking hand to my lips, let the waters drip over my tongue. Only I didn't feel water. I felt the heat. The prickling power that pierced into my skull, shattering with gold and silver light. Light and power and heat, burning down my throat like a serpent.

All the light in the world.

And then, darkness.

CHAPTER TWENTY

The godchild was born in the tangled roots of the World Tree. She was pure and clean, born of stone and starlight, and a single, withering root clung to her navel. She did not cry; she did not stir; she was as still as statuary. When the elders came and brought her down, she curled within their arms, wrapped tiny fingers around their wrists. They christened her in the river Vinderis, a drop of water on her brow—the kiss of gods and destiny. When she finally opened her violet eyes, they named her Freyja, Hrafndottir—daughter of raven.

When she finally opened her eyes, they knew the end had come again.

The words drifted through my mind as I floated in the darkness. They sounded like Munin's, but the raven was nowhere to be seen. The world was too dark, the shadows too deep. Until I blinked, and saw her. Blink, and a spot of light. A pale pearl in the darkness, a glowing gem.

There.

And maybe it was magic, or movement, but the shape grew

larger. Until I hovered, bodiless, beside the baby girl. Her skin fairer than porcelain, colder than snow. The roots coiled around her, a knotted crib. A twisted tomb.

And then there were hands reaching toward her. Plucking her from the roots, the tuber on her navel snapping with a crack, the sound of metal on flint, the spark of a beginning. The speaker held her to his chest, his face illuminated by her light, his little fallen star. His face was grizzled, his skin mottled as earth.

The ravens on each shoulder, larger than the girl.

The patch over his eye, a cloth of spider's silk.

He looked at the raven on his left.

"Go to her, Munin. Guard her memories. See she stays safe."

And the white-eyed raven bowed his head, then took off in a flurry of feathers.

"You, Hugin," the Allfather whispered, turning to his other avatar, "the godchild is your charge. Train her. Teach her. Give her your wisdom."

This bird bowed and leaped, and in a curl of shadows transformed into a man with ink-black robes, his face hooded. He reached out for the child, his bony, clawlike fingers curling around her with tender care.

"Protect her," Odin said, smoothing the girl's brow. "Her destiny is far from kind."

The Allfather stepped back, into the shadows, and with a ripple of water, the trio was no more.

"Again," he snapped. His anger made her flinch.

The girl went through her motions, twin daggers slicing the

air so fast as to be invisible. Sweat beaded her skin as she spun and flipped, dodging enemies in her mind's eye. She refused to show weakness or exhaustion; with each cut, each turn, she kept her focus sharp, her motions intentional. She didn't shake, even though I could feel the exhaustion aching in her limbs. She didn't pant, even though I felt the burn of air in her lungs.

Hugin stood a few feet away, robed and hooded as always, and he would take nothing less than perfection. Her mentor knew all things. And that meant he knew her to her core. If she gave less than everything she had, she would be there for days. She didn't want to repeat that accident. She wanted to be finished. She wanted to return to Bragi. . . .

Hugin grumbled something and waved his hand, and suddenly she was not alone. Shadows swirled around her, twisting into wraiths with claws like rapiers, their long, sinuous limbs slashing through her defenses.

Freyja gritted her teeth but said nothing. She fought harder, both against the shadows and against the fatigue that wrapped around her.

"Do not let your attention waver, Freyja," Hugin said. His voice was more crisp than I'd imagined. Munin sounded like the rumble of waves, the depth of the ocean. Hugin was clearer, higher-pitched. Poetic.

Despite her tiredness, she fought hard. The shadows didn't die or disperse, but their ethereal nature didn't keep them from harming her. Soon, she was covered in slashes. Not once did she scream. She wouldn't give Hugin that satisfaction. She lunged toward another shadow, slashed it in half, only to watch it rethread and reach out again. Its taloned hand wrapped around her neck, forced the breath in her lungs to stillness. It squeezed, and her throat was millimeters away from collapsing.

Hugin held up a hand. The shadows paused.

"Remember how this feels," Hugin said as he walked forward, tracing a slow loop around her like a shark circling its prey. "This agony. Notice the pain in your body, the fear in your mind. And notice how your mind reacts." He knelt by her side. Her wide eyes tried to catch his but, as usual, she couldn't see him through the depths of his robe. "Notice the resignation. As your breath slows and your heart hammers. As your brain tries to calculate any means of survival and finds there are none. You are accepting defeat."

Hugin watched the whites of her eyes turn red with a detached sort of fascination.

"You must fight to the bitter end, Freyja." He sounded sad. "Even now, you should be struggling. You should be trying to kill that which cannot be killed. Anything less, and you have failed. You know the price of that failure."

He snapped his fingers, and the shadows vanished. Freyja fell to the ground, her gasp a death rattle. Her wounds closed in the next heartbeat. But the pain, and the self-hatred, didn't vanish at her defeat. Because she had brought this on herself. If she had stayed focused, he wouldn't have summoned the illusions. He wouldn't have had to show her this lesson. Again.

Hugin stood and walked away.

"Again," he said, still facing away. He didn't summon any more demons for her to fight. He didn't turn around.

She forced herself up on shaking legs, then picked up the daggers she'd dropped in her fall. She tried to force down the disappointment, to temper it into something she could use. Something beyond anger or need. A detachment, a single-pointed focus. She began moving through her forms again.

Hugin still didn't turn around.

"Let this be a lesson," he said. "Only pay attention to that which is worth paying attention to. Once you have proven that you are worth *my* attention, I will turn around. Perhaps then you will be finished. Perhaps not. Let your goal not be to finish. Let your goal be to be worth something in my world."

She bit back the pain. I felt it in my own chest. Knew it all too well. To be good enough. To be worthy. Wasn't that why I'd sent myself to Islington? Not just to escape Brad's memory, but to prove to myself that I was better than he was? That I deserved more?

Freyja continued her motions. I watched.

I watched until even I forgot that anything else existed.

The boy with stars on his brow waited for her in their shared house. It was a small thing, the hut, but it was hers. She hadn't been granted much in this life—not even her own life—and the cottage felt like a home. It was carved within a thick root of the Tree, dangling above eternity like a hornet's nest, with no ladders or bridges to reach it.

"I thought you would never return," Bragi said. He sat before the fire, his harp between his knees. The music had gone silent the moment she stepped through the door, and oh, had she considered lingering just outside, listening to his notes dance through the silence like a cloud of fireflies.

"Today is not that day," she said. She tried to keep her voice light, but it was difficult. Hugin had drilled her for hours after he'd sent the shades after her, and lectured for hours more on duty and diligence. Nothing she had not heard since she had ears to comprehend, but that didn't make the listening any easier.

He plucked a few notes as he stood and walked toward her, the sound hanging in the air like gossamer.

"And we are blessed for it," he said. He drew her into his arms, and despite everything—despite the training that taught her never to be weak, never to feel love, never to know anything but duty—she let herself fall into his embrace. As always, he smelled of earth and cloves and something sharper, the birth of a spark. She wrapped her tired arms around him and let the day fall away. "He is growing harsher," he muttered into her ear.

"Because she grows older," she replied. "She is nearly ready."

He was silent for a moment as he held her, one hand twining delicately through her hair. She wanted to cry. That surprised her. She hadn't cried since she was summoned to the human world to kill Kaira's lover. It wasn't the act that had shaken her though; it was Kaira's own pain at the violence done. The Shadechild had been hurt deeply from the sin and the sacrifice, and for some reason that pain echoed through Freyja like a dissonant chord. Kaira didn't just hate the boy: Kaira hated *herself* for wanting him dead. Kaira hated Freyja for the act of vindication.

"Come," Bragi said, pulling her from her shadows. "Listen. I've composed something new."

Despite everything, a smile played across her lips as he drew her across the room to sit at his feet by the hearth. She loved him more than ever in that moment. Not only for the way the firelight played over his red curls and hazel eyes, or the way his fingers curved over the harp as gingerly as they'd curled around her. She loved him for his innocence. For his ability to see the blood on her fingers and love her anyway.

For his sheer determination to deny the future that loomed on their horizon.

But Bragi was a god. Immortal. For him, the future stretched far longer than she would ever know.

He played. And when his fingers caressed the harp strings, she closed her eyes and let the warmth of his music fall over her. It unknotted the muscles clenched tight in her limbs, soothed the ache from welts left by her shadowed attackers. She drifted in the golden melody, let her mind dance between the roots of the World Tree. And when he sang, her heart blossomed. She lived with the weight of so many worlds on her shoulders; under the influence of Bragi's song, she felt light. She felt more like a bird, and less like the stones on which Yggdrasil slept.

She didn't know how long she floated within his music, only that eventually it came to an end, signaled not by the ebb of music but by his hands on her waist. Her eyes fluttered open, the last strains of music still dancing in her ears. He knelt before her. His smile. Oh, that smile—the reason she had fallen in love with him as a child. He had looked back then exactly as he did tonight.

"That was beautiful," she said.

She brushed her fingertips over his forehead, delighting in

the constellation that glittered to life at her touch.

"Our music is only just beginning," he said, his smile turning mischievous. He leaned in and kissed her, and the next melody in their song began.

There should have been noise.

That was her only thought as they stood in the circle and faced one another.

There should have been a coliseum, like the ruins on earth. There should have been a crowd to make this a spectacle. Instead, there was only her and Bragi and the raven on a nearby root. No jeering. No war drums. No incantations.

The silence made it so much worse.

Bragi knelt before her.

She'd demanded he stand. To fight. But he refused. He carried no weapon save for his smile, and that cut deeper than her blades ever could. Because to him, she was still a savior. To him, she was still worthy of love. To him, this entire ritual was an honor.

"Get up," she choked. "Get. Up."

Hugin watched it all impassively, his raven head cocked to the side, talons digging clean furrows into the root on which he perched. She felt the darkness closing in on her, the terrible weight of the Underworld. Perched on her shoulders like the raven that brought her here.

"I humbly offer myself to you," Bragi said. Even now his words were melodious. "Let my gift aid in our quest for eternity. With my life, may the World Tree thrive."

She could barely see him through the tears in her eyes. And she couldn't decide if that was better or worse—to see him like this, so dumb and serene, or to remember him singing her songs.

Damn it, Hugin. How could you?

Because in all his teachings, the damned raven had said nothing about this sacrifice. But she should have known, shouldn't she? The Norns demanded a sacrifice from any who wished to ascend the Tree they stoically guarded. Why should she be any different?

And she knew, with a terrible twist of guilt, that she had brought this all upon herself.

Hugin had warned her not to love. To think only of duty.

She had let herself find comfort in Bragi. She had let him become a different sort of meaning. And now that he was the most important thing to her, he was the one she must destroy to succeed. The very act of loving him had made him a target.

"I can't," she whispered.

Even though Hugin said nothing, she felt the whip of his admonition the moment the words left her lips. She had stopped using that phrase years ago. Nothing good ever came of it.

He wasn't the one who spoke against her though.

"You must, Freyja," Bragi said. "Please. I offer myself willingly—"

"Then you are a fool!" she yelled. She wanted to say worse—so much worse—but her thoughts were thick. Even in the worst moments of her training, she had not felt pain like this. Or fear. Her hands trembled. She had no hope of holding a dagger, let alone wielding it, even if her prey didn't flinch from her cut. "You will vanish, Bragi. You won't be reborn. You will . . . you will . . ."

"Be with you," he whispered. "Always."

"But you won't. We both know that."

There was no reincarnation for a god thus sacrificed. There was no immortal ghost. There was only memory. And if she failed, even that would die.

Even his words played at the lie—his sacrifice would do nothing for the World Tree. Only mortal blood and worship nourished it. The gods were merely the tenders and caretakers. Bragi's blood would spill for nothing but the pleasure of the Norns. Only for the act of ritual. It was pointless. His death was pointless.

Like everything in her life up to right now. None of it had been hers. Not even him.

"I love you, Freyja," he said, and that hurt worst of all. "Let those be my final words. Let that be what you remember. I love you, and for that I am eternally thankful."

She wanted to scream. She wanted to hit him, to force him to run. Or to fight. She wanted him to drive her own dagger through her heart in defense. But she knew he wouldn't. Just as she would never make it from this clearing without his blood on her hands. The Norns needed their offering. And the Underworld needed its savior.

For some reason, she thought of the girl. Her vessel. *She has a name. She has a life.* And in that moment, those facts hardened her. Filled her with flame. Kaira was a girl. Kaira was a pawn. Just like her.

She had watched the goings-on in the mortal world, had seen Kaira's friends get killed as some unknown deity manipulated its mortal host. She had felt the girl's pain. And her fear. And her fledgling love.

But they were both pawns in this game. For that, Freyja wanted to denounce the gods, to stab herself in her treacherous heart. She almost did, too. But what would that do besides delay the inevitable? Kaira's life would be forfeit, and more blood would spill because of her inadequacy. The Tree would falter, but eventually, a new godchild would be born, and the cycle would begin again.

There was only one way to end it.

She looked at Bragi. His resolution wavered as he watched her. Waited for her.

She stepped forward, her heart turning to iron. To ice.

"I love you, Bragi." She knelt before him, then took a blade from her belt. "And I accept your offering. May it nourish the Tree." She dropped her voice as she laid the dagger across his throat. She didn't take her eyes off his. He wouldn't be alone in this, even though she would be alone after.

"May your death be the altar on which the gods kneel."

His eyes went wide, but whether it was from her statement or the slice of her blade, she did not know. She held him there as his life bled out onto the ground. As his blood coated her dagger and hands. And with every drop of blood, his body faded out, just as her resolve grew stronger.

When she stood, the body of her lover was no more, just a cloud of dust that spiraled off into the ether like the stars on his brow that would no longer light her way.

His blood coated her hands, sticky and pungent of cloves. Like the Tree's sap. She wanted to break down. She wanted to burn the world and spite them all. Today she would do only one of those things.

"Bring me to them," she said, turning to her winged mentor. The raven nodded, then took off into the air. She folded the shadows around her, let the feathers meld from her body, and followed behind.

She did not think of her lover's soul.

She thought only of the girl who would help craft her revenge.

CHAPTER TWENTY-ONE

"I thought you were dead."

Freyja's words jarred me from my stupor, or the vision, or whatever the hell it was. I stared at her, warring with the memories and emotions that clashed in my head. Her memories. Her emotions. At the end, there, I'd stopped remembering I was watching. I had *felt* her pain, heard her thoughts. Like she was becoming part of me.

I'd spent forever holding her off, and in those moments, I learned what it felt like to give in.

Oddly enough, her pain wasn't much different from mine.

As I stared at her, I couldn't find the same anger as I'd had before. I'd seen what she'd gone through. Or part of it, at least. And I knew she was as angry about all this as I was.

"I'm not dead yet," I muttered, knowing she wouldn't catch the reference. I pushed myself up to sitting. It took a moment for me to realize that the movement didn't make me wince. And that I was, in fact, very much alive and very much intact. The slash on my back was healed, and the poison in my veins had faded. I scrambled to my feet and looked around.

The snow was gone. The canopy of roots was gone. And Mimir and his well were definitely gone. I looked at the earth beneath my bare feet—black stone, not a root at all. We were clearly still in the Underworld—the roots tangled all around us, fading off into glittering shadows—but it was impossible to tell just how deep or far.

It is what you make of it.

I pushed aside Mimir's words and the lingering traces of Freyja's memory. If she could read my mind, I didn't need her knowing that I had just seen so deeply into hers.

"How are you still alive?" I asked.

She shrugged. "I am not so weak as you. Also, they weren't after me; I was just in the way. You're welcome for that."

"Why would they want to kill me? Aren't I the savior or whatever?"

She smiled slowly. "That is yet to be seen—so far, you've only fallen headfirst into danger. But . . . savior or no, you are still a mortal. There is a reason your blood and prayers fuel the Tree: your very existence is sustenance for the creatures of this place. It has been a very long time since a living mortal entered here. Your life is like a flame, and to those so used to living in the cold and the dark, that warmth is a gift to be coveted." She began to walk, heading toward wherever the hell Chris had flung himself. "As for the harpies, well. They're vicious beasts. They don't care who they kill, so long as they taste mortal blood. I'm sure you discovered their garb of choice."

I nodded, fighting down the shudder at the image of all those transposed faces, the skin tight and decaying. . . .

"How far are we?" I asked. I wanted to ask about Bragi, or Hugin, or the other creatures we might run into down here. But that was the only question that didn't feel like opening Pandora's box.

"Not far now," she said. Roots arched over her, reminding me of the architecture of a Gothic cathedral.

"How did you find me?"

"If you hadn't noticed, we're tied to each other. I couldn't lose you if I tried."

I wasn't certain if it was just my imagination, but it seemed like the more we were around each other, the more her mannerisms and dialog sounded like mine. It was actually a little disturbing. It kept reminding me that we were two halves of the same coin.

"That's not an answer," I said. "I mean, what if I lose you again?"

"You won't."

"But *if*. I don't have a weapon and I don't know where the hell we're going, besides, well, *Hell*. So if we're separated, I'm screwed."

She pulled a knife from her belt, tossed it in the air, caught it by the blade without cutting herself, and handed it over to me. I didn't take it.

"You know that won't do me any good." I made sure to glare at her as I said it. I mean, I knew which side went into your enemy, but that was it. After seeing the harpies, I didn't think a dagger the size of a kitchen knife would do me any good. "I need to know how to find you."

She didn't withdraw the knife.

"Take it."

If she wanted a staring contest, she was going to get it. She shook her head.

"You're impossible, Kaira."

It definitely wasn't my imagination—she was using my name more often.

"I can find you because of my training," she said. "But you don't have eighteen years to spare, and I can't risk you getting killed in my absence. So take the damn knife."

I relented and took the knife. I didn't know the first thing about using it. But I had to admit—having it made me feel better.

I glanced down to my pajamas. I couldn't exactly slide the knife into the waist of these. Not if I wanted to keep all my blood in. Freyja slid out of her jacket and handed it over.

"When can I do that?" I asked.

"What? Be chivalrous?"

"No. The clothes thing you did earlier. You know. Manifesting them."

"I'm a creature of the shadows," she replied. "I can bend them to my will. You're mortal. It will take more training than we have time for to teach you."

It wasn't much of an answer, but I took the coat and slid into it. I grimaced at the sensation—even though she'd been wearing it, it was as cold as ice. I hid the dagger in an inside pocket, which seemed to be made for just such a thing.

She began walking again, and I hurried to her side.

"You know where we're going?" I asked again.

"Down." She looked at me. "What has changed about you?"

"What do you mean?"

"You're taking initiative. You aren't fighting me—*this*—off. What has changed?"

I kept my mind clear.

"There's something about nearly getting killed by flesh-wearing nightmare creatures that changes your perspective, you know? Not to mention, you were gone for a very long time. I was able to examine my life and decide that you were my best chance at survival. The future war notwithstanding."

Her eyebrow rose. There was something in that movement that reminded me so strongly of Ethan, I almost cried. Where was he, in all this? Freaking out, if I knew him. I thought of our nights at the café—would we ever get another evening at T'Chai Nanni again? The last few months, I'd been silently panicking because I'd known our time together was nearing its end: Graduation loomed, and the future was hazy. But this wasn't the finale I was planning for.

There was no way this was going to be a future I wanted.

"I was gone for a few moments," Freyja said, drawing me back to the present. It was so easy to get lost in thought down here, like the very act of being in the Underworld made you reminisce. . . . "The harpies vanished the instant you fell. I thought they'd chased after you, and I followed. But you were perfectly fine. Somehow."

I knew that expression. She wanted me to explain myself. But I was very, very good at suppressing things, and this was nothing compared to suppressing *her*. I ignored the unspoken question and focused instead on the changing scenery. The roots grew thicker, not in size but in number, and the shadows were lightening in shades of violet. And in the distance, I heard the unmistakable roar of water.

"You are hiding something," she said. It wasn't necessarily a probing statement.

Now it was my turn to shrug.

"I guess I'm just interested in knowing more about you. Seeing as, you know, you're going to take over my body when this is over with."

"I think you've already proven that I'm not taking over your body anytime soon."

But wasn't she? Or was she just not trying as hard as she should have been? It felt like sharing a studio apartment with a stranger. Only . . . that wasn't the right analogy either. Because the more I thought about it, the more this particular space seemed built for two.

"You know what I mean. You've been watching me forever. I've known you a few days. We have to save the world together. So, I guess I figure we have catching up to do. You know . . . goals, dreams, boyfriends. Girlfriends?"

She paused.

"You've seen him, haven't you?"

"Who?"

"Don't play stupid. It doesn't suit you. Mimir. That's how you survived the fall. He found you. I should have known." She rounded on me. "What did he show you?"

"Nothing."

"You can't lie to me, Shadechild. What did he show you?"

She stepped forward, and I was acutely aware that of the two of us, she was the one who knew how to use a weapon.

"Things!" I said. I forced my voice down. "He said I needed to understand you so we could work together. That's it. He showed me a few things to prove it."

There was an anger in her violet eyes I hadn't expected. But I knew that look well. It wasn't just hatred; it was fueled by hurt.

"He had no right."

"And you had a right to watch me?"

"To help you."

"Well, maybe I can help you."

She laughed bitterly. "Can you raise the dead?"

"No. But I can help you avenge him."

For a moment she just stood there, looking me up and down. Assessing.

"No one can avenge Bragi's death. He is gone, and there is no use mourning his loss. He invited it," she said. I could tell she didn't fully mean it. Especially since we both knew, if she hadn't met him, he never would have been placed on the offering block. "But perhaps, in finding your lover, we can save you the same fate." Then she turned and continued walking.

I didn't dispute her word choice this time. Chris and I might not have had the same length of connection that Freyja had known, but I was starting to realize that I wanted to.

I wanted him to become someone I didn't want to lose. Which meant I had to find him first. And somehow kill the god that wanted his life.

"Wait," I said, the thought stalling me in my tracks.

"What?"

"Down here, we're separate. I mean, you aren't in my head or body or whatever."

"And?"

"Is the same true for Chris?"

"I would imagine so."

"So they're separate. Him, and the god?"

She noticed my train of thought.

"Perhaps."

"So we can kill him. Here. Without touching Chris."

She smiled. I couldn't tell if it was pleasure or bloodlust, and this time I didn't care to make the distinction.

"Perhaps you have found a way to avenge Bragi after all," she said.

"I want to do it."

"What?"

"The god. I want to be the one who kills him."

"You are a mortal girl with no training," she said. "And he is a godchild who has been taught to fight from the day he was born. What chance do you have?"

"He's the reason we're down here. He's the reason Chris resorted to . . . to this. I want to be the one to kill him."

"I will not agree to such a thing," Freyja said. She had to raise her voice; the roar of water was louder, and the air was damp. "I won't risk everything for your pride."

My heart fell.

"But," she continued, "if the opportunity arises, I will indeed let you be the one to strike the killing blow."

"Thank you."

"And here I thought you'd lost the taste of blood after your ex."

If it wasn't for Chris's image in my head, I would have stopped cold. Because at her words, I swear I heard Brad's laugh echoing through the falls.

"This is it!" Freyja yelled out. The roar of water was nearly deafening here. It wasn't my imagination, either—there actually *was* a roar coming from the falls that tumbled into and out of the shadow, tumbling against nothing, save for itself. A roar like guttural anger. A roar laced with screams.

I didn't know what I expected when we neared the falls. Maybe something like Niagara, or some dark rain forest pit. After a few more minutes of walking through a low tangle of roots that barely passed over my head, the roots above opened up and we stood on a ledge that jutted from them like an offering tray. And I realized we were far, far away from the bottom. I mean, I heard crashing water—surely that meant that somewhere, farther down in the shadows, there *was* a bottom. Right? The water cascaded down in front of us, a rushing, frothing spray that seemed to glimmer and roil. I couldn't see through to the other side. I looked closer.

Scratch that. I didn't *want* to see through to the other side.

What I did make out was enough. There was no mistaking the shapes twisting and screaming through the water as they fell. Bodies. Thousands of them. Tumbling through the darkness with naked flesh and muffled agony.

"You can't be serious," I muttered. If the Underworld was

what you made of it, who had made *this*? It seemed straight out of some Greek punishment. Here was Styx, carrying the damned through Hades.

"Everyone's hell is different!" Freyja yelled. She stood at my side, staring at the water with contempt. And fear. "But some ideas take hold in humanity, and they cut deeper fissures in the fabric of this place. Ideas become permanent. Myths become reality."

"And these people . . ."

"Are spending eternity as they expected to. We cannot change their fate."

I watched a young girl tumble past me, her skin so pale, it was almost translucent.

"Is Chris in there?"

"No. He is deeper. And this will take us there faster than walking."

"You can't be serious," I repeated. My brain was too far gone to be witty. So many people. So much pain . . . it seemed to call out, to resonate.

"I am," Freyja said, looking to me. "Remember, you're the one who wanted to save him." She smiled. It looked forced. "I assume you saw my training. If you learned one thing, let it be this: Stay focused on your goal. Focus on that, and nothing else. Do not be distracted. Do not be waylaid. Myth is filled with men and women who lost sight of their goals and thus perished. Think of Chris. Think of his return. Hold this above all things."

I opened my mouth to say I *was* focused. Find Chris; kill the bastard responsible for this.

Then she shoved me off the ledge.

My heart fell into my throat as I tumbled through the air. As I hit the water, as my body went numb. As something grabbed my ankle and pulled me into the torrent, and the rest of the world vanished to water and memory.

CHAPTER TWENTY-TWO

"You look beautiful."

"Thanks," I replied. Gods, what was wrong with me? That he could say that and I'd feel my chest rip and tighten, half contented, half terrified. Because I knew what it meant. "Beautiful" was a contract. An obligation as well as an entitlement. "You look . . . handsome."

He laughed and sidled in closer. We were at his place, in the living room, and his parents had given us those annoying looks parents do when they "give you some room" while clearly insinuating that they'll have an ear to the wall in case any funny business happens. It made my skin crawl.

But I was also grateful, because it meant he couldn't try anything.

Except for this. Except for leaning in just a little bit closer, his arm draped over the sofa behind me like he was blocking off an emergency exit. One leg was on the coffee table, and he was so close, I could smell his breath. My heart still hammered. Even though he was being "perfectly respectable" and not looking at anything but the TV. Brad knew I was uncomfortable with intimacy. And he was okay with that.

Which should have made me more comfortable with his brand of closeness.

In truth, it just set me on edge.

The movie was a blur on the television. How was I supposed to focus on the screen when he was so close? When I knew what the movies wanted me to do—to lean in and snuggle against him and wince away at all the scary parts, bury my head against his chest so he could laugh and rustle my hair and use that as an excuse to touch me? When in truth, I wasn't scared of the shitty slasher movie. I was scared of the boy I was supposed to be dating, which was beyond stupid, since he had literally never done anything to warrant it.

My mother told me to honor my intuition.

My intuition was shit.

"You're tense," he muttered.

"Scary movies do that," I lied.

He chuckled.

"Want a massage? Or we can watch a chick flick—"

My heart stopped with the idea of a massage. "No. This is fine." My voice squeaked. Damn it. It wasn't for the reason he probably thought.

The last thing I needed was an "emotional" movie around him. Because then he'd really think I was broken when I didn't cry at the right parts. Or he'd want me to melt against him once the sappiness kicked into gear. To be like a normal girl.

That was the trouble. I never reacted properly. Not to him. Not to movies. Not to friends. Not to life. It was like I was playing the wrong role, placed in the wrong body. I just never seemed to fit.

"Well, just let me know," he said. He leaned in a little closer.

"Brad . . . ," I began, my words edging on warning.

"I'm not going to do anything. Trust me."

I couldn't tell if it was a plea or a demand. It didn't matter. It didn't. I should have wanted to. But I couldn't. Because I felt so screwed up, I couldn't imagine any relationship with me ending in anything other than disaster.

He reached over with his free hand, and I had a terrible moment of thinking he was going to put a hand on my leg, but he only grabbed the popcorn from the coffee table in front of me and placed the bowl in my lap.

Blink. Shift.

"So you don't date? Like, ever?" Elisa asked, grabbing some popcorn from the bowl on my lap. She lay sprawled on my bed beside me, her limbs draped over or next to mine, her pajamas smelling of lavender and detergent. Our whole room smelled like that, since we'd just done laundry together.

"Nope," I replied. I didn't want to admit that the slasher film we were settled in to watch was one I'd already seen. Because then she'd ask who I saw it with, and that wasn't a conversation I wanted to have with a girl I'd only known a week.

Though, after a week of living together and having a dozen

different Islington "firsts"—first visit to the Dark Note, first all-night movie binge, first time having her model for a sketch before we both burst out laughing—she knew me better than anyone back home.

"What about your student mentor, Ethan?"

"Ethan? No. Boy's gay."

"Could be bi."

I laughed. "Like you?"

She threw a kernel at me.

"What, you want me to prove it?"

She leaned over and puckered her lips. I giggled and pushed her back.

"If we make out, we can't be roommates! You read the rules."

She sighed dramatically and leaned back. I continued.

"No one in my school was out about being bi. And the one gay kid I knew kept it quiet."

She sighed and leaned back.

"Bi erasure at its worst," she said. "But yeah, I had a girlfriend last year. We split when I found out I got in to Islington."

"For how long?"

"A few months. It got pretty serious."

"And now you only talk about boys," I ventured.

"Because there are male dancers here and holy shit, have you even seen how flexible Kyle is?"

"And we're sure he's straight?"

"Mostly. Honestly, I don't really care if he also likes boys. Just so long as he likes me. Which he does. Because I have first-hand experience regarding his flexibility."

She smiled and stared off dreamily. I started to laugh.

"You move fast."

She shrugged. "Love is a game and I plan on winning. Which is why I still think you should—"

"Nope."

"Not even—"

"Especially not."

"And you've never—"

I silenced her with a look. She knew that look. I was pretty certain all girls knew that look.

"Oh."

That was all she said. And as she leaned against me and went back to snuggling me, I knew that was all she'd ever say. It was how I knew I was safe with her, how I knew that all this was okay. The closeness—physically and emotionally—didn't feel like a danger. She'd never press too hard or demand too much. Probably because she had been in my shoes too.

Up until the point they'd been coated in blood.

For the first time in my life, I actually felt like I was doing what I was supposed to be doing. Being who I was supposed to be. And as I held her closer and listened to the softness of her breathing and closed my eyes to ignore the movie I hated because of Brad, I gave my thanks. Because life was finally throwing me a bone.

Things were finally going right.

Blink.

"Just when I thought it couldn't get any worse," Ethan said.

He slouched against me in the hall in the visual arts building.

There was maybe an hour until sign-in, and there were a dozen places we could have been hanging out. But we were there, in the arts hallway, sitting on top of our coats and staring at a student's interpretation of an Escher painting—made of toothpicks.

He wasn't talking about the art, or the cold hall and the snow drifting outside.

"Boys suck," I said.

"Yes, but this one sucked so well."

I laughed so hard, I started to tear up.

When I finally got the laughter under control, I squeezed him closer. "I thought I was supposed to be the one comforting you."

"You are. You're here. That's all I need."

"No. You need a boyfriend who doesn't take you for granted."

"I thought you'd stand strongly in the 'you don't need a boy-friend' camp."

"You don't. But when do you have one, he better damn well be worth it."

Ethan sniffed and buried his head against my scarf.

"He could have at least told me."

"What? That he was going to cheat on you with a freshman flautist boy? Fuck that."

"It wouldn't have been cheating if he told me."

"Now you're just defending him."

"I'm trying not to feel like shit. And if I make it my fault, I can hate myself a little bit less for ever trusting him."

His words hit deep. For a moment I couldn't say anything. Could only sit there and try to force out Brad's face. His scent.

His hands on my hips and the cold wall against my back. *Can you ever forgive yourself for trusting him? For ignoring your instincts?* But I pushed it away. Down. This was about Ethan and his stupid ex, Stephen.

"New rule," I said.

"Celibacy?"

"We aren't talking about me," I said. "No. No more dating theater kids. They're trouble."

"Too much drama."

"Badum-cha."

He sighed.

"I'm starting to think you're right."

"Of course I am."

"No," he said, pushing himself to sitting so he could look in my eyes. "About dating. About boys in general. It's too much trouble and you just get hurt."

I shrugged and looked away. I'd never told him about Brad. But my strict aversion to dating was enough to fill in the blanks.

"Next year will be different," I said. I didn't know who I was trying to convince. "We'll be older and wiser, and everyone knows seniors get more action than the rest of the school combined."

"I don't care. I'm swearing off men. You're all I need."

He wrapped himself around me.

"I love you, Kaira," he said.

Brad had said that to me once. After a few weeks of dating. After a dinner at our one nice restaurant in town.

I'd told him *thanks*. Because I didn't like lying. To anyone other than myself, at least.

"I love you too," I replied now, and, closing my eyes, kissed him on top of his head.

Shift.

"And in the end," the voice said, "your love will spell his death."

His voice sent chills down my spine. I knew it. I remembered it. How could I forget it?

I tried to make him out in the gray, but there was nothing there. Nothing but cold and shadows and the rushing water. Or perhaps there was something, in the corner of my vision, like a watermark. An inverted stain, a lightening of the dark. I couldn't make him out, but he scared me. He scared me more than Brad or Freyja or death ever could.

"You think you have come so far," he said "You think you have learned. How to love. How to move on. And it all amounts to nothing. Because in the end, I will kill them. Everyone you have ever loved. They will all die at my hands. And I will let you watch."

I felt him sweep his hand, felt the gray world ripple, and then I was back at Islington. Only it wasn't the Islington I'd left.

I couldn't fight the scream as I ran over to Elisa, who was sprawled on a bench with an arm over her head like she was posing for some dramatic painting. Only her other arm was missing, her legs bent at odd angles, and I could tell from the way her hair fell that part of her skull was collapsed.

"Elisa, no," I choked. Tears clouded my eyes and I wiped them away.

"There is no fighting it," the shadow whispered behind me. Not vengeful. Pleased. "This is what the gods will."

242

"No . . . I won't let them."

His voice was cold, so cold, even against the silent snow. I tried to hide my eyes and look away from him, from Elisa, but then I saw Oliver. Or what was left of Oliver. Hanging from a tree by a slimy red noose that wasn't a rope . . .

I retched and closed my eyes. Felt his frozen hands curl over my neck.

"Don't worry, Shadechild. You will be with them soon enough."

CHAPTER TWENTY-THREE

Hands on my neck, on my arm, and I tried to push them off even as something heavy thudded against my back. Tried to scream, but something filled my lungs. And then the hands moved to my chest, pressed hard. Water burst from my mouth. I gagged, kept vomiting up the cold, putrid water. My eyes shot open. Freyja knelt over me, her hands still on my chest, her eyes intent on mine.

"I threw you into the River Styx to bring you down here. I did not intend for you to try to drink all of it."

"What was that?" I asked. It felt like my throat was made of salt and sandpaper and something metallic. Almost like blood. Very old blood.

"What was *what*?"

I didn't try to move. I didn't want to roll over. I didn't want to start moving again. The images I'd been shown burned so brightly in my mind. Not like visions. Not like magic. Like truth. I *smelled* the decaying bodies at Islington, tasted the death in the air.

244

"What I saw," I said, gasping.

"I don't know what you saw." She leaned in closer, her eyes tightening. "How strange. I can normally read you like a book. But I cannot see anything from the river."

"I saw . . ." I shook my head. I didn't want to tell her. I didn't want any of it to be real. It was probably all some magic of the Underworld anyway, some ancient Greek torture—see the people you loved. And then see them taken away.

So why did I see Brad?

It didn't make any sense and, honestly, I didn't want it to make any sense. I was done with this place. I wanted to be back in my room in my world, curled up with Elisa or Ethan, worrying about art.

"Remember where we are," she said. "Remember your goal. Focus on that, and nothing else."

But could I even have my goal? That return to normalcy? Or whatever my version of normal was. Hanging out with Elisa. Painting my heart out. Complaining with Ethan. Hell, even flirting with Chris . . . It all seemed impossible. If what the waters had shown was true, it wouldn't matter anyway. They were all doomed to die.

"What did you see?" she asked. Her hand went to my shoulder.

I wanted to shake her off. Instead, I forced myself to sitting and looked around, letting her hand linger. We sat on the sandy banks of the river, everything bathed in a grayish light. The waters were as still as satin, a faint glint on the surface making it look like liquid steel. No bodies screaming for eternity.

No shadowed figures trying to drag me under. Behind us—away from the river—the sand turned to cobblestone, the horizon paved and gray and fading into fog. It was like being in an overturned bowl, everything obscured at the domed edges. Even the sky was the same gray haze, with black roots breaking from the cloud cover like alien tendrils.

"The end," I whispered. I tried to force out the images that crowded in my mind.

"You saw the war?"

I shook my head.

No. No, I hadn't seen the war. I'd seen those images before, the fire and chaos, the fields running red. This was different. This hadn't been war. This had been cold and calculated bloodshed. This had been personal. This had been malicious.

"That is impossible," she whispered, and I realized my thoughts had been trailing, and that she had once more followed them like bread crumbs.

"What?"

But our relationship was far from a two-way street. She shook her head, and whatever thoughts she had, she kept to herself.

"What? What is it?"

"It is none of our concern. Not now." She took a deep breath, as though trying to center herself, which just made me feel more off-balance. She was keeping something from me, and no matter how hard she tried to compose her face, I knew that it wasn't good. "We must stay focused. This place will try to deter us. You."

"Then where is he? Where's Chris?" I hated to admit that there was a note of panic in my voice. Because he certainly wasn't nearby, on the river, and I couldn't stay here any longer. I needed out before I lost my mind. Before I lost my way. I wasn't made to fight harpies and travel the Underworld or fight a war. I was made to drink tea and paint and spend my nights dreaming up a normal future: traveling the world and displaying my pieces in exotic galleries, drinking fancy drinks in mismatched ceramics at bourgie house parties, wearing strange dresses and fierce makeup, and making small talk about annoying artistic trends while Ethan cracked jokes at my side.

This wasn't supposed to be my life.

None of this was supposed to be my life.

My thoughts spun. I sniffed, tried to turn the panic into something I could use: anger or frustration or at least some sort of resilience. I needed one of those if I was going to find Chris and kill the god that wanted to overtake him. If I was going to ignore the weight of what was left unsaid between him and me— if I was going to ignore that my visions had meant something. And that that something was too terrible for her to mention.

Freyja didn't answer. She stood instead and helped me to my feet. Her silence set my nerves on edge.

"Freyja, where is he?"

She nodded to the cobbled expanse. "He is there, among the other suicides who thought they deserved punishment for ending their lives." She bit her lip, and for the first time since I'd known her, she looked tentative. "Be careful where you tread."

"Why?"

Again, she didn't speak. But when she walked forward, toward the stony horizon, I learned why.

The place wasn't paved with normal stones. It was paved in faces. All ages, all races. All of them facing upward, faces contorted in silent screams, concrete or stone surrounding their heads, hiding their ears, binding them to the earth. Like something only Dante could have dreamed up.

The sight hit me like a blow to the chest. I couldn't take a step forward. Doing so would entail stepping on someone's face, and even though they were silent, I knew they were alive. Or conscious. Or whatever you were when stuck down here.

How was I going to find Chris down there? The cobblestones stretched out into the horizon, flat and unchanging, and there was no way to figure out who was who until you were right on top of them.

Freyja stood there, staring out at the skulls with a look of disgust on her face.

"This is terrible," I whispered.

"I never said my world was kind," she replied. She looked to me. "Is your own world not the same?"

I could tell she wasn't just speaking of my own experiences, but of the ones I'd seen in her history. I didn't know . . . I'd always hoped that the idea of eternal punishment was a human one, that when you died, there was a white light no matter what. But that clearly wasn't the case.

"Are they stuck here forever?" I managed to ask.

She looked uncomfortable.

"Everyone's hell is different. Everyone gets the afterworld they expect. That is, perhaps, the most dangerous facet of myth and religion: What humans believe, the afterlife creates. Perhaps these souls will eventually find salvation. Perhaps they will never escape their torment. All I know is, there is no divine force to pluck them from their misery. They must find that salvation themselves. They must save their own soul. Otherwise . . . it is best not to think of it."

But there was something bothering her—I could tell that much. And I didn't like the feeling that she was holding back. It made my stomach flip.

"What is it?" I asked. "What happens to them? If they don't get out?" I found, the moment the words left my lips, that I didn't actually want to know the answer. It was one thing to stay up at night, worrying about death and the afterlife. It was another to be staring it in the face.

"Everything fades," Freyja whispered, her words sending chills over my skin. "Even eternity must end."

She nudged the sand with her foot. "I believe . . . I believe that there was once no shore. Only the condemned buried along the banks of the Styx. But over time . . ."

I wanted to vomit. I wanted to leap out of the sand. But of course, there was nowhere else to go.

"These are people."

"Were."

"But their souls? What happened to them?"

"I am not a god, Kaira. I do not know the workings of such things. All I know is that even the sand nourishes the World Tree, so perhaps they are reborn once the process is complete."

It wasn't a time for theology, but I found myself unable to move forward. The idea that *this* was eternity paralyzed me.

"That's horrible."

She looked at me.

"That is Creation. The Tree gives birth to the worlds, and from its fruits all living things are born and nurtured. And, like leaves, they in turn give the Tree life. When their time comes to fall, they are pulled back into the Tree, become transformed, perhaps to be reborn, perhaps not. In life and in death, all things nourish the Tree, and the Tree nourishes and *is* all things. It does not care about what we believe. It only exists to exist. Everything else is our projection."

There was a lump in my stomach that made me want to scream, that made me want to run away from everything I saw and everything I was hearing. This couldn't be true. I'd been raised to believe in many gods, to believe that there were divine forces that took interest in human life. But to think that this was real, that everything in Creation was simply *this*: a life cycle. A mechanical, thoughtless circle that birthed worlds only to harvest them when they died . . . It was horrible. There was no white light. No great kindness.

God didn't give a shit. Only mortals did.

I opened my mouth to ask more, but no. I didn't want to know. I didn't want to think about God or Creation or what happened when something immortal died. I wanted out. I didn't care if I was lying to myself: I wanted to go back to pretending that everything was okay and the only thing I had to worry about was finals.

"How do we find him?" I asked.

Again, she didn't answer right away.

"Freyja, how do we find him?"

She sighed.

"You won't like it."

I said nothing in response.

"The souls are brought in from the river," she finally said. "The first were laid here, at its edge. The newer are farther on . . ."

"You mean we have to walk over there. Over *them*."

Her nod was solemn.

My stomach churned as I looked out at the faces. To be bound like that for eternity, staring up at a sky as bleak as limbo, unable to move or scream or blink . . . I couldn't imagine such a fate. Didn't want to. But another part of me wondered . . . even if I didn't truly believe suicide deserved an eternity of torture, would I have suffered a similar fate? If Munin hadn't rescued me, would I be out there as well, waiting for time to turn me to dust just so the misery would end?

This could have been my future. My afterlife. And somehow, in the face of all this, what I'd been given seemed a whole hell of a lot better.

I stared at the poor soul trapped in front of me. The flesh was barely there—thin paper stretched over harsh cheekbones, the lips pulled back to reveal ivory teeth, her eyes open and darting about madly. Irises the palest blue, the whites bloodshot. It was grotesque and beautiful and terrifying, and I thought I could stare at that face for eternity. Wondering who she had been. The life she had lived. Wondering why she had decided to end it, and if she would ever receive liberation or simply become dust like the rest.

Wondering if I could actually save Chris from this fate, or if we were already doomed.

Wondering if it was worth it, any of it, when we were just cogs in this divine machine.

"Kaira," she said, and for a moment I thought it was the bound woman, calling my name from the depths of her past. Instead, it was Freyja. She stood closer to me, one hand on my shoulder. "We need to get you out of here," she said. She was looking at me like she was worried. Why was she worried?

She lifted my hand and held it before my face.

"You're starting to fade," she whispered.

It took me a moment to realize what she meant. Her delicate white fingers against mine. I wasn't translucent. So why was my skin paler than usual? Why did it feel like, if I pressed hard enough, I could push my hand right through hers?

"I feared this would happen," she said. She squeezed my fingers, like she was trying to get more life in me. "Mortals aren't built to be down here. Rather, they aren't meant to enter and leave. We have to get you out of here. Before we can't."

I looked around.

But how . . .

There were too many bodies out there. Too many lost souls. How would we find Chris?

"You are connected," she said. She turned me to face her. "Kaira, listen to me. Remember what I said about holding your goal above all else. If we are to save him, you have to focus on Chris, and solely Chris."

"But . . ."

"You are the only hope of finding him down here," she said. "I brought us to where he was kept, but you must be the one to find him. You two are connected, whether you call it fate or love or just foolishness. You dove into the Underworld to follow in his footsteps—there is a thread between you, and if you don't use it, we will wander lost down here forever."

But there wasn't a pull in my chest, no golden thread guiding me to him. There was just the emptiness, the cold press of a ceaseless eternity. There was no way I could find him, no tug that would bring me closer to him.

I wouldn't give up, though. Not when we were here, not when we were so close. Not when both of us—no, all three of us—had already lost so much.

If I couldn't find him, I would make the Underworld bring him to me.

"This place is what you make of it," I muttered, the mad prophet Mimir's words rasping through my mind.

Maybe Freyja had heard it before—maybe she knew exactly where the words had come from—because she didn't ask me to clarify, just nodded and stared out at the skull-capped horizon.

I closed my eyes and thought of Chris. I thought of the way he looked at his paintings when he was absorbed in his work, the way he never broke eye contact when we spoke. I thought of his hand in mine as we walked through the woods, his words leaving trails in the air, a trail of bread crumbs I could follow to the ends of the earth.

A trail I would follow to the ends of the earth.

And then I could feel him there, at the edge of my awareness— the linger of his touch, the trace of his heat, the curl of his breath. Just the memory made my pulse race, but not in a bad way. There was part of me, deep and protected, that wanted him in my life. That didn't just want to save or protect him, but wanted him to be closer. *Needed* him to be closer.

I need you here, Chris. I need you.

I envisioned how it would look, the painting of the two of us: our hands held, the snow fading into the white of the canvas, the sky azure and void of ravens. I let myself brush in the colors, the strokes of his arms, our fingers, his russet hair. I painted him closer. As he was meant to be. As *we* were meant to be.

There wasn't a rush of power or a whir of shadows. Freyja didn't gasp or clench my arm. And so, when I opened my eyes, I fully expected to have failed.

I thought I had.

The horizon still stretched endlessly before us, covered in the faces of the damned. But when I turned around, the river was nowhere to be seen. I turned back to Freyja; she wasn't looking at me. Or the horizon.

"You've found him," she whispered. She pointed down, only a few inches from where my feet had been.

At Chris's face.

I scampered back, suddenly aware of the sensation of skin and bone beneath my bare feet, at the cut of teeth against my heels, the squish of cheeks and eyes. I froze, clutching Freyja, as though she could lift me above all this. All the pain and torture that stretched around us, that pooled at my feet. But I didn't take my eyes off Chris's face.

It had only been a few hours since I'd seen him.

He looked like he'd aged forty years.

There were white patches in his hair, and his skin had lost its golden luster, pulled down into halftones of white and cream and tan. His eyes, once so piercing, now only darted around, crazed, bloodshot. Like he was searching for something.

A small, vain part of me wanted to think he was looking for me. But I knew that—even if that was the case—he needed a whole lot more for salvation.

"What do we do?" I asked, my voice swallowed up in the dead silence of the place. "Can we dig him out?"

"No," she said. "If we are to drag him out of here, we must enter his hell. You must convince him to leave it."

"Why wouldn't he want to?"

She looked at me, and her gaze shot straight to my heart.

"None of us believe we are worth saving from our crimes, Kaira. You above all others should know that."

She was right. How many times had I tried to convince myself that I deserved what had happened to me? That I deserved to be punished—for what I had done to Brad, and what he had done to me?

"There is plenty of room in hell for martyrs," Freyja said, her hand suddenly on my wrist. "But if you wish to escape here, you cannot be one of them. And neither can he."

She knelt, and guided me down.

"Just remember," she said. "It is his hell, not yours. Do not let it become your own. If you forget, if you get dragged in . . . there is nothing I can do to bring you back."

"What happens then?" I whispered.

She didn't answer, just looked down to the sea of mute faces around us. That was answer enough.

"Remember your focus," she said. "You found him. Now bring him back."

Then she guided my hand down, pressed my palm to the side of Chris's cheek. I'd just registered the stubble, the cold flesh. And then the world faded in a wash of shadow.

CHAPTER TWENTY-FOUR

Sand burned beneath my feet, sharp and acrid and infinitely more hellish than the landscape I'd escaped. There was no sun in the sky, just an angry, reddish ochre hue that radiated through my veins, made my blood boil. No hellfire, though.

No Chris, either.

Or Freyja.

I turned on the spot, stared out at the landscape. I smelled seawater, farther out. The promise of coolness, of moisture. Just the thought made sweat break out over my skin. Made my throat turn to cotton. I needed to find water. The desert stretched, but the promise of water pulled me toward the horizon. Why had I come here? To a land that wanted to kill me. A land that wanted to turn me into a husk. Water called. I had to find it. Had to find . . .

Focus.

The word rippled through my mind like a mirage. The horizon rippled as well. A spot in the sand. A fleck of gold and flesh.

"Chris!" I yelled, and the moment the word left my lips, the sand around me shifted, fell and rose.

Walls of sand erupted around me, blocking Chris from view. I struggled to my feet, the sand suddenly thick, viscous, wet. My hands came up red.

Vomit rose in the back of my throat, but I didn't try to wipe the blood and granules off on my pajamas, didn't let out a yelp. He was out there. Down here. *Focus*, I thought.

I didn't think anymore. I ran.

Sand churned thick beneath my feet, every step labored, every footfall slurping into the grit and blood. I kept my eyes forward, darting in the direction I thought Chris had been, though it was impossible to tell where I was, where I was going. No sun to guide my way, no sound, save for the sand. I ran. Gargoyles of the same young girl topped the walls, her eyes crying seawater and blood, rivulets streaming down the walls, swirling at my feet. She was familiar. I'd seen her. How had I seen her? *Her hair, swirling in the seawater, her skin paler than moonlight. "Her life for yours, Endbringer."*

And I gasped as the sand collapsed around me, as air flooded to water, and I was swirling, sinking, drowning. It was cold, so cold, ice dripping through my veins. The only warmth was in my chest. My lungs burned. I had to breathe, had to breathe.

"Just let go," she whispered. The drowning girl. She floated before me, her short hair a halo, her eyes as white as pearls. *"Let go, and the pain will go away."*

I knew her then. Bri. Her name twisted through my mind as seaweed tangled around my ankles. How did I know her name when she didn't say it? For some reason, her presence made me calm. It was okay. It was okay to die. She was dead, and she was okay.

The water was cool, but it was no longer uncomfortable. Only my chest hurt. Only my breath.

It only hurt to try to stay alive.

She knew. She knew the truth. She had died to save someone. I would die to save someone. But who? Who?

Her brother.

Chris.

Focus.

"*It isn't worth it*," she said, her voice suddenly older, angrier. Bri was close to me now, her hands on my neck. "*There's no point in trying to save him. I tried to save him, and look where it got me. Look where it got him. He still ended up here. He's still hurting. Because of you.*"

She squeezed, and the last of my air burst from my lips in a torrent of bubbles.

"*Let go. Let go. You're only going to hurt him.*"

"*You deserve this. You deserve to stay down here, to suffer, as you've made him suffer. You'll only make him suffer. You are doomed to destroy each other. Even if not, you could never love him, and that would destroy him just as assuredly.*"

No. No, I was going to save him. We had both done too much hurting.

We didn't deserve this pain. No one deserved this pain.

Water flooded away, a wave that dropped me to the cold stone floor in a heartbeat, leaving me gasping and shuddering. My neck ached and my lungs burned, but Bri was no longer there. No one was there.

Just a circle of ink on the tile floor of the classroom. A stool at the ink's edge, beside an easel, beside a painting of ravens and blood.

I scrambled to my feet and stood in the center of the circle. Blink, and there he was, sitting at the easel, his hand holding a brush of bone. Chris.

He sat there, rocking, and muttering something I couldn't hear but that I fully understood. The pain. The fear. I knew it like the shadows of my own heart.

I took a step forward. I had to get him out of here before his nightmares could catch hold again. I had to get us both out of here before I forgot what I was doing in the first place.

Another step forward.

"Chris," I whispered. He didn't move or flinch, just kept rocking back and forth. Had he heard me? And what was that noise, that growing wail? It sent chills down my spine. *We have to get out of here. Now.* "Chris," I said again.

And then I heard his laughter.

Chris turned from the stool, and as he did so, light peeled from his body, curled out into golden threads and wings. I stepped back, but he was faster. The glowing god grabbed my arm before I could take a second step. His name burned from the back of my throat, a hatred older than the blood in my veins boiling to the surface.

"Heru," I whispered. Had I heard the name before? Or was it part of me, like Freyja? A rivalry not even the gray of the Underworld could diminish.

He smiled. Even though he'd worn Chris's skin only moments

before, there was no sign of the mortal boy in that look. That was a smile of razors and blood. I knew then that he was nothing like Freyja. There was no mortality there, no soft side to play to. He *wanted* to be a tool of the gods. He wanted to make the world worship him.

He would want me to beg.

I reached for the knife in my jacket, but his other hand caught my wrist before I could manage.

"You really think it could be that easy?" he asked. His touch burned. I held in the pain, though. I wouldn't let him see me hurt. I wouldn't let him know I was scared. "You, a mortal? Killing a god?"

"You're no god," I replied.

"Perhaps not yet," he replied. "But I will be."

He flung me to the ground. It hurt. The pain of it reverberated through my bones. I heard someone whimper. I looked over.

Chris. Sitting just outside the circle of ink, hands pressed to his ears as he watched in terrified silence. Had he been there the whole time?

"You think you can kill me," Heru said, drawing my attention back to him. But part of me stayed focus on Chris. On what I hoped was the *real* Chris. I had to get him out of here. Above all things, I had to get him out. "You think you have a chance. I would have hoped for more from the vessel of the Vanir. But they have always been cowering, worthless beings. I suppose that was a vain hope at best."

"If you kill me down here, you fail," I said. I had already pulled the dagger from my coat while he talked. I brandished it at him weakly, just like my threat.

He actually laughed.

"That's not how this works, Shadechild," he said. "The gods created us for bloodshed. I can still take the mortal plane without you there. The war will happen, with or without you as an adversary. Your blood only sweetens the deal."

He struck. So fast, I didn't see him move, just the flare of light, and then my blade was gone, skittered across the floor.

"I will kill you down here," he said. "I will bleed you dry until you are only a shell, until your bones are brittle and your skin snaps. And then, when you are almost gone, when your life has drained to the very last, I will make him burn you alive." He pointed to Chris as he said it. Chris flinched back. Closed his eyes.

Chris, come on, Chris. Don't hide from me. Don't hide.

I opened my mouth. Called out for him to help.

If he heard me, he didn't register. Heru just laughed again and stepped forward.

How was he here, when Freyja couldn't be? How could this be the end? I had come so far. So far.

Heru kicked me in the ribs. Hard. I grunted and curled over. Another kick landed on my back, right against my kidney. I couldn't help it this time; I screamed.

"Oh, I forgot how good this feels," Heru said. He leaned in, put one burning hand on the side of my face, forced me to look up at him. "That is what makes us different, you and me. We were both born for bloodshed. But I revel in it. I delight in the gifts I was given. The gifts I can *take*."

He flung my head back. It ricocheted on the tile, made stars

dance across my vision. My fading vision. I struggled to my feet.
I couldn't end down here. Wouldn't . . .

Another kick. I screamed again. Screamed Chris's name.

I couldn't find the dagger. It didn't matter. But I couldn't find it.

"Your lover won't save you," Heru said. "He has already been
broken. By what he has done. By what *you* have done."

He kicked. I flinched, rolled over, tried to roll away, but he
was before me now, his golden body piercing through my tears
like the unforgiving rays of Heaven.

"I must admit," he said, "Yggdrasil chose you well. You are
both broken. You are both worthless. You deserve each other."

There was a scream then, though not my own. Not one I'd
heard. And before Heru could react, Chris was there, and my
dagger was in Chris's hand, and the blade in Heru's back.

Heru yelled. Light spilled from behind his shoulder blades.
I didn't have time to watch. Chris grabbed my arm. Grabbed me
and pulled, and I tried to push myself. To run with him. To leave
here.

In the depth of all the pain, relief sparked in my chest as I
watched Heru fall to the floor.

We ran toward the door. Chris flung it open. Flung us both
through.

But we didn't step out into the land of skulls. Freyja wasn't
waiting for us by the River Styx.

We were in a circle of light. A circle of light surrounded by
heaving blackness. A circle of light broken only by a hospital bed,
half in, half out.

"What—" I managed with a gasp. Right before Chris pushed

me. The motion so quick, I didn't have time to register. One moment I stood there, and the next, I was on the bed, and he was strapping my arms and legs to it.

His eyes were rimmed red and his hands shook. But his grip was strong; he pulled the straps tight on my wrists, even as he looked to the shadows of the room. Even as the wails grew louder and his shaking grew stronger. As a metallic tang filled the air. Why was this happening? We'd defeated Heru. We had won. We should be back.

I struggled. Tried to struggle. But my arms and torso were already strapped to the bed—how? *How?*—and he had moved down to my ankles. I kicked. He caught my foot and slammed it to the bed, yanking a strap over it in one fluid motion. Like he'd done this before.

Fear laced through my chest like poison. I forced away Brad's face, his laughter. I forced it away, but I didn't have much force left. Brad laughed in the shadows, and I felt vulnerable in a way that I hadn't since he'd last touched me.

Focus, I thought, trying to keep the room from shifting back into the school bathroom, the night of homecoming.

"Chris, what—"

"Not again," he muttered to himself. "Not again."

He looked at me then, as he tightened my ankles.

"I'm not letting you do this," he said. "I won't let you make me hurt her."

He leaned in closer. "Change back," he seethed. "Change. *Back.*"

CHRIS

CHAPTER TWENTY-FIVE

"Change back," I grunted. I hadn't even realized my hand was on her neck until she started to choke. But it didn't matter, did it? It wasn't her. It couldn't be her.

It was just a trick. Just another trick.

He thought I would give in. I would be weak. He thought I could be tricked again. That I'd think that it was her I was rescuing, and not another illusion. Another lie. He would make me think I was safe. That I had fled. I had gotten away. But that couldn't be true, when we were still here. Still here together, so it couldn't be her. It was him. In disguise. He would trick me. Make my guard ease. And then he would strike. He would peel from her flesh or whisper in my ear, and I would kill her, the shell of her, the memory of her, and he would make me watch. He would make me laugh. He would make me delight in it.

Again. And again.

As he had.

As I had.

Every time, I delighted in it.

He had to be the reason I delighted in it.

"Chris," Kaira said, gasping. And there was something in her voice. Something that made me flinch back.

Something *warm*.

"No," I whispered. "No, no, no, no."

I stepped away, toward the center of the light. To get away. It couldn't be her. Not really. This was a trick. It had all been another trick, and the moment I believed it was real, Heru would come back. He would always come back. He wasn't dead. She couldn't be down here. I shouldn't be down here.

I should. I should.

My foot clanked against metal. I jerked around. Another bed.

"No," I said again.

My mother was on this table, my father at her side, and she was moaning, and the wailing was growing louder, like somewhere far away the hordes of the damned were screaming out my name. Like Hell itself was after me. I squeezed my eyes shut and clenched my hands to my ears because I didn't want to see it. Didn't want to hear it. But it didn't help. I still heard my true mother begin to scream. Still smelled her blood. Still saw her face constrict in agony as the wails grew louder. I couldn't hide from them.

Shouldn't hide from them.

This was your doing. The godchild is born in blood. You were born in blood. Death is the only life you know.

I deserved it. All of it. To remember. They deserved to be remembered. What they did. How they died. For me. From me.

"Chris," she said, but it wasn't my mother. It was Kaira. The phantasm of her.

I flinched back again from my name. I wouldn't fall for this. I wouldn't let myself believe things were safe. It would only hurt worse.

I'd only hurt her worse. That was why I had to keep her there. On the bed. So I couldn't hurt her. So she couldn't escape. If she escaped, I'd forget. I'd hurt her again.

"Damn it, Chris, I'm trying to save you."

Behind me, my mother began to wail. But she wasn't alone. I heard my sister crying out from beneath the waves, her words undulating like tides.

Tears formed, but I kept my hands to my ears, stared at the face of my sister in the darkness. *Help me, Chris. Why didn't you try to help me?*

"Go away," I said. I wanted to sob. "You're not real."

"I'm real, Chris." There was a note of fear in Kaira's voice. I heard her struggle against the bonds. But I didn't open my eyes. If I looked at her, I couldn't trust what I'd do. I could never trust what I'd do.

Even without Heru in my head, I couldn't trust myself. Even if I thought he was actually gone, that I'd managed to escape. I couldn't trust myself in his absence.

That made it worse.

That made it so much worse.

That was why I had to stay down here. Because I didn't need him urging me to kill. I was born in blood. I had already found my power there. I would use it again.

"You have to believe me, Chris," Kaira said. No, not Kaira—the memory of Kaira. Her demon. *She's not real. She's not real.* "I came to save you."

No, no, I can't be saved. Nothing can save me.

"I can't go free," I told her, told my sister. "For what I've done. For what I'll do."

"You can," she said. "I can help—"

"No!" I yelled, my eyes flashing open. I took a step forward, toward her, even as my mother screamed behind me and my dad called out for help. I pushed them away, pushed them down. My veins were filled with rage. For this. For all this. For myself. "I know what you are. What will you make me do this time? Kill you with my bare hands? How about I fall in love with you and then you rip out my heart while my sister watches? Is that it? Is that what you want? To make me believe it's okay, so you can hurt me?"

I was near her again. She hadn't moved from the bed. Hadn't transformed into anyone else.

Just her.

Just her, and my sister at the edge of the light, and my mother's muted screams behind us. What a group we were. Here for eternity. Here because I deserved nothing better than misery.

The girl pretending to be Kaira struggled again. She even *smelled* like Kaira—and what was wrong with me, that I could realize that? That I knew her down to her smell?

"Please, Chris. I'm trying to help you. I'm trying to get you out of here. We have to leave before Heru finds us."

"There is no out of here!" I yelled, and my hand was on her

wrist now. How did that happen? When had I moved? When had the anger overcome? "Don't you get it? I can't escape. This isn't a place. It's all *right here*." I pointed to my head with my free hand. "I'm never getting away from it. I figured it out. I figured it out, you know that? This is what I've done. This is what I deserve."

She shook her head, made the bed shake. Or maybe the nightmare was shifting again. What would it be this time? My sister and I playing in the toy room while it flooded? My mother—my real mother—and my father on their wedding day, her stomach ripe and ready to burst? Or perhaps it would be more of this— Kaira, right in front of me, trying to save me, only to end up dead at my hands.

"Chris—"

"No!" I yelled. "I loved her, damn it. I won't let you use that against me. I won't."

I looked at her, tears in my eyes. I hated her for this moment of clarity. I hated myself for earning it.

"Do you know how many times I've watched you die? How many times I've killed you?"

She shook her head. Her own eyes were wide. Like she was scared. She *should* be scared.

"A thousand times," I whispered. Tentatively, I brushed my fingers over her forehead, slid her hair behind an ear. "A thousand times. And every time, before the shock, there was such *happiness*. Don't you get it, Kaira? I want you dead. Some part of me. Every time I killed you, I felt *power*. And now you're just going to make me do it again."

I started to cry then. Because already I could feel my body's instincts taking over. It was worse than when Heru was whispering in my ear. This was me. This was all me. I couldn't hide from what I'd done or what I wanted to do. What I'd continue to do.

"Chris, I know you would never hurt me," she whispered. Her voice shook, but it was strong. She was just convincing herself. I know she was just convincing herself. "I came here to find you. Through Hell. To save you. That's where we are, Chris. This is the Underworld. You tried to kill yourself. To save me." She made a noise, almost like a sob, but I couldn't see her through the tears in my own eyes. "That's why you're here. Because you wanted to save me. Because you didn't want to see me hurt. And now I'm going to save you. You just have to let me out of here. . . ."

"You can't," I replied. *No one can save me from this. I don't deserve to be saved from this.*

"Yes, I can," she said.

I opened my eyes and tried to see her through the tears. *Let me go back to seeing my sister drown. Let me go back to the other pain. They were easier to get through than this.*

"I killed my own mother," I whispered. "When I was born. She died. And my parents never told me. *The child of the Aesir is born in blood, and through that blood he wields his power.* I can't live, Kaira. If I come back . . . I can't go back."

I saw it, the briefest flicker of concern. Of doubt. It flitted over her features like a shadow. Like a raven's wing.

"That was the past," she whispered. "And that wasn't your fault. Any of it. I know you don't want to hurt me. To hurt anyone."

"But I do. I'm not safe."

"Chris," Kaira said, her voice no longer gentle. It was demanding. "Only you can get us out of here. You're here because you think you deserve it. But you don't, okay? This is all an illusion."

"I *do* deserve it," I said. "I deserve all of it."

My mother started screaming again. Kaira groaned.

"Chris, come on. You can come back with me. None of this is real. None of it. We can leave here together, okay?"

"We can't. I'll hurt you. He'll make me hurt you."

"You won't. Trust me, Chris. I'm a big girl. I don't get hurt easily. Not anymore. Let me out, and we'll leave. Together."

I knew what she meant. I knew about Brad, about her horrible past. I never wanted to hurt her like that. I never wanted to hurt her in any way. That was why I had to stay here. To keep her safe. But I wouldn't keep her with me. I wouldn't relive her death again. I undid the straps holding her down, then stepped back. Back to the center of light in the room, back toward the sudden silence. I looked around. My mother was gone. My sister was gone. And so was the bed Kaira had been strapped to.

Now it was just her and me. Her and me in the circle of light, with nothing but Hell between us and redemption.

"Just go," I whispered. "Leave me."

She stepped forward. I stepped back. This made her hesitate. But she didn't move away. Against better judgment, she moved closer.

"Damnit it, dude, I'm not leaving you. Not after what I've been through to get to you." Her voice didn't hold the anger or resolve it had before. It sounded tired.

"I'm going to hurt you," I said, looking away. It wasn't a

threat or a promise. It was a fact. She needed to understand. If it *was* her, she needed to leave. I came here to save her. And that's what I was doing by staying. "Please. Just go."

"Or I'm going to hurt you," she said. "That's part of being alive. It happens."

"But not like this."

"Chris, come on," Kaira said again. "I . . . I need you to come back." She sighed. Like she didn't want to admit it to herself. But also like it was the truth. "I need you."

"I can't—"

Her lips found mine. A shock pulsed through my heart, a vibration that made the rest of the world still.

Something new welled up within me, sweeping away the pain and fear.

This would end in disaster.

But this feeling, this *power*, that felt worth the risk.

KAIRA

CHAPTER TWENTY-SIX

Kissing Chris was nothing like kissing Brad.

Brad had always been abrasive, fumbling; his tongue moved like a jackhammer the moment I'd part my lips, and his mouth was almost always dry. It felt like kissing a fish. With a jackhammer tongue.

Even in the world of the dead, Chris's kiss was infinitely different; his lips were warm, the perfect mix of soft but firm, and when I felt his chest expand against mine, my own lungs lit with heat. With desire. I had never liked kissing Brad. It had always felt like a battle for dominance. With Chris, it was opening up. Both offering. A mutual communion.

He wrapped his arms around me, falling against me, letting himself be heavy and light.

I hadn't planned on kissing him. I hadn't planned on saying I needed him.

But I did.

And I meant it. Both actions.

He had said he loved me. Had he meant that?

"Kaira," Freyja said behind me. Her hand was on my shoulder, and my happy little daydream snapped into reality. I pulled back from Chris and opened my eyes.

We were no longer in Chris's hell.

To be sure, we were still in the Underworld; a field of skulls paved the ground around us, stretching into a hazy infinity. But Chris was there, held in my arms, his forehead now nuzzled against my neck. I didn't want to admit how comfortable it felt, having him there. How natural, the scratch of his scruff against my skin, the warmth of his breath. He was warm. So warm. I wanted to fold myself around him and soak up his heat for eternity.

Gods, why was I so *cold*?

"You did it," I whispered. Then Chris leaned back and looked around. He didn't let go of me though. If anything, his hold tightened.

"What?" he asked. He sounded groggy, like he'd just woken up. If only this could just be a nightmare. When was the part where we woke up and everything was okay? "Where are we?"

"The Underworld," I replied. I tapped the ground with my foot, the one small tile in the entire landscape that didn't contain a skull. "And you, my friend, were just right here."

"I don't—"

"We can discuss this later," Freyja interrupted. "We must go. Now."

I shifted my body, slid my hand down to Chris's. It was the only thing that felt warm out here. The only thing that felt solid.

Chris's hand tightened in mine. He tried to take a step back, but the moment he did, he stumbled over a face and would have toppled had I not been beside him.

"Kaira. What is this? Where are we?"

"I already told you," I said. "We're in the Underworld." I tried to be calm, but Freyja's words had me on edge. I was acutely aware that Heru was out there. Somewhere. And injured. Unless that, too, was just some figment of Chris's inner hell . . . It wasn't a risk I was going to take.

Chris wasn't looking at me, though. Just as he wasn't looking at the faces beneath his feet. He was staring at Freyja like she was death incarnate.

And I guess, in many ways, she was.

"What is *that*?" he whispered.

It was stupid, that his words made me cringe. Not because I was worried about what Freyja would think or do, but because . . . because she was part of me.

That realization made me look at her with a completely different awareness. It also made me wonder what would happen on the other side of this journey. With Chris back in the land of the living, what would she and I do? Would we still be battling for control over my body? Or would this whole endeavor grant us a certain understanding?

"That," I said, trying once more to keep my thoughts in line, "is Freyja."

"I recognize her," he said. His voice was a low growl. "She was the one trying to control you."

"Was," I said. "But not anymore." I looked at her, raised an eyebrow, but she didn't catch my unspoken question. She was too busy staring at the hazy sky. "You can trust her."

"She's a god. We can't trust her. She's just trying to use you. Us. If you'd seen—"

"We don't have time for this," Freyja said. She looked back down, stared between the two of us like she was tired of babysitting. "We must get moving."

"I'm not going anywhere with you."

"Chris," I said, squeezing his hand to remind him I was there. "She's on our side; it's—"

"No!" he said, pushing me away. "You can't believe her. She's just like him. She just wants to use you."

"We really can't be doing this right now," Freyja said. "We have to get out of here."

"I won't go back."

His words were steel. I stepped to the side and looked at him, a knot of fear in my chest.

"What?" I whispered.

He wasn't looking at me. He was staring straight at Freyja, his hands balled into fists.

"I'm not going back with you. I know what you want. I've seen what you'd have me do. You're no different from him. You only want to kill. I'm not going to let you use me like that. I'm not going back."

"Chris," I said. I tried to keep my voice level. I saw a glimpse of what he'd been dealing with in his own hell; I couldn't blame him for being reticent. But I didn't have time to fill him in on the blanks. "I just came through the Underworld to get you. What the hell do you mean you aren't coming back with me?"

"He's still out there," he said. He didn't break eye contact with Freyja.

"We really, really don't have time for this," Freyja said. "The Aesir is not here. Which is precisely where we should be. *Not here*." She leaned in. "Even if we aren't attacked, neither of you will last much longer down here. We must leave now."

"We attacked him. In *there*." My words were hesitant. "Is he gone? Trapped?"

"It is not important. None of it will be important if the both of you fade out before we reach the mortal world. The Aesir is the least of our worries."

But I knew her by now. I knew she didn't believe it, not really. But I also knew her explanation wasn't for me.

"I'm not going—" Chris began, but I rounded on him.

"Shut up," I hissed. "Do you trust me or not?"

He opened his mouth, then shut it again. His eyes searched mine. Those eyes . . . they glimmered gold, but they were so muted. He looked like a washed-out painting.

"I do," he said finally. I'll admit: It made my heart flip over.

"Then trust me in this," I replied. "Heru is gone; he can't hurt you, and he can't make you hurt anyone else. And if he isn't gone, I'll handle him. But look"—I held up my hand, to show him how pale I'd become, how translucent and frail my skin had gone—"we're already fading. Any longer, and we'll be worse than dead. Don't let him win. Don't leave me. Please."

He looked like he wanted to argue, right up to my last plea. Instead, his whispered words were a spear to my heart.

"I just don't want to hurt you."

So unlike Brad. So why did my ex's words echo within Chris's?

"You won't," I replied. I tried to grin, felt it falter, and looked back to Freyja to hide it. "I have a goddess if you get out of line."

He didn't respond. I didn't press him. It took all my self-control to keep Brad's face out of my head. I needed to get out of here. I needed to get to a place where we could think straight.

"How do we get out?" I asked her. I'd jumped into the River Styx to get here, and there was no way we were going to swim upstream. . . . I couldn't imagine there were elevators in Hell.

"There is only one way up," she replied.

"And how's that?" I didn't like the inflection in her voice. Like she knew a terrible secret she couldn't quite hope to share.

She didn't answer right away. Her violet eyes shifted from Chris, to me, and then back again. Was I wrong in what I was seeing? Freyja could read my thoughts, and right then, I thought I could *feel* hers. And if I was right, she was bitter. And envious. When she answered, however, her words were deadpan.

"You already saw how to return to the mortal world," she said, her gaze returning to me. "The same way I ascended. By making a sacrifice to the Norns."

My stomach clenched. Another sacrifice?

She had killed her lover to come to my aid. But I had come down here to rescue Chris—surely the Norns or the gods or whatever wouldn't make me give him up. They weren't that cruel.

Then I remembered all the myths and fairy tales.

Of course the gods were cruel.

They were rarely anything but.

We also didn't have a choice.

We followed her, mute, Chris's hand firmly in mine. He didn't speak, didn't even seem to be himself. He stumbled along at my side, watching the horizon, a grim expression on his face. Not like he was worried we were going to be attacked. But like he knew it would happen, and he was ready to die when it did. Despite the warmth coming from his hand, he felt like a shade of himself, the barest echo of a memory, as though I hadn't actually rescued the boy I cared for. I'd just pulled forth the idea of him.

He mumbled something. It took me a moment to catch it.

"It won't work."

"What?" I asked. I nearly stopped, but Freyja's pace didn't allow for it.

"It won't work," Chris said. "It never works. Think of Orpheus. He failed. Right at the end, he failed. All the heroes fail."

My stomach twisted with the thought. He was right—I couldn't remember a single myth where the hero brought back the loved one. Orpheus failed to bring back Eurydice. Persephone stayed in Hades.

"Yeah, well," I said, trying to kick my dull thoughts into gear. "Those stories are about men. I'm a girl. I'll get shit done."

He laughed. Slightly. But it honestly felt like the sun coming out from behind the clouds. If only for a moment. Then the clouds drew back over, and he was silent and reserved once more.

Still. It gave me hope. Down here, that seemed as rare and necessary as ambrosia.

Every step, I expected the heavy clouds overhead to part, for harpies to screech down from the sky and attack. I expected the faces below our feet to wail, to drag themselves up from the soil, because surely it couldn't be this easy. Surely the Underworld would try to keep us down. Or I expected Heru, that golden god that bore Chris to do this, to split the skies and take back what he had tried to steal from me.

I wanted to believe we had trapped him in Chris's hell. But I knew better. I wasn't that lucky.

The silence that cloaked us, that only grew thicker with every passing yard, made my hair stand on end. Not only because of the sound our feet made as they slapped on flesh. But because I knew, if the Underworld was letting us off so easy right now, something terrible waited ahead of us.

This place was what you made of it. And millions of people had collectively made this world a land of misery. There was no way we'd be let go without a catch.

All the heroes fail. Chris's words were a mantra in my head, one I desperately wanted to quell, but that only grew louder in the silence.

I wasn't a hero, though. I was just a girl. And I would succeed. *I would succeed.*

I wasn't going to let my story end this way.

It felt like we walked for an eternity.

It felt like it was over in the blink of an eye.

One moment we were walking over human skulls.

The next, our toes dug into sand.

The River Styx raged before us. It should have filled me with relief. Instead, it just made my pulse race with dread. So close. So close. And that meant we were still so far.

I shuddered when we neared the water. The memories of what I'd seen in there were still fresh in my mind: all those bodies, littered around Islington like fallen leaves. And the presence . . . the voice that chilled me to the bone. Maybe it was just some wayward god from down here, trying to scare me away.

So why had Freyja seemed so concerned by it?

There were so many things I wanted to ask her. And Chris. And right now was not the time for any of it. It was going to drive me insane.

"Where do we go now?" I asked. There was no way I was jumping in there again. No way.

Again, that look from Freyja, that guarded expression that made me rail against the fact that she could see into my mind, but she was still an enigma to me. I expected there to be a boat to ferry us across—where was Charon, demanding coin for passage?

"Down." Her word dropped like a drachma into the waters, swallowed up into nothing.

I looked into the water. My heart dropped to my feet as Chris's hand clenched tighter in mine. Tighter, and yet it still felt like he was fading away.

"The water leads to the base of the Tree," she continued. "It is there the Norns rest."

"I'm not going back in," I whispered. I didn't want to see the shadowed figure again. I didn't want to smell the innards of my friends rotting in the air.

She sighed. For the briefest moment, I thought maybe she would respect my reluctance.

"We have no choice. We cannot make it on foot. Not anymore."

She took my hand.

She didn't ask if I trusted her. I didn't ask Chris if he trusted me. He didn't even seem to register what was happening. Freyja dragged us toward the river. Then she leaped, and we fell in behind her.

Shadows.

I panicked. I didn't want to be back here. Back with the shadowed man in his shadowed robes, the owls watching.

But then I realized—I was *realizing*, and wasn't that better than before, when I'd lost myself to the illusion? *I'm tumbling through the river. I am holding Chris's hand. Soon, Freyja will pull us from here, and this will be a bad dream.*

"But what if she doesn't?" came a voice. His voice, harsher than snow, colder than the void. "What if this isn't an illusion but the truth?"

He appeared from the mists, or maybe the mists disappeared from him. But he stood there, in the dim streetlamp, in the alley, and the world was heavy. Heavy as my limbs. As my empty hands.

I am still holding Chris's hand. I am still safe.

"Oh sweet Shadechild," the figure said. He didn't move toward me, but his every word was the sharpening of a dagger. I cowered back and stumbled against something. Something that cried out.

I turned on my heel, looking at the child at my feet. A baby. With dark skin and dark hair, clean as crystal. A raven's feather clutched in her palm.

"Did you ever wonder," the figure asked, "why she calls you that?"

I shook my head. Backed away from the child now squirming on the concrete. It was cold. So cold. How was she still alive?

"Because you were born in shadows," he whispered, right behind my ear. "That is the game they play, the gods. They create their spawn, delight in their cleverness. The Aesir's avatar killed his mother coming into existence, as the Aesir wanted their hero to sow blood in his wake, to make the world bend knee. But you . . . the Vanir had darker desires. They wanted something else. A different sort of worship. They don't want blood. They want to seep into the consciousness of every mortal, the shadow to the light—the constant fear and reminder of mortality. They don't want humans to tremble in fear. They want mortals to bow in subservience, to the inevitability."

The figure moved past me, knelt down to the child. To me. His robe was gray and mottled, like a snowy owl, like snow itself. I swore I saw the nubs of wings protruding from his back, but when I blinked, they were merely folds of fabric. I knew him then. The same figure I'd seen behind and within Jonathan.

The same figure Freyja was sure she'd banished.

"And so they crafted you, sweet one. Have you never wondered about your history? Your own flesh and blood?"

He stroked the baby's forehead. I wanted to scream at him to stop, but I couldn't move. Couldn't open my mouth. Ice froze my veins, even as the snow began to fall around us like broken prayers.

I *had* wondered. When I was younger. When I learned I was

adopted. I'd loved my mother and father, but the moment they told me the truth, I felt the rift. I wasn't theirs. Not really. And according to them, I'd never truly know. My biological mother had left me with no word, no way to be traced, at the doors of a hospital. I'd been taken into the system, and my adoptive parents had taken me in soon after.

But I hadn't let myself wonder for too long. I knew it was a dangerous road to travel. My adopted family had shown me love. It was more than my blood had ever done. I wasn't going to throw that in their faces by being indignant or demanding information they didn't have. The past was the past. I preferred leaving it there.

"This is your history, Shadechild. Child of the shadows. You were crafted from darkness the moment the godchild was born in the roots of the World Tree. You were her compliment. And like her, you have no family save for the Tree itself. No relatives. No blood."

The figure stood and turned to me. I couldn't see his face through the shadows of his hood. I stepped back anyway. I didn't want to see that face. I didn't want to let him in.

I looked back to the child.

"You want to have a future," the figure said. "You think you can win this little battle. But you have no future, Shadechild. You have no family. No reason to defend. Those who love you only do so out of pity, and those who help you only do so to further their own desires."

A raven appeared then, bleeding from the shadows, like ink pouring into water. I knew him immediately. Munin. The raven cocked his head to the side, seemed to study the child. Me. And I knew, in the deepest recesses of the Underworld, the Allfather was telling Hugin to watch over Freyja. To turn her into a weapon. While Munin turned me into a sheath.

More shadows curled around the baby, coalescing into a blanket as black as night. Munin clutched the blanket in his beak and unfolded his great wings, and then silently, effortlessly, took off into the darkness, disappearing into the sky like a mirage.

"Why are you showing me this?" I whispered.

"Because you wish to have a future. You wish to save humanity. Why? When you have no past. When your humanity is itself an illusion? You have flesh and you have blood, yes. But you have no ties to mankind. There is no future for those like us, Shadechild. We are nothing but names in the book of history—a purpose served, and a life unlived."

Those like us? I shivered. And not from the cold. "You don't know anything about me."

He laughed. The sound of an unfurling avalanche.

I'm going to have a future. I'm going to save Chris, and then we're done. Heru is gone. The battle is avoided. I've won. And now I can have a normal life. . . .

"With a god of the Underworld in your head?" he asked. "If you believe that, you are not the girl I thought you were. She will not rest until she has felt vengeance. There are reasons she can see into your head, but you cannot see into hers. If you knew half the things she felt . . ."

He stepped up to me, placed a frozen hand on my shoulder.

"You will kill everyone you love because of her. The future I

289

showed you, that was not my doing. But hers. Yours. The world will run red with her anger. The loving life you desire will never be yours. She would never let you have happiness, not when she was denied it."

I thought of what I'd seen in Mimir's well. Freyja and Bragi. Her love's sacrifice. And I thought of the resolve in her heart at the very end. The desire to scorn the gods. To make them pay.

"Why are you here? Why are you telling me any of this?"

"Because I am tired of being played by the gods," he said. "And if you had any sense, you would be as well. Remember this, when I am proven right. She will never be your savior, and you will never be his. You are nothing but shadows, Shadechild. Shadows and regret. And that is the only future you will ever know."

He turned, then, and stepped away. Into the pooled light of the streetlamp. Into the center of the circle.

"The battle nears," he said. "But not the one they expect. Prepare yourself, Shadechild. The end comes."

Deep in the shadows of his cowl, I could feel the coldness emanating from his smile. Then he spread his arms, and his cloak spread like wings, and in a gust of snow and pearlescent feathers, he was gone.

Leaving only the circle in the snow. Only the drifting feathers. Only the light.

Only the words echoing in my head, the ones I'd seen written in ink and blood.

The Tree will burn.

CHAPTER TWENTY-SEVEN

I knew where we were before I even opened my eyes. I could feel it humming through my veins, everything vibrating, less of a noise and more of a sensation stuck in my bones, drawing me forward, calling me by name.

I opened my eyes and nearly wept. How could I describe such beauty? In all its simplicity, how could I understand its perfection?

The heartroot of Yggdrasil stretched down before us, glistening dark like ebony and silk, the skin of it as smooth as the face of the stars. It was larger than a skyscraper, stretching down through the shadowed expanse of the world and into a lake that formed from the pooling tides of the river beside us. The water's surface flickered in the low light like stars swirling around their cosmic nexus. I blinked, and realized there *were* stars swirling over the lake. Stars like fireflies, in purple and green, and they danced over the water in patterns that seemed to breathe prophecy.

We stood on the beach, the sand finer than flour and as dark as coal. It felt like standing before an altar.

Everything was quiet. Heavy. Expectant. And yet everything was filled with energy, a movement that pulled at my heart.

The potential. This was the potential for everything.

This was where Creation began.

This was where Creation would end.

I didn't even look over at Chris: his hand was still in mine, and I could feel him staring in awe. I didn't speak to Freyja, because words seemed sacrilegious here. I could feel her emotions too—the fear, the duty, the resentment. She had sacrificed her lover to be here, to ascend. She had sacrificed everything to come to me, to fulfill her duty. Our duty. Our martyred duty.

In the smallest corner of my mind, I held on to the memory the river had shown me. The doubt. But that was fleeting. That was fading.

The Tree will burn.

No. That was impossible. The Tree was all. The Tree would last for eternity.

The Tree *was* eternity.

One couldn't kill God.

I could have stood there, staring, forever. As if standing there would answer all my problems. As though at any moment, the Tree would speak through my veins, and I would know the secrets of the universe. I would know how small my troubles were. And I would feel peace. Because we stood at the feet of Creation.

Because we *were* Creation.

Of course I would lay down everything for this. How could I have ever thought I would do anything else? How could Freyja have ever believed she could overturn the will of God?

As if she'd heard me—of course she'd heard me—Freyja broke the dream.

She stepped forward, her feet dipping gently into the sand as she walked toward the lake.

The moment her foot touched the lip of the water, a dozen of the floating lights swarmed her foot, curled around her sole. She continued walking, and the lights continued to coalesce around her feet, dispersing whenever she stepped up, swirling every time she touched water. Like they existed only to hold her up. Her gait was smooth. Steady. The lights danced around her, casting shadows and color over her pale skin. She walked on the water's surface as though she were a savior. As though it were as simple as breathing.

I turned to Chris. I wanted to tell him something. Anything. *I'll protect you. We're safe now. We can be together.* But the hum of the heartroot was too great, and the silence around us too sacred. Instead, I guided him forward and hoped he would feel at least a small amount of that reassurance, that promise. His fingers were like porcelain in mine. I wasn't too late to save him from the shadows in his own heart. I wasn't too late to save him from his inner hell.

Even though I knew he would carry it with him forever.

I would be there to help guide him out. Forever.

The faerie lights descended the moment my feet touched water, buzzing and filling my limbs with a pleasant sort of static. I almost laughed after the first step. I was walking on water. I was performing a miracle. And yet, here, it felt like nature. Like all the world was a miracle, and there was nothing that could be seen as mundane.

We walked, hand in hand, and it felt like moving through a dream. Every step made the Tree's vibration grow stronger, louder. Heavier. My reflection stared back at me when I looked down, the water still swirling, and I couldn't tell if it was the waters moving beneath the surface or simply the dance of the lights. Down there, I swore I saw the cosmos stretching for eternity. I swore I felt it in the blood pumping through my veins, a map of my own inner workings.

Freyja didn't speak when we stopped beside her, before the root, fireflies still buzzing around our feet, my toes just barely registering the coolness of the water I stood upon. Warmth radiated from the treeflesh, and the vibration was so loud, so thick, my teeth vibrated in my skull. My blood frothed in my veins. The root was so smooth up close; it reflected the fireflies like an obsidian mirror. My heart ached, to be this near.

The Tree was God.

The Tree was All.

And in that moment, the Tree was calling to me.

Freyja nodded. Maybe to my thoughts, maybe as an indication. I couldn't speak. Words wouldn't make sense here. She reached toward the Tree. My hand mirrored hers, and Chris was close behind. Without speaking, all three of us placed our hand to the Tree.

We reached toward God.

The Tree reached back.

We floated in darkness, suspended on threads of shadow and whispers. The vibration was less intense in here, but my bones still hummed with power. Chris was beside me; I could see him from the corner of my eye, even though I couldn't move my limbs. I couldn't panic. I felt nothing. We floated in the darkness and I felt only calm. Peace.

Then the shadows faded, or a light grew, and I felt something new in the space of my chest.

Awe.

They were before us. The whole of the cavern arched around them, a cathedral of gray and black that spanned stories and centuries, a temple of twisted stone. No, not stone—treeflesh. Walls of root and tendril curled and curved around us, twisting and carved in filigree and archways, like the chancel of a cathedral, everything ebony and muted light.

The three Norns existed in its center. The nexus of the nexus. The beating heart of God.

Even if Freyja hadn't told me what they were, I would have known. They were like nothing I'd expected, nothing I'd seen in storybooks, but that was a distant thought, a different memory. These were the three weavers of fate, of creation. And for all their terribleness, they were beautiful.

I couldn't judge their sizes, even though they were hundreds of times larger than myself. Their heads were oblong, like potatoes, the flesh mottled and thick and pale, their eyes lost to skin, their lips the mere shadow of a space. Their bodies hung below their necks, limp and clothed in rags that dangled far into the abyss, their limbs long and frail, trailing like spiderwebs. But what use did they have for movement? From the tops of their heads sprouted a lacework of antlers. The bone curved and curled above them like crowns, twining into the treeflesh, into the antlers of their sisters, and the roots mirrored, twisting around bone, into skull. They were one and the same, the Weavers and the Woven, the cosmic and the conscious. In the most distant corner of my thoughts, perhaps, I would have found them terrifying.

Instead, I wept at their beauty.

They were the guardians of the world, tenders of the Tree. They had woven me into existence. And they would snip the threads of my life when it was time.

How had I ever feared death, when it was such a tender choice?

We didn't speak. We didn't have to. I knew what they needed. A sacrifice. Something more precious than life itself. Freyja had given her lover to rise to the mortal world, but Chris was far too young in my life to be worth such a cost. I searched my heart. What would be the hardest to give up? Not a lover, or a family member. Not a memory, though I had many I wished to lose. What had carried me through my life? What did I need to survive as much as breath?

"Your art."

The words filtered through my mind like the deepest strings of a cello. And for the first time since being by the heartroot, I felt a trace of fear.

My art?

No. No, I couldn't.

It was the one thing that had carried me through the darkness, the one thing that allowed me to wake up every morning. When I was depressed, I drew my demons and better horizons. When I was having anxiety attacks in public high because I wasn't popular enough, or outgoing enough, I found solace in the back art studio, surrounded by paint and other outcasts. I didn't just send myself to Islington to define myself: I went there to protect myself. My art was how I expressed, how I coped, how I integrated. I couldn't give it up. Without it, I was nothing. Life was nothing.

I could only imagine days without it. Rambling through life with no spark, no purpose, no *passion*.

What use was there to being alive, if there wasn't art within it? If everything was muted gray and empty? Like a drained corpse.

No. Like a concrete slab. A tombstone.

Art was creation.

Without it . . . without it, it would be like remaining here, in the Underworld, forever.

Anything else. Let it be anything else.

Despite the fear, despite the fact that every cell in my body screamed otherwise, the response that drew through my bones silenced all doubt, a surge of water to my growing fire.

"You hold your skill above all things, even yourself. And that is how we know it is what you must sacrifice."

My heart was numb, but the spark I had, the spark that was left, burned bright with rage.

This was Chris's fault. I'd followed him down here to save him, not to play the martyr. Why was I the one who had to sacrifice something, when this was his journey?

"He shall also sacrifice," the voice said. *"It is not your place to decide the cost."*

No. It wasn't fair. Freyja hadn't mentioned this when I followed him down.

Give up my art?

What would I have left?

Chris, I thought. *You'll have Chris.*

I felt him there, beside me. Maybe I should have asked if he was worth it. Maybe I should have questioned. Maybe I should have listened to Freyja and let him drown.

But deep down, I knew this was right. This was what I was meant to do. Art had been my life up until now. Chris . . . he might not be my everything, he might not be my entire future, but his life was important. To me, I thought, it could be even more important than art itself.

I looked over at him. He stared at the Norns, tears in his eyes, his lips moving wordlessly. Just the sight made my heart swell. He was worth this. He was worth this.

Right?

I didn't say yes, but my heart answered for me.

I blinked, and the middle Norn floated before me. Only she was human now, her flesh glowing like a star. She looked like my mother. She *was* my mother—the raven hair, the fierce eyes, the proud smile. And I saw, then, the other two sisters. The Maiden on her left, with hair as fine and lush as silken thread. The Crone on her right, her hands gnarled and holding sheers cut from Time. And the Mother, my mother, she smiled.

"Your sacrifice has been accepted."

She reached to my chest. And when she placed her hand where my heart should be, my body and soul unraveled in trails of red silk.

I gasped at the pain, at the ecstasy, as infinity opened within my veins.

As the world wove itself anew.

CHAPTER TWENTY-EIGHT

Freezing water.

The pressure instantaneous, the cold to my bones. But I was sinking. Struggling. Swimming. Toward him.

Chris was below me, his pale face barely illuminated by the light.

I swam farther. My lungs burned.

How long had I been down here?

How long to get back up?

I kicked. Wished I had Freyja's magic or strength, but I only had me. And I was shutting down.

Our fingers touched. His arm held out in offering. His eyes wide. Seeking.

Growing wide.

Losing light.

Fingers touched.

Latched.

CHRIS

CHAPTER TWENTY-NINE

Fingers touch.

Cold

presses. And she

is angelic, weightless, the light

around her body a halo. Her lips

whisper bubbles, whisper my name. And I feel

the stirrings, the rightness, to reach

out, to ascend.

I reach.

Until

I see him. Behind her

wrapped within

her halo

a ghost within her glow.

Heru.

Reaching beside her. His smile
a dagger, his hands blood.

I will never leave you.
He says.
She says.

No.
We've come so far.
She's come so far. For me.
But I can't. I see the blood
in his eyes. The promise
in his hands.

My lips part, water
floods in. Her hand clutches
mine, as Heru's light
slides down my throat
as darkness folds
and here, in the depths, I
am not alone.

I will never be
alone.

CHAPTER THIRTY

There was darkness. And then there was light.

It slammed against me, harsh and hard and cold. I coughed, and the last dregs of lake water spilled from my lungs. I turned over in the snow, tried to blink in my surroundings.

Sky.

Snow.

Ice.

Blood.

Kaira.

Kaira. She lay in the snow beside me, facedown, her hand still clutching my wrist, and somewhere out there people were screaming, people yelling and running toward us, but here—right here—there was only the silence. Kaira wasn't moving. Kaira wasn't moving. And when I put a hand on her temple, she was colder than the snow beneath my bleeding hand.

She was cold. So cold.

She wasn't moving.

Everything else was moving, but she was not.

I didn't know what I was doing, and yet, I did.

I reached through my blood that pooled around us, turning the slush pink. I reached into the power and pulled.

Heat flared under my palm. Light like sunshine poured from my fingers. The power. The heat. I wrapped it around her, heard snow hiss and pop as her skin steamed, as her thin pajamas dried.

The power wanted to consume her. Wanted to ignite the cotton of her shirt, crisp the carbon of her hair. But I shuddered and wrestled the power down. My power was blood. My power was blood.

And blood was what gave us life.

She groaned. Tightened her grip on my fingers. Opened her eyes.

Her violet eyes.

"Chris," she whispered.

I felt the flicker of a smile on my lips.

Then I heard another voice.

"Burn her."

I let go of the power. Let go of her hand. Behind us, the dark water churned. I could hear it calling me. To end it. To end it. I should have ended it.

Heru was still there. Waiting. He'd been waiting all along. And I knew then that I couldn't escape him. Not even in death.

Kaira sat up. Her eyes—were they violet? Or was that my imagination?—darted from me to the hole in the ice. She didn't ask how it had gotten there. Didn't ask how I had warmed her. I watched her watch me. Waited for her to break into crows.

Waited for blood to stream from her eyes. But she only reached out and took my hand. Her skin was still cold. Far too cold. Or perhaps mine was simply too hot.

"We did it," she whispered. Her finger traced the healed scar on my wrist. And in that moment, Heru's voice disappeared. I could feel him, at the very edge of my awareness. But he stood outside the circle. So long as Kaira was here, with me, he would always stand outside the circle.

I wanted to open my mouth to thank her. I wanted to apologize.

I wanted to forget what I'd seen—I remembered running out here, running from the visions. I remembered drowning. I remembered what lay beneath.

And I remembered what I had given up to return.

The words for everything knotted in my throat. She didn't seem to mind.

Instead, as the fishermen from their huts surrounded us, she leaned forward and placed her fingers on my cheek. On my temple. On the back of my head. She pulled me closer.

"We did it," she said again.

Then her lips touched mine, and even though they were cold, even though every inch of her was snow, I felt my chest blaze. Felt her pulse quicken. Felt my blood mirror hers.

Even though we'd both trudged through death, I'd never felt more alive.

KAIRA

CHAPTER THIRTY-ONE

It should have felt like the happy ending.

It should have felt like everything was going back to normal.

The scary part was, it all did. It all seemed like it was going to be okay. And that scared me more than anything else.

The fishermen came and wrapped us in blankets and took us back to the school. Nurse Bettie saw to Chris and me, but ultimately decided that we didn't need to go to the ER. Despite having been drenched in the lake—for what had, apparently, been only a few seconds—neither Chris nor I showed any signs of hypothermia. She said it was a miracle. Especially since my cold had broken in a heartbeat. Despite being a little too cold to the touch, I was *as right as rain.*

We were still told to stay in the nurse's office overnight.

Separate rooms. Of course.

As for the cover story, well, that was harder to figure out. Mainly because she didn't remember Chris coming into my room, just as she didn't remember me chasing after him. No one did. So, once we figured out what everyone *didn't* know, we threw together the stupidest lie we could. We had gone out for a walk because I needed fresh air. The ice cracked, we fell in. And that was that. It shouldn't have been that easy. But it was.

"I still think you're insane," Ethan said. He sprinkled more red pepper on his pizza before taking a huge bite. The five of us were in the lobby of the nurse's office—Ethan, Chris, Elisa, Oliver, and me. Chris sat on the bench beside me, his thigh resting against mine. Oliver and Ethan were cross-legged on the floor. Elisa sat a little bit apart. Watching us. I couldn't tell if she was skeptical or approving of the fact that I was willingly sitting so close to a boy. And that I was, on occasion, nudging him with my shoulder.

There was something in Chris's look, though. Something wary. He knew something. He was hiding something. But I hadn't had a chance to ask him what.

"What?" Oliver continued. "You never break the rules?"

Amazingly, Ethan actually blushed.

"Of course I do," he said. "Just not the ones that keep me alive. It's the *fun* ones I break."

"Like no sleepovers with significant others?" I ventured.

Again, his ears reddened, but he nodded anyway. It was easy to think everything else had been a bad dream, that *this* was reality. The whole of reality. But even now, trying to feign normal, I knew that wasn't the case.

"Let's be honest," Ethan said, staring me right in the eyes, again with that wary, albeit impish, expression. "I'm not the only one who will be breaking the sleepover rule."

I nearly choked on the slice of margherita pizza I was chewing on. It felt like I hadn't eaten in days.

Apparently, I hadn't.

Gods, there was a lot I needed to catch up on.

Chris didn't say anything. He hadn't said anything the entire night, beyond a few short answers to all the obligatory questions: *How are you feeling? Okay. Are you hungry? Sure. Do you want to postpone your thesis? Maybe.*

He looked older. Haunted. And even though he seemed to light up when I was near, the moment others were around, he closed back in on himself. It scared me. I'd sacrificed so much to bring him back. What if I hadn't succeeded? What if I'd just brought back an impression of him, and left the spark of the boy I loved behind?

But it wasn't just the way Chris acted around me that threw me off. It was the way he studiously ignored Ethan. There was definitely something between the two of them. Something that made them dance around each other like they shared a horrible secret neither could express.

Earlier, I'd tried asking Chris about what had happened while I was "sick," once Nurse Bettie had left and I'd snuck into his room. (Sneaking around seemed ridiculously easy now. For some reason, I had no doubt that if I didn't want to be seen, I wouldn't be. This was proven when I walked right by Bettie without her saying a word.)

Chris's answer had chilled me to the bone. Which was an omen in and of itself, since I didn't seem to feel cold anymore either.

"It was worse than you could imagine," he'd said, looking me

straight in the eyes like he always did. Then he'd looked away. And he wouldn't say anything else.

Not even when I asked if he'd felt Heru since we'd returned. Especially not then.

That told me more than an answer. Maybe things weren't back to normal. Maybe that was just another lie.

In any case, I didn't think there would be any rule-breaking tonight. At least, not the kind Ethan expected. I didn't want to jump Chris's bones.

I wanted answers.

As did Freyja.

She was the other member of our dinner party. But she didn't speak. She sat in the shadows, invisible to everyone but me. And maybe not to Chris, from the way he kept looking to the corner of the room when he thought no one was watching. Freyja watched us all in silence, and I couldn't tell what she was thinking. Did she feel vindicated, for helping me save Chris when she couldn't save Bragi? Or were the visions from the River Styx more prophetic than I wanted to believe?

I refused to think she was sitting there, plotting.

I refused to think that everything had been in vain.

"It won't matter much longer," Elisa said. It took me a moment to realize she was talking about breaking rules.

It felt like a curtain dropping—the mood in the room immediately suffocated.

"What do you mean?" I asked. Ethan and Oliver looked down. Elisa kept staring at her uneaten pizza. "Elisa. What do you mean?"

My hackles rose. I'd had too much prophecy lately. This couldn't be another one. This couldn't.

"They're closing the school next week," she said.

Instantly, my appetite vanished. I dropped my pizza to the plate and stared around. None of them would meet my eyes. Not even Chris, who now seemed worlds away. Had he known? Or was this new to him as well?

"That's not possible," I said.

"Apparently it is," Elisa replied. "Enough parents were calling in, trying to get their kids out. The authorities started getting involved. . . ." She sighed, poked at her pizza. "This place is no longer safe."

How could I have expected anything else?

People had died. And even though I wanted to tell everyone that it was safe now, no one would believe me. I had a handle on the goddess in my brain. We'd banished Heru, at least for now—Chris seemed to have it under control. We weren't going to fight each other. No one could force us.

The worst was over. The great war would never come.

So why, when I thought that, did I remember what I'd seen in the River Styx? The visions of Islington, and all my friends slain? The figure in a cloak of owl feathers, promising a battle I couldn't foresee or stop?

They had just been visions. Just visions.

Just some awful torture thrown up by the Underworld.

We had fended off the end.

I wished I was naive enough to believe it.

"So what happens next?" I whispered.

Ethan shrugged.

"We transfer back to school at home," he said.

I looked to him. To Chris. To Oliver and Elisa.

They were my family. *They* were my home.

This was supposed to be the happy ending. I looked to the shadows, to Freyja. And I remembered my sacrifice. I had given up my art to come back. But giving up Islington wasn't what I'd meant. I thought of going back home—of graduating not with my best friends, but with people who hadn't been there for me, false friends who turned their backs when I needed them the most. I thought of dropping in on classes I didn't give a shit about. The art classes wouldn't hold a candle to what I'd experienced. I wouldn't have "Islington Arts Academy" on my diploma.

And I wouldn't have these guys around. I would have to be there on my own.

"I can't go back." I hadn't even realized the words had left my mouth until Chris put a hand on my thigh.

"It will be okay," he replied. It was the first time he'd sounded like himself.

Except it wouldn't. And we both knew it.

Nothing was going to be okay. And not for the reasons my friends expected.

The blank page stayed as clear and virginal as snow.

I stared at the sketchbook, a piece of charcoal in one hand, a mug of cooled tea in the other. It was midnight. Past midnight. I had the girl's room of the nurse's office to myself. I didn't want to have it to myself. But I didn't want to sneak over and find Chris, either. Not yet. Not right now. Because he would just remind me of what I'd given up.

Now that Islington was closing, even sacrificing my art seemed pointless. Chris and I would be going to different states. I would probably never see him again.

It was all for nothing. I'd saved the boy, and I couldn't even keep him.

I wanted to scream. I wanted to rip the page to shreds. I wanted to run outside and yell at the top of my lungs, because this couldn't be happening, *shouldn't* be happening.

Mostly, though, I wanted to draw something. Anything. Because that was the one time I felt like myself. The one time I felt like I had some control over the mess of my life.

My hand hovered over the sketchbook page.

Inspiration never came.

"What did he give up?" I asked the shadows.

As expected, Freyja stepped forward. We had barely spoken since coming back up here. There were so many things left unsaid. I didn't want to puncture that dam. Right now, ignorance was mostly bliss.

At the very least, ignorance was numb.

"That is not mine to tell," she replied.

Anger flared. I crumpled the coal in my hand and flung it at the wall. The coal—brittle and as light as a feather—disintegrated into dust. Not nearly as cathartic as I'd wanted it to be. I growled in the back of my throat as I stood and turned to face her.

"Was it worth it? Any of it?" I asked her. "I brought him

back so we could be together. I gave up my *art* so we could be together. And now I have nothing. Nothing!"

The last word came out as a yell, but fuck it. If Chris or the nurse on duty wanted to come in and tell me to shut up, they could damn well try.

Freyja just stared at me, her arms crossed at her chest. She was in the same leather as she'd worn while traversing the Underworld. But now she looked less like some fierce deity. She looked oddly mortal. Save for the eyes.

"We have much to discuss," she said. Her voice was calm, but there was a note to it that kept me on edge. "Your lover's deity . . . The Aesir survived the Underworld. I have felt him."

"So what?" I asked. "Chris isn't going to hurt me. Just like I'm not going to hurt him. You're not going to make us."

She stepped forward. I fully expected her to chastise me, to tell me I had to do my duty. The owl god had said she had a plan, one that would destroy everything I loved. She may have helped me through the Underworld, but I know she only did it because she needed me.

I'd told Chris I trusted her.

It hadn't been the first lie I'd ever told.

I just needed him to trust *me*. Because there wasn't anyone else to trust.

"I sacrificed my lover to find you," Freyja said. Another step closer. "I held him as he died, all so I could come here. So I could fulfill their prophecy. My destiny. *Our* destiny." She reached out, took both of my arms. "I swore, when he breathed his last, that I would do everything in my power to avenge him."

When she leaned in, I expected the anger. The rage. I did not expect the sadness.

"The greatest vengeance I could enact would be to help you live," she said. "With Chris. You have been given the chance I would have given anything for. He lives. In this world, with you. I will fight to protect that."

I thought of the river. This didn't line up with what the strange figure had said.

"But what about the Tree?" I asked. "What about the war?"

She shook her head.

"There will be other wars and others to fight in them. The Tree can last until the next godchildren are born. And I could care less for the fate of the Vanir. The battle is always coming. Let someone else fight it."

I wanted to feel relief, but I didn't think that was possible anymore. Everything seemed to have a hook. Every light, a shadow.

"What will you do?" I asked.

She let go of my arms and stood tall. "The Aesir will still try to use the boy. His god is not as understanding as I. You will need me when that time comes. We will keep him from hurting anyone else."

"Thank you," I said. It sounded stupid. I wasn't even certain I meant it. Did she expect me to just follow Chris to his hometown, or vice versa? And what would happen with college? I couldn't just be his shadow for the rest of his life, hoping the god that wanted to screw with him wouldn't rise up. I almost laughed. There were so many physical logistics to work out, so many mundane impossibilities . . . All of the divine shit just seemed like fantasy.

"Of course," she said. "This is the life you have been given. I will ensure—"

A knock at the door cut her off. I looked toward it. Maybe the nurse had heard me talking? Before I could answer it, the doorknob turned and the door swung open. Slowly.

Chris stood on the other side.

He stepped in, his gait awkward and jerky, like a marionette's. He was in only his boxers. Despite everything, I blushed. He clearly worked out.

"Chris, what are you—?"

And then his eyes locked on to mine. His golden eyes. I stumbled back into the room, into Freyja, who caught me just in time.

"You," I seethed. "Heru."

Chris smiled. It wasn't his smile. Daggers and blood.

"Relax, Shadechild," he said. "I am not here to fight. Not yet." The smile didn't fade. Any wider, and I expected Chris's lips to crack. "I bring the Endbringer only to relay a message."

"Speak," Freyja said. Her hand was tight on my arm. The other hand, I knew, was gripping a dagger.

"First, know that I am not done with the boy. He thinks he can control me, that I am his whipped dog. Let this be proof that he is wrong. He is mine. And he will always *be* mine." Chris took a step forward. "Second, I must thank you for bringing him back to me. I learned much while he was in torment. Much about you. And much about the world."

"One more step, and I will kill you." Freyja's words were ice.

Chris stopped. The god manipulating him laughed.

"Oh, how I wish I were only here to taunt you. But I bear a message. One you have been too dull to hear. You may not want to fight." He nodded to me. "*You* may have found a way to control her. But the Tree will have its war. One way or another, there will be blood."

He stepped forward again, until he was only a foot or so away. His heat was unbearable.

"Tell her, Vanir," he whispered. "Tell her the truth in what she saw. In what you know to be true. There is a third." He chuckled. "There is a third, and Ragnarok comes."

Chris crumpled to the ground. A light turned out.

I dropped to my knees beside him. He was burning up. When my hand touched his forehead, he moaned.

"Freyja," I said, looking up to her. "Freyja, what was he talking about?"

But she didn't meet my gaze. She stared at the empty doorway, biting her lower lip. I was about to ask her again, when she opened her lips and spoke.

"I had hoped," she whispered. "I had hoped it wasn't true. That we had curbed the threat before it rose." She looked at me. Her violet eyes seemed lost. "The god your professor had been sacrificing to. The one we tried to banish. He is the same as the one you saw in the River Styx. And he is trying to rise and fight."

"But I thought . . . I thought there were only two? The Vanir and the Aesir, to fight this war and nourish the Tree. Just like you said."

"He is not of either race. This god . . ." She trailed off, looked away. "At the end of times, the Tree creates a third. Not to nourish the world, but to destroy it. Entirely."

"Why?" I asked.

"Because the Tree has deemed that it is time for humanity to end. From the ash and the blood of the old world, a new Tree will rise. And a new world. Harkened in by the god that brought the old world's destruction." She paused, and her next words were a whisper. "Hugin said nothing. He knew . . . he knew I would not have fought if it were to bring this about."

"How do we stop it?" I asked.

"We don't," she replied. She looked at me, and her eyes were filled with tears. "There is no other way. Ragnarok is the end of everything, Kaira. And no matter what we do, no matter what we try, everything you know and love will die. The Tree wills it."

ETHAN

CHAPTER THIRTY-TWO

"It wasn't supposed to end like this," I whispered to the ceiling.

Oliver was curled up beside me, his chest rising and falling slowly to the rhythm of his sleep. He'd been out cold for hours. Everything had been turned upside down since Jonathan had died. My roommate had already left, and no one cared that Oliver was staying the night. I nuzzled against his neck. The sex had worn him out, but I couldn't sleep. I couldn't stop thinking of Kaira, alone in the nurse's office. Of Chris, and what he'd shown me that afternoon in the snow—the flame in his palm, the glint of gold in his eyes. I had told myself it was a trick. Some magic trick he'd gotten online.

But I hadn't been lying. I knew something was wrong. And I knew it was never going to be all right.

We'd had this plan, you know. Go to college together. All three of us. Get an apartment off campus and paint the walls in graffiti and fill the living room with throw pillows, the cupboards with tea directly imported from T'Chai Nanni. Candles and books and art supplies everywhere. And a practice room for Oliver, of course. When we graduated, we'd move to the country a train ride away from New York or somewhere big. We'd have a mansion. Separate wings. We'd grow old there together. And our fade-out would be on the porch in our rocking chairs, drinking mimosas and reminiscing about the good old days.

Now our picturesque future was smeared.

Go home. Re-enroll in public school. Get the rest of our credits that way. Graduate. And pray all the colleges we applied to would still accept us, even if we hadn't graduated from the esteemed Islington.

All I could think of now was the guest bed at Kaira's. The scent of the patchouli incense her mom used, the breakfasts of Earl Grey and toast. What the fuck were we supposed to do? I couldn't go home. And I couldn't move in with her. Even if I could, Oliver wouldn't be able to join. He was from Florida; Kaira lived in Ohio. It wouldn't work.

Nothing was going to work.

Tears blurred the corners of my eyes.

Everything had turned to shit. And it wasn't even just the school. Kaira had seemed . . . different. Everything Chris had said ran through my brain. He was worried she was . . . I don't know, possessed or something. Seeing them there, together, though . . . it made me think that maybe he was the one who had fallen prey to something darker.

What the hell was I even talking about? I didn't believe in that shit.

Not really.

326

Not anymore.

Except you do.

Gently, I pushed myself out from under Oliver's arm and tip-toed to the bathroom. I didn't turn on the light. The nightlight was enough.

I couldn't breathe. It felt like all those years ago, when I'd tried to kill myself with that plastic bag.

When I *had* killed myself with that plastic bag.

I'd felt my heart stop.

I'd seen the light. Or something.

And then I was back in my room, and the bag was no more. Just the memory of my suffocating lungs to haunt my dreams.

My lungs burned as I gripped the edge of the sink.

I wasn't currently having a panic attack, though. I knew how those felt.

This was just waking life. That made it worse.

This wasn't supposed to go this way. We were supposed to be happy. Together. All of us.

"I wish we could go back to the way we were," I whispered to my pale reflection.

You can.

The voice came from nowhere. From inside. I knew that voice.

It was the voice that had told me it wasn't yet my time.

My reflection blurred in the effervescent light. Became a figure robed in pale white, a feathered hood pulled over its head.

Draw a circle, he whispered into my limbs. *Draw a circle, and we can fix everything.*

327

ACKNOWLEDGMENTS

First, and always, my deepest thanks to my fabulous agent Laurie McLean at Fuse Literary. She has been my knight in shining armor every step of the way. Without her knowledge and encouragement, this book would still just be a scribbled page in a forgotten notebook.

Next, to my editors extraordinaire, Michael Strother and Nicole Ellul—and the entire Simon Pulse team—for turning this story into a true work of art.

To my mother, for helping me leave the nest before I knew what it meant to fly; I couldn't have done any of this without you. To my father, for inspiring my love of books and adventure. And to my brother, for showing me what dedication truly looks like.

To Will Taylor, for helping me fine-tune both this book and my life. And being the sparkly unicorn to my . . . opposite of a sparkly unicorn. At least in terms of writing.

To Interlochen Arts Academy, for giving me a boarding school experience worth writing about.

To my Seattle writing team—Danielle Dreger, Kristin Halbrook, and Danny Marks—for keeping me on track. Or at least caffeinating me.

To my LA writing family—Kirsten Hubbard and Sarah Enni—for keeping my world alive with dust and stars.

To David Levithan, for being the most amazing friend, confidante, and travel conspirator.

And finally, to you, my dear readers, for being a constant source of inspiration.